THE TEMPLAR DETECTIVE

AND THE

SATANIC WHISPER

A TEMPLAR DETECTIVE THRILLER

Also by J. Robert Kennedy

James Acton Thrillers

The Protocol	*Sins of the Titanic*	*Keepers of the Lost Ark*
Brass Monkey	*Saint Peter's Soldiers*	*The Tomb of Genghis Khan*
Broken Dove	*The Thirteenth Legion*	*The Manila Deception*
The Templar's Relic	*Raging Sun*	*The Fourth Bible*
Flags of Sin	*Wages of Sin*	*Embassy of the Empire*
The Arab Fall	*Wrath of the Gods*	*Armageddon*
The Circle of Eight	*The Templar's Revenge*	*No Good Deed*
The Venice Code	*The Nazi's Engineer*	*The Last Soviet*
Pompeii's Ghosts	*Atlantis Lost*	*Lake of Bones*
Amazon Burning	*The Cylon Curse*	*Fatal Reunion*
The Riddle	*The Viking Deception*	*The Resurrection Tablet*
Blood Relics		*The Antarctica Incident*

Special Agent Dylan Kane Thrillers

Rogue Operator	*Black Widow*	*Extraordinary Rendition*
Containment Failure	*The Agenda*	*Red Eagle*
Cold Warriors	*Retribution*	*The Messenger*
Death to America	*State Sanctioned*	*The Defector*

Templar Detective Thrillers

The Templar Detective	*The Unholy Exorcist*	*The Black Scourge*
The Parisian Adulteress	*The Code Breaker*	*The Lost Children*
The Sergeant's Secret		*The Satanic Whisper*

Kriminalinspektor Wolfgang Vogel Mysteries

The Colonel's Wife   *Sins of the Child*

Delta Force Unleashed Thrillers

Payback	*Kill Chain*	*The Cuban Incident*
Infidels	*Forgotten*	*Rampage*
The Lazarus Moment		*Inside the Wire*

Detective Shakespeare Mysteries

Depraved Difference   *Tick Tock*   *The Redeemer*

Zander Varga, Vampire Detective

The Turned

THE
TEMPLAR
DETECTIVE
AND THE
SATANIC WHISPER

A TEMPLAR DETECTIVE THRILLER

J. ROBERT KENNEDY

ISBN: 9781990418433

First Edition

For Wessel Gordon.

THE TEMPLAR DETECTIVE

AND THE
SATANIC WHISPER

A TEMPLAR DETECTIVE THRILLER

"I do not fear Satan half so much as I fear those who fear him."

Saint Teresa of Avila

"The will is a beast of burden. If God mounts it, it wishes and goes as God wills; if Satan mounts it, it wishes and goes as Satan wills; Nor can it choose its rider... the riders contend for its possession."

Martin Luther

AUTHOR'S NOTE

This is the eighth novel in this series, and for those who have read the others and embraced these characters as so many of you have, please feel free to skip this note, as you will have already read it.

The word "detective" is believed to have originated in the mid-nineteenth century, however, that doesn't mean the concept of someone who investigated crime originated less than two hundred years ago. Crime long predated this era, and those who investigated it as well.

The following historical thriller is intended to be an entertaining read for all, with the concept of a "Templar Detective" a fun play on a modern term. The dialog is intentionally written in such a way that today's audiences can relate, as opposed to how people might have spoken in Medieval France, where, of course, they conversed in French and not English, with therefore completely different manners of speaking, and of addressing one another. For consistency, English phrasing is always used, such as Mister instead of Monsieur. This does not mean they will be speaking to each other as rappers and gangsters, but will instead communicate in ways that imply comfort and familiarity, as we would today. If you are expecting, "Thou dost hath

1

offended me, my good sir," then prepareth thyself for disappointment. If, however, you are looking for a fast-paced adventure, with plenty of action, mystery, and humor, then you've come to the right place.

Enjoy.

PREFACE

During the crusades, a number of monastic orders were formed, the most famous of which were the Knights Templar. There were other orders as well including the Knights Hospitaller, the Lazarists, and many more.

While in the Holy Land, they fought the same enemy, but as their numbers grew, so did their rivalries. Power, wealth, jealousy, influence. These were but a few of what came between knights sworn to serve God and their Lord Jesus Christ, as they were, after all, men, with all their flaws, no matter how pure of heart they struggled to be.

The conflicts between the orders were often on an individual basis, with fisticuffs in the streets, but more critically, the rivalries became political, fought in the royal courts throughout Christendom.

So, for them to unite in a common cause, the threat they faced must truly be dire.

Like a battle against Satan himself.

Outside Gien, Kingdom of France
AD 1298

Perrot Roussel prostrated himself on the floor of the large chamber, his face pressed into the hard rock as those around him did the same. The cavern carved out of the mountains near his home by forces unknown reverberated with terrifying incantations spoken in what he could only assume was Latin, a language he only heard at church but had never learned—the Church didn't want its flock capable of reading the Bible. That was left to the priests that guided them spiritually.

Priests who guided him no more.

He hadn't been inside a church since last year. Instead, every Sunday he came here, and each week more of the villagers attended with him. They had no choice. Satan held dominion here, and it was he whose voice they now heard, a terrifying, demonic rumble unlike anything he had ever experienced nor imagined. And the words he and those surrounding him repeated over and over sickened him.

"Satan is my master, and I pledge my soul to him."

Perrot was a God-fearing man, always had been and thought he always would be. Yet here he was, worshiping the Devil, though not by choice. None of them were here by choice. Satan had stolen their children one by one and demanded dominion over their lives in exchange for their safe return someday. He would do anything for his son, even burn in hellfire for eternity, but they had been given an out.

Tribute and recruitment.

Everyone here donated a portion of their crops, a portion of their wares, depending on what they did for a living. One tenth, the same as the Church demanded. At least here it served a purpose other than supporting the Church—it was saving their children's souls as well as their own. Unfortunately, just as with the tithe the Church demanded, the tribute was breaking him financially. At least with the Church, when you were unable to pay, you were just frowned upon and encouraged to make it up. Here you had no choice.

Tribute must be paid.

He would never forget when his good friend Jeban had been unable to pay. He had pleaded with those who served Satan in this realm for mercy. He had nine mouths to feed and that 10% was something he could never afford to give up otherwise his children would starve. The following week, Jeban's missing son lay on the altar at the front of the chamber.

Dead.

It had been heartbreaking, horrifying, and terribly effective. No one had missed a payment since. Everyone came with something, no matter how small, and this satisfied God's fallen angel. There was no accounting, as long as something was paid in tribute.

The final words were spoken and the voice of the dark under-lord fell silent. The vibration in the floor as he spoke from his domain below them settled and everyone rose. He brushed off then retrieved his purse from under his robes, carrying the tribute gained from the sale of one of his prized cows. He had been forced to sell her before he would have wanted, but he had nothing left to give, nothing left to sell. She was smaller than she should have been, which meant a lower price, a price already hurt by the fact there were few left with any money in his or the surrounding villages. Everyone was hurting, though many didn't know why, many not yet forced into the circle of Hell he now found himself in.

But they would soon be drawn in.

It was inevitable.

Satan was all-powerful and God had abandoned them, for if He hadn't, surely He would never let such evil reign over so much innocence.

Unknown Location, Kingdom of France

Adam Bouvet slowly walked the long row of converted horse stalls. Each held four lost souls, children who now belonged to his master. His master. He shivered at the thought. The first time he had heard his master's voice, it had shaken him to his core, everything he had ever heard in church, anything he had ever doubted, was instantly truth. The Devil was real. Evil walked among them, and only the purest of heart were safe from the dark one's influence.

Something he wasn't.

He wasn't a good man. He never had been, and was likely condemned to burn in Hell for eternity for what he had done on God's creation. So, he had capitulated. He hadn't even bothered protesting. There was no point. If he were to suffer eternal damnation, defying Satan while alive was foolish—it would only make his punishment all the more harsh. Perhaps in serving him, he might be granted some small mercy in the afterlife.

Yet none of that made his task any easier. He and the others here like him were condemned to watch over the child prisoners, an ever-growing number, each child taken to be groomed as one of Satan's future soldiers.

7

And as the evil one's power spread across the land, new children arrived daily. What was remarkable was that no one had noticed, no one had noticed the growing darkness, no one had noticed the evil spreading throughout the kingdom.

No one was fighting back.

But was there any way to fight back? This was Satan. The only one who could beat him would be God Himself, and if God were allowing this to happen, surely it was punishment for man's sins. Could this be the end time spoken of by his boyhood priest? Could this be the beginning of Armageddon where there would be one final battle for the souls of mankind and the righteous would be raised into Heaven to enjoy paradise at God's side while those like him were condemned for eternity?

The thought gave him nightmares. He hadn't had a good night's sleep since he first heard that voice rumbling through the cave, a portal to Hell that allowed Satan to not only recruit the innocent, but communicate with those who served him in the realm he was forbidden to tread upon.

Bouvet didn't want to be part of this, not really, but he was hedging his bets, serving the evil one in the hopes of a better damnation, while secretly praying God would win out in the end. He was on the wrong side of this, of that there was no doubt, and he should do something to fight on the side of good, but who was he? He was a petty thief and nothing more. He had picked the wrong pocket and had been caught and thrown in a jail far worse than what these children enjoyed. He and several others had been plucked from the hellhole they had been suffering in and taken on a long carriage ride with no windows, then shown into a cavern lit with torches, an altar at the far end, the surface large enough for a grown man to lay upon. It had been terrifying, but then came the voice. He shivered and his chest ached, for he knew what so few did.

Evil did walk among us.

Satan was real.

And he served him.

He closed his eyes for a moment, standing in front of the first stall he was assigned, and gathered himself. His terror was one thing, but that written on the faces of the children he was now about to see was something far worse. He wasn't a good man. He had seen things. But these were innocent children. They had done nothing wrong, nothing to deserve this.

And there was nothing he could do about it.

He smacked his walking stick against the stall, several startled yelps the response. He opened the gate, revealing the smaller cages inside, stacked two-by-two, four sets of wide, terrified eyes peering out at him, their cheeks stained with tears, their bodies covered in filth. It was heartbreaking even to him, and he had always considered himself one who was unconcerned with such things.

"All right, everybody up! Clean out your beds then line up for breakfast. You have a busy day ahead serving your master."

He unlocked the cage, swinging the door open, freeing the four boys from their personal prisons. They set to work cleaning their stall, a daily ritual made all the more necessary by the fact it was four humans here rather than a single horse. There was something about the stench of human excrement that was far more disgusting than anything a horse produced.

He moved on to the next stall, rapping on the gate before opening it. Three sets of eyes peered out and he frowned, stepping forward and rapping on the fourth cell. "Wake up!"

Nothing.

Another rap.

Still nothing.

He took a knee and bent over, peering inside, and cursed. The cage was empty. He stood and tested the locked gate that covered all four cells. It swung open and he cursed again. "Who opened this?"

Nobody answered, all three of the remaining prisoners scurrying to the rear of their cells and out of sight. He examined the lock closer and shook his head as he realized what had happened. The four cells, stacked two-by-two, were constructed of wood. The metal gate across the front was bolted to the wood on one side, with the lock attached to a ring bolted to the other. That piece of wood where the ring was attached was dangling freely, still connected to the lock. The wood was broken, and since it was newly constructed, it wasn't from rot or fatigue.

He grabbed the hanging piece, examined it closely, then got back down on a knee, peering into the cell of the missing prisoner. A small stone lay on the floor, one edge of it chipped away into a crude blade used to saw at the wood from inside. He gently ran it across his palm: It was dull. It must have taken days, if not weeks of effort, done at night when the guards were few and mostly sleeping on duty.

This was bad.

He stabbed a finger at the three remaining children. "You three stay here!" He stepped out of the stall, closing the gate, then turned to Raimbaut, the other guard assigned to this particular barn. "One of the prisoners is missing."

Raimbaut spun toward him. "Are you serious?"

"Yes. He cut away the lock."

"What are we going to do? If they find out, they're going to punish us."

Bouvet eyed him, incredulously. "You're not suggesting we cover it up?"

"Why not? Just say he died and we got rid of the body. It wouldn't be the first time one of them has died."

Bouvet stepped closer to Raimbaut, lowering his voice. "But there was always a body. This time there isn't."

"We'll just say he was diseased and we got rid of him to make sure it didn't spread to the others."

Bouvet grabbed at his temples, squeezing them in frustration with the stupidity standing in front of him. "Don't you get it? You're attempting to deceive our master, and remember who our master is. It's not the man who owns this estate, it's Satan himself, who is as all-knowing as God. He already knows that boy escaped and he already knows you want to cover it up." He stepped back, staring up at the heavens to beseech his master for forgiveness, then corrected himself, staring instead at his feet and the hellfire that burned far below the ground he stood upon. "Forgive me, Master, for listening to this treachery. I am your humble servant and I will always do the right thing. Satan is my master, and I pledge my soul to him."

He gave Raimbaut a look and the moron's eyes narrowed. Bouvet pointed a finger firmly at the ground, and Raimbaut's eyes finally shot wide as he figured out what was expected of him.

"I'm sorry, my Master." Raimbaut lowered his gaze, clasping his hands in front of him. "I...I don't know what I was thinking. I guess...well, I guess I didn't want to disappoint you with our failure. I humbly beg your forgiveness and promise I will never waver in my duty to you again. Satan is my master, and I pledge my soul to him."

This satisfied Bouvet. "Good. Now let's go let them know. Perhaps we can still find the wretched creature."

Unknown Location, Kingdom of France

Christian crouched, shivering in a ditch by the road that ran in front of the largest home he had ever seen. He had no idea where he was. Nothing looked familiar. All he knew was it had been several days' ride to get here in the back of a carriage with eight other children, some of whom he recognized from his village. He had no idea what was going on. He was only ten years old. But he knew it was wrong. It was evil.

Every day men in dark robes preached at them, teaching them to worship Satan, that Satan was their protector, and that service to their new master would gain them their freedom and save the souls of their parents from eternal damnation. Most of the children were convinced that what they were taught was the truth. Even he had faltered, for as they said, if God and the Lord Jesus Christ were their protectors, why would they be there?

It was the night they took Estienne away that changed things for him. It had happened after dark. Estienne had screamed, begging not to be taken, and in a heartbreaking testimonial of how effective the preaching had been, he begged not for God's help, but Satan's. His mind, spirit, and soul had been broken. Everyone had woken to the screams, and Christian remembered gripping the bars, cocking his ear, pushing it through the metal as far as he could to hear what was going on.

The pleas had continued as Estienne was dragged out of the barn that had been their home for months, then a sickening cracking sound silenced the cries, and everyone had remained still in shock as they all strained in vain for any sound from their friend.

But none came.

It was the next morning when they received confirmation of their worst fears, the guards informing them of his execution for failing to serve his new master well. They had all worked harder from that day forward, laboring in the work barn, toiling away at various tasks, laundering clothing, polishing jewelry, weaving cloth, sewing garments. Every day they toiled from dawn until dusk, and new barns were constructed as their numbers grew. He had no idea what was truly going on here, though he was certain his father would know.

Whatever it was, it truly was evil.

No one good or God-fearing would treat children like this, would murder children, would force them to toil day in and day out.

A shout rang out behind him, followed by several more. "A child has escaped!"

He gulped, his heart hammering. He rose, sprinting along the ditch as quickly as his little legs would take him, desperate to put as much distance as he could between himself and those who served Satan.

Who would never be his master.

De Rancourt Family Farm
Crécy-la-Chapelle, Kingdom of France

Sir Marcus de Rancourt tapped the final nail in place, the honor left to him, the bulk of the work done by his squires, David and Jeremy, with his loyal sergeant Simon Chastain directing them in his usual gruff manner. The extension to the small farmhouse was now complete, adding four more bedrooms and allowing them to repurpose the area from one of the existing rooms so as to expand the kitchen and main living area.

Their family was growing rapidly. The barracks they had built now housed the four of them, plus young Thomas Durant when he was visiting. Eventually, some of the male children would be old enough to move in there as well, but for now, the matron of the farm, Lady Joanne de Rohan, insisted all children must sleep in the house, and with the arrival of Madeleine Rabot and her orphaned niece and nephew, the house had become overwhelmingly cramped. Joanne ordered an extension be built and it was delivered, the last nail secured, the final window, made of glass, a gift from Sir Denys de Montfort, whose recent wedding had unleashed a previously unknown generosity.

Life was good here, far better than he ever would have expected. He was a Templar Knight, not a farmer, not a father figure to half a dozen children, not a caretaker and provider for three women. So much had changed since his sister died and left his niece and nephew in his care. The farm had become a haven for victims of heinous crimes that had left them orphaned, destitute, outcasts. And now they were a family, everyone doing their part, no matter what their station once was. From nobility to misfits, all had a home here, and though he wasn't serving his Lord in the way he had assumed he would for the rest of his life, he was content with the knowledge that he was still serving.

Tanya, the farm's mastiff, raced around the new addition, sniffing every surface her nose could reach, as his niece rushed over, staring up at him.

"Uncle Marcus, can I go pick my room?"

He smiled and patted Angeline's head as Joanne gave him a look indicating what his answer should be. "That's not up to me, sweetheart, that's up to Lady Joanne. I'm sure she already has room assignments all picked out for everyone."

"All right, but I don't want to share with my brother anymore. Boys are stinky."

Marcus chuckled. "Yes, we are, aren't we?"

His nephew Jacques stuck his tongue out at his sister then took a long sniff of his armpit and grinned, his expression suggesting it smelled like the freshest of flowers.

Joanne rushed at him with a wagging finger. "Don't make me force you into that bath again, Mister."

He scurried away, squealing as she reached for him. He evaded her grasp and disappeared around the rear of the home.

"Is it finished?"

Marcus turned to see Thomas Durant and his fiancée, Isabelle Leblanc, striding up the laneway. She was breathtakingly beautiful, though she was a farm girl through and through. She did little to capitalize on her beauty and never hesitated to pitch in whenever needed. She would make a fantastic wife for young Thomas, who was developing into a fine young man despite his troubled youth. Marcus looked forward to the day when the two of them finally married and started their life together.

A day rapidly approaching.

Marcus smiled at them. "All done. The only thing that remains is the fight over who gets what room."

Joanne slapped him on the arm. "Don't say things like that! The children will think they have a choice."

Simon grinned. "Don't worry, David and Jeremy know they're staying in the barracks."

Jeremy made a face at him and the children giggled.

Isabelle hurried around the three walls of the new addition. "It looks wonderful. This will make everyone's life so much easier." She turned to Joanne. "I hope you've chosen the finest room for yourself. You deserve it."

Joanne batted her hand. "Oh, I don't need much. Beatrice and I have become accustomed to sharing."

"Perhaps another addition is needed then."

Every man within earshot that had contributed groaned. Marcus put an end to that nonsense. "Perhaps next year when you two build your matrimonial home on your father's farm, you can build in some extra space."

Isabelle took Thomas by the arm. "I think we'll be needing the space for our own children."

Thomas blushed, still the shy one.

"So, what are you two up to?" asked Joanne.

"I'm here to see him off."

Thomas nodded. "Yes. The farm work has been finished, so it's time for me to return to Paris and get back to work on Mrs. Thibault's books. If I leave it too long, they'll be a complete mess."

Beatrice growled. "I wish you didn't have to work for such a beastly woman."

Thomas shifted uncomfortably, staring at his shoes. "She's really not that bad once you get to know her, and she's changed a lot over the past year."

Marcus agreed. "She has that."

Beatrice dismissed the defense. "She's still a scoundrel, taking advantage of the poor."

Thomas shrugged. "Where else are they going to get the money they need?"

"From far better people than her, I can tell you."

Thomas shrunk away from her tone, never comfortable with confrontation, and Isabelle jumped to his defense. "When have you ever known nobility to lend money to the poor?" She looked at Joanne, askance.

Joanne caught it. "I'll have you know that when I was part of that society, we donated generously to the Church and to various charities."

"Well, it's one thing to help feed and clothe the poor, but that does nothing to help a man earn a living or fix his house. Those things all require money, and a hot bowl of soup can only be traded for so much."

Marcus held up a hand. "Enough of this. There are too many opinions on this and they're all strong. There's no point tearing ourselves apart over the actions of a woman who isn't even related to us."

Joanne officially ended it. "You're right, of course. Thomas has a job that pays him well, and through his good work, no one is overcharged, and by all accounts, he's tempered Mrs. Thibault's leanings. And that can only be a good thing. And Isabelle, you're correct, food and clothing does little to keep a man in business, or weatherproof his home. Charities help those who've already fallen. Money lenders, no matter how unscrupulous, help those who've faltered get back on their own two feet. And if I ever had money again, it's where I would direct it."

Marcus glanced up at the sun, taking note of its position. "Well, Thomas, if you intend to reach Paris by nightfall, you'd best be leaving now."

"Yes, sir. Does anybody have business at the fortress who perhaps would like to accompany me?"

Marcus suppressed a smile. Thomas had proven he wasn't a coward, but he also wasn't a brave man. Marcus could respect that. The young man was still slight of frame, though he suspected that a few years of working on the farm would cure him of that. But nothing would cure him of his fear if he were always accompanied by a trained Templar for his journeys between here and the city.

"Why don't you take Tanya with you?" suggested Beatrice. "She's always underfoot anyway. A run to the city would do her good."

Tanya bolted over to them at the mention of her name. Marcus pointed at the ground and the massive beast sat panting as she stared up at him, her tail wagging. "Would you like to go to Paris with Thomas?" She barked and it made him wonder how much she truly understood. She barked again and he reached down and scratched behind her ears. "I think she'd like to go."

Simon chuckled. "If I let you scratch me behind my ears, can I go too? Anything to get away from the smell of shit."

Marcus laughed, his sergeant definitely not built for the farm. "Don't worry, Sergeant, you won't have much time left to suffer. I'm due at the fortress in two days regardless, and you'll be accompanying me."

David perked up. "And us?"

"I'm afraid not. There's too much work to be done here, and I don't want the women and children left alone unless it's absolutely necessary."

David hid his disappointment well with a nod, but Jeremy groaned. David swatted him, silencing the youngest of the four servants to the

Templar Order, who was by no means a young man anymore.

Marcus turned to Thomas and Isabelle. "Then it's settled. Tanya will go with you if you so choose."

Thomas stared at the massive creature and Marcus had to wonder who the young man was scared of more, the dog or those he feared lay in wait for him on his journey home.

Joanne eyed him. "Well, out with it. You're about to be a husband and soon a father. With those types of responsibilities, you can't take this long to make a decision over trivial matters."

Thomas flinched. "I'll take her."

Simon grinned. "Excellent! One less source of shit."

Unknown Location, Kingdom of France

Horses' hooves clopping from behind had Christian diving to the ground, his little heart slamming with terror. He had made his escape in the dark, but now it was bright out, and judging by the rumbling of his stomach, it was well past breakfast if not lunch. He pressed his body into the side of the ditch, praying whoever approached wouldn't spot him in the tall grass. As the sound grew near, he realized there were at least two horses, and a conversation was taking place that he couldn't make out. He held his breath, struggling to remove any source of motion the two sets of eyes might spot.

"I'm going to kill that little urchin when I find him."

He recognized it as Bouvet, one of the guards that watched over them during the day. Christian's bladder let go, the warmth momentarily comforting against the cool ground before the shame of soiling himself washed over him.

"The overseer said to bring him back alive."

Bouvet growled. "Fine, I won't kill him, but he'll get the flogging of a lifetime, I swear it."

The other man laughed. "You're right, the overseer never said anything about what condition we had to return him in."

The conversation faded with a cackle of laughter from both men, leaving Christian sobbing in the ditch, lying in his own filth, uncertain as to what to do. Should he leave the road that might take him to someone who might help but where those searching for him were likely to be, or should he take the slower route over the land where he might encounter no one, good or bad?

He squeezed his eyes shut. "Please, God, help me!"

A gentle breeze blew over him. He pushed to his elbows to see the grass surrounding him bending forward along the path of the road. It was a sign, a sign from God, telling him to continue along his chosen path.

Salvation must lie ahead.

En Route to Paris, Kingdom of France

The deeper Thomas fell in love with Isabelle, the harder the goodbyes became, and though he had his reservations about taking the massive Tanya with him, he was enjoying her company. While he never liked making the journey between Crécy-la-Chapelle and Paris alone, he did feel safer with her, though it didn't compare to traveling with Sir Marcus and Simon in their full Templar regalia. He was armed only with a dagger—a sword would be useless in his hands, for he knew not how to wield it, though David and Jeremy had begun teaching him the basics. It was simply something he could never see himself becoming adept at. He wasn't a very physical person—he preferred to use his mind to think his way out of a problem.

Traveling alone on a valuable horse with only a dagger for protection made him a target to ruffians that might lie in the woods on either side of the road. Tanya made a good deterrent, her sheer size enough to strike fear in most men, but he always breathed easier the closer he got to Paris. The traffic continually grew, and once one reached the outskirts, scores of people on foot, on horseback, and in carriages provided protection through numbers.

The danger was here, where no one else was in sight, halfway between his two homes. He always urged his steed on a little faster and struggled to pass the nervous time as he always did, by talking to himself. But with Tanya at his side, he spoke aloud, his voice comforting in that it helped drown out any sounds that might be coming from the trees.

"I can't believe I'm going to be married soon. I never thought I'd see the day. Did you, Tanya?"

She looked up at him and barked.

He sighed, his shoulders slumping. "If only she didn't live on a farm. It's such a hard life. I was never meant for that. What do you think, Tanya? Do you think I'll ever make a good farmer?"

She barked then bolted ahead, disappearing into the ditch and the tall grass filling it. Thomas tensed, reaching for his dagger and gripping the hilt. He peered ahead but couldn't make out anything. He reached Tanya's position and all he could see was her tail wagging and her head dipped below the grass as if she were sniffing at something.

"Come on, girl, let's go."

Tanya poked her head up and looked at him then barked, the massive head disappearing below the grass once again.

"I said, let's go!" It was as firm a voice as he could muster without rehearsal, and it had no effect, merely eliciting another bark. He wasn't as familiar with dogs as some, but didn't sense any fear or anger, and he was certain a wagging tail was always a sign of happiness or excitement. He groaned and dismounted, casting a wary eye over his surroundings. No one was within sight.

He stepped down into the ditch, the grass reaching his waist. "What have you got there, girl?" He gently pushed Tanya aside and her rear end swung out of the way. Thomas squinted as he spotted something curled up in the grass. He wasn't sure what he was looking at, and at first he thought it might be an injured animal, but then he noticed the clothing and gasped.

He dropped to a knee and reached out. "Are you all right?" A whimper was the only response. It was a child, but what would a child be doing out here in the middle of nowhere? He put a hand on what he assumed was a boy's shoulder. "It's all right, I'm not going to hurt you. Where are your parents?"

The head raised and a filthy face stared up at him, tears pouring from piercing blue eyes. "I-I don't know."

"You don't know? How did you end up here?"

"I ran away."

Thomas smiled, remembering his youth and several of his own escapes that always ended when he grew hungry. "We should get you back. They're going to be worried about you."

The boy vehemently shook his head, scurrying away. "No, I won't go back! You can't make me go back! They're evil! They'll kill me!"

Thomas chuckled. "I highly doubt your parents are going to kill you for running away."

Again, the young boy shook his head. "No, not my parents."

Thomas eyed the boy. "If not your parents, then whom?"

"Those who serve Satan."

A shiver rushed through Thomas' body. He couldn't recall the last time he had heard the name outside of church. "What do you mean, 'those who serve Satan?'"

The little boy cringed. "It's forbidden to talk about them. We're not even allowed to look at them. They wear long dark robes with hoods."

"Then how do you know they serve Satan?"

"Because we were told they did."

"By whom?"

"By him."

24

"Who is 'him?'"

"Satan," the boy whispered, his entire body shaking, his voice quivering.

Thomas regarded the clearly terrified boy. What he was saying was nonsense, yet regardless of how he felt about the boy's story, the child clearly needed help. He extended a hand. "Come with me. I'll take you to my home and we'll try to figure out how to get you back to your parents."

The boy stared at the hand and slowly reached for it before finally grasping it. Thomas gently pulled him to his feet. He smiled down at the boy when he suddenly wrapped his arms around Thomas' legs, holding him tight before the grip finally eased. The child slid slowly to the ground and Thomas chuckled as he realized the wretched creature had fallen asleep.

Thomas picked him up and walked back toward his horse. The poor child was clearly in dire straits. The question was why? His story was too fantastic, clearly that of a child who believed the greater the lie, the more believable it must be. He had likely run away from home or perhaps an orphanage, but there were no answers to be found here. His only choice was to bring the child to Paris with him then hopefully get the truth when he realized he was safe.

Thomas turned to Tanya. "Well, girl, it looks like this journey is turning out a lot more interesting than we expected."

Tanya barked then sniffed the boy's face, her tongue darting out and lapping at the dirt, yet another lost soul now under her protection.

Unknown Location, Kingdom of France

Bouvet and Raimbaut both stood in front of their superior, their hands clasped in front of them, their heads bowed, their chins pressed against their chests. They had been unable to find the escaped child, and it was now clear he would never be found. It was time for their punishment, and he feared failing the antichrist meant certain death. The man they referred to only as "Milord" stood in front of them, his face covered by a horrifying mask, clearly modeled after the dark one himself. It was a visage that Bouvet couldn't bring himself to look at, for every time he did, he suffered from horrific nightmares for days as he became consumed with the realization of just who he was serving, who held dominion over his soul.

The man stood in front of them, his hands clasped behind his back as his piercing eyes glared out at both of them from behind the mask. "You realize how serious this is, how much difficulty this could put us in, how this could interfere with our plans?"

"Yes, Milord," they both echoed.

"Our master is displeased, very displeased."

Bouvet shivered and Raimbaut dropped to his knees, clasping his hands in front of his face. "Please, please forgive us, Milord. It will never happen again. I swear it, I swear to God—"

Their lord slapped Raimbaut hard. "You swear to who?"

Raimbaut's jaw dropped in horror. "To our master, of course, not to that pretender God," he spat.

"Then pray to our master."

Raimbaut hit the ground, his face pressed into the mud as he spread out his arms, prostrating himself to their master, repeating the incantation over and over. "Satan is my master, and I pledge my soul to him."

Bouvet clasped his own hands in front of his face. "Milord, may I too pray for forgiveness?"

But his wish wasn't to be granted. "No. Someone must be made an example of for this failure."

Tears filled Bouvet's eyes. "Please, I beg of you. It wasn't my fault. I only discovered it. I wasn't on duty when it happened."

"Yet you yourself said it must have taken days. How many times did you fail in your duty?"

"But I wasn't the only one!"

"Why should all be punished when one is sufficient? The others shall learn from your pain."

The word sent shockwaves of terror through his body. What were they going to do to him? What did he mean by pain?

"Twenty lashes!" shouted the lord, and several of the dark servants rushed forward, grabbing him under his arms and leading him away. He was lashed to a post that stood in the middle of the cluster of barns and his tunic was torn away, exposing his bare back. The one who would deliver the sentence, the executioner, a man whose face needed no mask for it was disfigured enough, an entire side of it burned long ago in some incident Bouvet had no doubt was hellish, approached.

His punisher, half beast, half man, slowly circled the post, dragging the whip behind him on the ground as he cackled with glee at this fresh opportunity to inflict pain on those who had no doubt made his life horrible. "You have failed your master, you have failed your lord, and you have failed yourself. Do you deny this?"

Bouvet shook his head. "No, I deny none of it. I accept responsibility for my failures and I willingly hand myself over to my master's servant for punishment so I and the others responsible can learn from our mistake."

"Well said." The beast paused, staring him in the eyes. "Most merely beg for forgiveness, but you have heart." He sneered. "Which will make this all the more enjoyable." The hideous creation stepped out of sight, the only indication he was still there the dragging of the whip in the mud and his slow cackle.

Then all fell silent.

He finally noticed the dozens of people standing around, a few of the more senior with smiles, the rest like him, relief written on their faces that they weren't the ones receiving the punishment today. He had been in their position before and had never taken pleasure in what he witnessed. It was barbaric, and the first time he had seen it, he'd sworn he would never let it happen to him. Yet here he was in the position he had promised he would never be.

Helpless.

The beast inhaled deeply and Bouvet clenched his jaw tight, squeezing his eyes shut as he braced for what was to come. The creature exhaled as the whip whooshed behind him, then a moment later lashed at his skin, the snap as it reached its target at the exact right time the sign of a skilled practitioner. It was so loud it rang his ears, but that was nothing compared to the pain that overwhelmed him. If he had to suffer through nineteen more of these, he couldn't see how he would possibly survive, for the first stroke was never the hardest—it was always just a test to see if the one delivering the punishment was standing at the perfect distance to deliver the maximum effect with the whip at its highest speed just as it snapped.

Another inhalation followed by a grunt, the whooshing of the leather, then the snap as his back was once again torn at. He cried out this time, but there was no shame. A third strike and this time the blood flowed down his back. This was when it got bad, this was when tear upon tear shredded the skin. This was when the blood could flow too freely, when his spine and rib cage could be exposed, where a man could die before the final blow was delivered, and if he didn't, could die days or weeks later of infection from wounds that refused to heal.

Another blow then another, his cries now joined by whimpers as the tears flowed. This was no time to be a man, no time to be tough, and there was only one thing he could think of to say.

"Satan is my master, and I pledge my soul to him."

Another blow, another cry, and then another prayer shouted for all to hear.

"Satan is my master, and I pledge my soul to him!"

Another blow, this time the pain unbelievably excruciating, something more than skin damaged. A blinding white light caused his head to jerk back and he stared up at the heavens and thanked the Good Lord for one final mercy as a lost soul was gently welcomed back into the flock.

Approaching Durant Residence
Paris, Kingdom of France

The boy had slept almost the entire way to Paris. If he had run away, it was clear he wasn't from the city, his wide-eyed wonder at everything around him betraying the fact he had never been in a city before. It meant he was from a village or town, likely a village, and unfortunately that meant countless possibilities. Thomas hadn't asked him any questions except for his name. Christian. Thomas had instead spent the time answering questions as excited fingers darted out at everything in sight until they finally reached his humble home in the slums.

"Is this your home?"

"Yes."

"Wow, it's so nice!"

Thomas stared up at it, much of the front recently replaced after it had been intentionally burned. It did look nice compared to most of those surrounding it, though he wouldn't say it was necessarily nicer than most farmhouses he had seen. They were simply different. It was wedged into a long line of buildings, mixtures of homes and businesses that to the inexperienced eye of a youngster made it look far bigger than it was.

He loved it. It was his family home, after all, where most of his life had been lived, all of his memories, good and bad with his parents having happened here. But it was also where his mother had died, where his father had been murdered, and where he had nearly starved to death before Marcus and the others had saved him.

Thomas dismounted then lifted the boy off the horse. He rapped on the door then opened it rather than just walk in on Enzo, the massively muscled and misshapen creature he now called his friend and protector while working for their boss, Simone Thibault. Enzo was her enforcer, his sheer size and menacing nature enough to terrify any delinquent borrower. But as Thomas had discovered over the past year, the beastly man was grossly misunderstood and painfully lonely. Their friendship, however unlikely, had brought a lot of joy into Enzo's life and a lot of peace into Thomas'.

Enzo now lived in Thomas' home, which meant it was safe. No one would dare enter for fear of encountering the famously protective man. It meant the home was lived-in, secure, and Enzo had a welcome place to come home to at the end of a hard day of enforcement.

"Enzo, it's me, Thomas. Are you here?"

"In the back," rumbled the man's impossibly deep voice.

Christian shrank behind him, terrified. "Is that Satan?"

Thomas laughed. "No, that's my friend Enzo, but be forewarned, he's very large and very scary looking, but he's our friend and will do anything necessary to protect us. Understood?"

The wide-eyed boy nodded unconvincingly.

Thomas stepped inside, ushering the boy along with him. Tanya burst through the door and disappeared in the back, a happy reunion with Enzo taking place out of sight. "We have a guest," announced Thomas.

"Oh? Who?" The floorboards creaked as Enzo approached.

"A young boy I found on the road to Paris. I've offered him shelter and our assistance in finding his parents."

Enzo appeared and Christian gasped, darting behind Thomas. "You'll have to forgive the lad. He believes Satan took him and other children prisoner."

Enzo's eyes narrowed. "Satan?"

"Yes. Come, Master Christian, and meet Enzo, my good friend."

Christian poked his head out from behind Thomas. "You're sure he doesn't work for Satan?"

Enzo laughed. "Though I may look as if the Devil himself placed me on this earth, I can assure you I'm a God-fearing man, just like I'm sure you are. Don't let my size and face scare you."

Christian stepped out slightly, Enzo's deep but gentle voice soothing the terrified soul slightly. "What happened to your face?"

Enzo shrugged as he took a knee in front of the boy. "I was born this way, but I assure you I'm one of God's children, so God must have wanted me to be like this for some reason." He smiled at the boy, pointing at the disfigured face. "Want to touch it?"

The boy's eyes bulged. "May I?"

Enzo shrugged. "Why not? It's not like it hurts. It feels normal, it just doesn't look normal."

The boy tentatively reached out and Enzo leaned forward slightly. A single finger touched the cheek. "Squishy."

Enzo reached out and touched the boy's cheek. "Just like yours."

Christian giggled and reached out with both hands again, mashing Enzo's face. Enzo reached out and did the same, and soon the two of them were laughing uncontrollably with Tanya barking and circling them, attempting to get in on the fun.

"I'm going to get our things then bring the horse down to the stable," said Thomas.

Enzo looked up. "I'll take care of that."

Thomas waved him off. "No, you get to know the boy. I'll be back shortly." He stepped outside and unpacked the horse as he slowly unwound from his long, tense journey. His plan tonight had been to relax with Enzo, eat a good meal, and sleep in his familiar bed before returning to work for Mrs. Thibault tomorrow. But now those plans had been torn asunder by the responsibility thrust upon him by God—find out what horror had truly befallen this young child.

It was a responsibility he couldn't possibly imagine measuring up to.

Unknown Location, Kingdom of France

Bouvet woke, the blinding pain still radiating from his back. He was completely spent and had lost his will to live. He prayed for death, or to at least pass out once again from the pain. This wasn't the first time he had awoken since his punishment. The last half-dozen blows he hadn't been awake for, the Lord's small mercy having protected him from the final horrors that had no doubt done most of the damage.

His first recollection was being cut from the pole. He had collapsed to the ground and passed out again. His next was in his barracks, Raimbaut and one of the others pouring buckets of water over his back in an attempt to clean his wounds. The final memory was something he was certain he had dreamt. It was a woman's voice, a young woman, an angel sent from Heaven, he was certain.

And she was outraged at what she had seen. "Take him to the house immediately and send for the doctor!"

He was certain it was a dream, it had to be, yet as he forced his eyes open, he found himself in unfamiliar surroundings, in a bed more comfortable than any he could have ever imagined.

"Don't move." It was the same voice, the same angelic voice. He couldn't disobey her instructions even if he wanted to. "What did you ever do to deserve such treatment?"

He couldn't see her. She was somewhere else in the room. "I failed my master."

"Surely my father wouldn't order such a thing."

His heart hammered. "Father?"

Could his angel actually be a demon, the daughter of the Antichrist? But if she were the dark lord's daughter, then she would know what her father was capable of and wouldn't be asking such a question. Something else was going on here. In all his time serving his new master, he had never heard of anyone taken into the estate, or even approaching it. But now he was inside. It was unlike any home he had ever seen. Whoever lived here must be impossibly wealthy if they lived like the king.

The cluster of buildings he and the others called home, some old, most new, were set well back from the large house on the hill, almost out of sight of the home, with its own access road and a fence surrounding it, clearly delineating the residence from the operation run on the property.

And it was forbidden for anyone to leave without permission.

Footsteps rounded the bed and she came into sight. She was the sweetest thing he had ever laid eyes upon. Long curly blond hair, the whitest of skin as if never kissed by the sun. Vivid green eyes that demanded to be stared into, yet simple clothes covered by a smock stained with blood.

Blood he assumed was his.

She sat on the edge of the bed. "Now, tell the truth. Why did this happen?"

"Because I failed my master," he repeated, uncertain as to what else he could possibly say.

She firmly shook her head. "I refuse to believe that my father would

35

order such a thing."

"Not your father, but my master."

"But you work on my father's estate, do you not?"

He shrugged, immediately regretting the movement as a jolt of pain surged through him and he winced.

She reached out. "You must lie still, as perfectly still as you can while your wounds mend."

"I don't know who your father is."

"Yet you work on his estate."

"Perhaps your father works for my master."

She giggled, a hand darting to her mouth as if the very notion of her father working for anyone was ridiculous. "I can assure you my father works for no one. The king barely holds dominion over him."

"Who is your father?"

She opened her mouth to answer then stopped herself. "Perhaps I shouldn't say. You work on the estate yet don't know his name. There must be a reason for that."

He was desperate to know the answer, but he didn't dare press. He was here, receiving care no one else in his position had ever received, and it would be key to his survival. "Perhaps that's best."

She smiled. "Yes, I think so. What are you doing down there?"

His eyes narrowed slightly. "You don't know?"

"No. Father sent Mother and I away two years ago so I could study in Bologna. Mother..." Her voice cracked. "Mother fell ill and passed, so I returned home. I just arrived yesterday. When I heard your screams, I, of course, went to investigate and found what had happened to you."

"Will I live?"

She frowned. "That, I cannot say. The doctor said if you make it through the week, then the chances are good. You're under my care now. The nurse who will be dealing with your wounds arrived earlier, and our doctor will check on you daily. I will do my best to save you from this wicked assault. You have suffered on my family's property, and I swear I'll get to the bottom of what's going on."

He reached out and grabbed her hand, staring her in the eyes. "Don't. If you interfere, he will kill you."

"But this must be stopped. Men cannot be treated this way."

"You don't understand. If you interfere, he *will* kill you."

"Who is 'he?' Who do you keep referring to if it's not my father?"

Bouvet closed his eyes and he let go of her. "If I tell you, he'll know, and we're forbidden to speak about it to outsiders."

A gentle hand brushed through his hair. "You can tell me. I won't tell anyone else, I swear."

"But he'll know."

"How could he possibly know? We're alone in this room."

"He's all-knowing. He's all-seeing." He opened his eyes, filled with tears. "You just don't understand."

She squinted at him. "Do you mean God?"

"No." His eyes darted to the floor beneath them and her eyes widened. She recoiled in horror as she rose from the bed and stepped back, putting a goodly distance between them.

"You don't mean…"

"Yes. He is my master, and I dare not betray him."

She rushed from the room, the door slamming shut behind her, leaving him to wonder what fate he now faced. He had been saved from pain by God, of that he was certain, but had it merely been a punishment so that he would suffer a torturous, prolonged death? Had it not been a reprieve at all, the Good Lord instead punishing him for his betrayal, for his deserting Him?

And as he continued to show his loyalty toward the evil one by not betraying his confidence, had the angel of mercy been withdrawn? Would he be tossed back into the stables to suffer the painful death he deserved, or had the shock merely been too much for her, and she would return in time to help save his life?

And perhaps his soul before it was too late.

Durant Residence
Paris, Kingdom of France

Thomas leaned back in his chair, marveling at how much food young Christian managed to shovel into his mouth. It was clear the boy was starving, though he didn't appear emaciated. "Did they not feed you where you were?"

Christian swallowed. "Breakfast and dinner, but I haven't eaten in over a day, and I definitely haven't eaten like this in months."

Enzo regarded him, halting his assault on a chicken leg. "Months?"

Christian shrugged. "I don't really know how long it's been. One day is like the other. They let us out of our cage, we clean up the stall, then they feed us, then they put us to work. And then at the end of the day, we have prayers, we eat, then are locked back in our cages for the night."

Thomas eyed him. "Prayers? I thought you said these people worshipped Satan?"

Christian vehemently nodded. "Yes, but they're not prayers to God, they're prayers to…" The boy hesitated, his eyes finally darting briefly toward the floor. "Him."

Thomas still wasn't convinced that this wasn't all an elaborate lie the boy had concocted to cover up for some perceived terrible sin. Yet as the evening continued, the boy's story had never wavered, and as he grew more comfortable with them, he freely answered questions. Thomas finally broached the subject they had been avoiding. "What would you like to do?"

Christian grinned. "Keep eating?"

Enzo laughed. "I like this one."

Thomas smiled. "No, I mean, you're welcome to stay here while we figure things out, but ultimately, you need to go somewhere. Where would you like to go?"

Christian paused. "Home."

Thomas was relieved to hear it, though it certainly did contradict his own theory that the boy had run away from home and had concocted this lie. "So, you want to return to your parents?"

Again, a vigorous head nod.

"Good, then we'll try our best to get you home as soon as possible."

Christian stared at him, his eyes wide. "No, I can't go home!"

Thomas eyed him. "But you just said you wanted to go home?"

"I *do* want to go home, but I can't. That's where Satan lives."

Thomas and Enzo exchanged glances. "What do you mean that's where Satan lives? I thought he was at this place you ran away from?"

"No, the people that serve him are at the place I escaped from. But Satan himself is actually outside of my village, near our farm."

Enzo dropped the chicken leg on his plate. "Have you actually seen him?"

Christian twisted in his chair and stared at the floor for a moment before his gaze abruptly switched to the ceiling. Heaven versus Hell. "No, but I've heard his voice. We all have."

Thomas took a sip of his wine. "And what makes you think it was Satan?"

The boy clasped his upper arms, embracing himself as he shivered. "Because no man could make that voice. It was pure evil." He sniffed. "The first time I heard it, I soiled myself." He stared at Enzo then Thomas. "And so did the others! A lot of the others! I wasn't the only one!"

Thomas smiled and reached out, patting the boy on the shoulder. "It's nothing to be ashamed of. I'm quite certain that if I heard the Devil's voice, I too would lose control."

The boy sniffed hard. "That was the last time I saw my home."

Thomas folded his arms as he leaned back. The story was becoming far too detailed to be concocted by the mind of a child. "Why don't you tell us everything from the beginning?"

"Does that mean you believe me now?"

Thomas wasn't sure if he did, but he was certain the child did. He decided the best way to continue the flow of information was to at least pretend. "Yes."

The boy smiled and faced him, his meal forgotten. "Me and some of my friends were playing in the fields. We had finished our chores when we saw a man in black robes. He called for us and we were curious because we had never seen him before, so we joined him. He asked us if we wanted to see something that would make our friends envious. We said yes and followed him to a cave entrance not far from the village. We went inside and found a large chamber. It was lit with torches and had some sort of table at the front like an altar you'd see in church. There were other men inside in the same black robes. I couldn't see their faces because they had hoods covering them. They had us stand in the middle of the cave then suddenly there was this voice, like a whisper, but loud. It was…terrifying."

Thomas leaned forward. "What did the voice say?"

"He said, 'Who dares enter my dominion?'"

Enzo was all in, his plate shoved aside. "What did you say?"

41

Tears rolled down Christian's cheeks. "I said nothing. I s-soiled myself, but so did Henri and Mario."

Thomas reached out and gently squeezed the boy's hand. "And then what happened?"

"One of the other men told us to state our names, so we did. Then the voice asked, 'Do you know who I am?' We didn't so we all shook our heads. I think I might have said, 'no,' I don't remember."

"Then what happened?"

"He said something like, I am the fallen one, once God's favorite, but, umm, forever condemned to the hell that…" Christian thought hard, then his eyes widened. "That lies beneath the feet of man, punishment for my hubris by an unjust, unloving God." His eyes narrowed. "What does hubris mean?"

"Think arrogance."

"What does arrogance mean?"

Thomas eyed him. "You remembered all that, and don't know what arrogance means?"

Christian shrugged. "One of the older boys in the carriage remembered and explained what it meant."

"And he didn't explain hubris?"

"He said arrogance. I didn't ask because I didn't want to look stupid."

Thomas chuckled. "It means to think highly of oneself. Anyway, it doesn't matter. What happened next."

"I can't really remember much more because it was then that I realized who was speaking, that it was Satan himself. That's when I fully lost control and really soiled myself. He said something about how he now owned our souls and those of our parents, and that we would serve him and were to follow the orders of the men around us. That's when they flipped their hoods back and revealed their faces. But they weren't men at all!" He burst into tears, his entire body trembling. "They were beasts! Demons!" His chin slumped into his chest and his cries turned to a whisper. "I'm sorry."

Thomas' eyes narrowed, wondering what the boy had to be sorry for, then he heard something. He leaned slightly to his left and saw a puddle on the floor, the poor child having once again soiled himself in terror—wiping away any doubt as to whether he was making up what he was saying.

A made-up story never terrorized the teller as much as this tale did this small boy.

Thibault Residence

Paris, Kingdom of France

Simone Thibault lay in her bed, fully dressed. Another day was about to begin and she simply wasn't prepared for it. She had no energy, having spent much of the night doing battle with a rat that had found its way into her bedding. They were disgusting, vile creatures, and she couldn't stand them, though they were part of life in Paris and there was no avoiding them. The best defense was keeping one's home clean with no food out to attract them, and to keep the structure in good repair, constantly inspecting for holes and patching them when found.

And several hungry cats.

She was fortunate in that due to her wealth, she had people that took care of such things for her, but because she lived surrounded by the squalor of her customers who couldn't afford such luxuries, the rats were a constant problem. She had the money to move to a finer part of the city, but had dismissed the idea. She could never fit in with the elite of Paris and those who ruled the kingdom.

Here, she lived like a queen. She had a fine home in comparison to those that surrounded her, fine furnishings, and she ate better than those she served could possibly imagine. It was a good life, though a lonely one. Her husband was dead and they had never had children, and due to the nature of her business, friendships were difficult.

Footsteps below brought a smile as the only friends she had in this world arrived for work—young Thomas Durant, who she had become to think of as a son, and her loyal servant Enzo, her protector, whom she could talk to for hours. Unfortunately, the poor man was too simple to participate in any such dialogue.

Yet they were company, and were here willingly.

She rolled out of the bed and stepped in front of the highly polished silver mirror, checking her reflection. She straightened herself up then unbolted the myriad of locks and bars on her reinforced bedroom door, her final line of protection should her enemies get past the guards. She descended the stairs and smiled at Thomas and Enzo.

"Thomas, my boy, it's so good to see you. How was the farm?"

Thomas shrugged. "All right, I guess."

She roared with laughter. "Oh, my boy, I can't see you ever being a farmer. Your place is here, working with the numbers, exercising that brilliant mind of yours. Planting fields and shoveling shit, those aren't for men like you."

Again, Thomas shrugged. "If I am to be with Isabelle..." His voice drifted off and Thibault reached out for his arm, squeezing it.

"Are there troubles?"

He shook his head. "No, of course not. We still plan to be married, it's just going to be a difficult life, though I'm assured I'll get used to it as I get better at it."

Thibault pursed her lips, regarding the boy and the upper arm she held. "Well, you do seem to have put on a little bit of muscle since I last saw you."

Thomas held up his still scrawny arms. "You must be seeing something I'm not."

She chuckled and tapped next to her eye. "Perhaps it's something only a woman notices."

A tiny face poked out from behind Enzo and she took a step back, startled, before quickly recovering. "And who do we have here?"

Thomas held out a hand toward the young boy. "This is Master Christian. Tanya and I found him on our way to Paris yesterday."

Thibault took a knee. "And you were all alone?"

The boy said nothing.

"Yes, he was alone, hiding in the grass in the ditch. He has quite the story to tell, and frankly, I'm not sure what to do about it."

"Well, perhaps if you tell me the story, we'll figure out what to do together."

"That's what I was hoping as well."

Thibault led them into her office and she sat behind her ornate desk, placed atop a platform that had her higher than anyone else in the room should they be seated in front of her, an intimidation tactic she had learned years ago, made necessary since most of those she dealt with were men raised to assume they were better than any woman no matter her station.

She listened while Thomas related the story as told to him by young Master Christian, the boy clearly uncomfortable and downright terrified at certain portions of the narrative. She took it all with a grain of salt, but as the plot thickened and neither Thomas nor Enzo gave any indication either of them shared her belief this was a tall tale told by a desperate boy, she paid closer attention. And as the details were laid out and she watched the boy from the corner of her eye, she came to the same conclusion Thomas and Enzo must have—no fiction, no matter how elaborate, should terrify its own creator.

This boy was telling the truth as he saw it.

The question was, what *was* the truth? Was Satan truly at play here, or was this a con meant to make simple-minded people cooperate when they normally wouldn't? The boy wanted to go home, but was too afraid to, since of course that's where he believed Satan to be. The tale told was clearly effective with him.

She folded her arms and pursed her lips as she regarded the young boy, fresh tears staining his cheeks. "Did Thomas tell the story correctly?"

Christian nodded. "Yes, ma'am."

She believed the boy, though wasn't certain of his story. Was Satan at play here? She didn't doubt the Devil existed. In her lifetime, she had seen unspeakable evil. If he didn't exist, and God held dominion over everything, then the things she had seen should never have happened. It was clear to her that either God did not hold dominion over everything everywhere at every time, allowing the Devil to practice his wicked ways, or God deliberately left openings for his fallen angel to test mankind. Whatever the reason, she had no doubt not only was Satan real, but his domain did extend into this realm, and if he were indeed at play here, there was no way in Hell she wanted to get involved.

Yet information was power. If she could determine where this cave was, where Satan had made his incursion into Christendom, and who these people were that served him not far from Paris, it might save her from future encounters she couldn't hope to win.

It was time to gather information.

"What's your full name, boy?"

"Christian Roussel."

Roussel Residence

Outside Gien, Kingdom of France

"Woah, that's enough for today." The massive ox came to a halt and Perrot Roussel removed the harness from around his neck. He collapsed in the soil he had tilled for hours, work made all the more difficult with the loss of a second son, his eldest, to Satan and those who served him. Everyone was suffering, but few dared speak of it. While he didn't doubt that the evil one was real and behind all the travails they suffered, he wasn't as convinced as some that he was all-seeing and all-knowing as God was.

Yet there was no denying his power. At least one child was dead—he had witnessed it with his own eyes. Scores from the village and surrounding area had disappeared without warning, and now some parents were even handing over their children in an effort to win back their souls all the more quickly.

What was happening, he had no idea. He was a simple farmer, but from birth he had been taught to be a God-fearing man, to obey the Ten Commandments, to never use the Lord's name in vain, to always be kind. Yet he was just a man who had failed in those efforts on many occasions.

He always confessed his sins as honestly and as earnestly as he could manage, but it obviously hadn't been enough. When he had been taken to the cave for the first time and had heard Lucifer's voice whisper at him through the darkness, it had terrified him to his core.

He couldn't resist.

He didn't dare resist.

The promise he clung to that his children would be returned when his debt was paid was all he could focus on now. The question he dared not ask was, what debt? Whom did he owe? Was it Satan? Did he somehow owe the Devil his due? Or was Satan really a means to an end employed by the Lord to exact a toll for past sins, and when he was punished enough, and the debt paid, his soul and that of his children would be released back into the loving embrace of their Lord and Savior?

"Perrot, where the devil are you?"

Perrot cringed at the choice of words. He recognized the voice. It was his cousin Gilles who lived a day's ride from here. He had given the name to the evil one's servants a month ago in exchange for not paying tribute. It had sickened him and he had thrown up several times that day, before and after giving the name, but he had seen what happened when some form of tribute wasn't paid, and he wasn't willing to have any of his children laid out on the altar, their body sacrificed, their soul condemned.

He rose from the dirt and waved at Gilles, still on his horse, approaching on the road that ran in front of his farm. "Cousin, how was your journey?"

Gilles dismounted then approached with a smile and extended hands. "Tiresome, but worth it now that I've seen your face. It's been too long, cousin." They embraced then Gilles stood back, admiring the freshly tilled field. "You've done a fine job, cousin, but where are the boys? Why aren't they out here helping you?"

Perrot hesitated. He could stop this now, yet could he? He had already given the name. The message had obviously been delivered otherwise his cousin wouldn't be here. And now that he was deep within the dominion undoubtedly controlled by Satan, was there any escape? This question was answered as he spotted two men on horseback, their black robes and hoods unmistakable, blocking the road leading away from the cave. "There is a problem. I need your help."

"Anything, cousin, name it."

He wanted to tell him to run, to save himself, to get away from this evil place, yet it would mean the certain death of one or both of his sons now in the hands of evil. "It's difficult to explain," he finally said, averting his eyes. "It's best to show you." He pointed toward the nearby hills. "It's just down here. Once you see it, you'll understand my problem."

They didn't have far to travel, so they walked Gilles' horse along the road, Gilles happily answering questions about his six sons, all healthy, all at least as old as his Christian. And all of whom could help pay his debt and release his soul and those of his sons from eternal servitude to the dark lord.

They reached the cave and Gilles tied up his horse then followed Perrot through the dark passage and into the chamber.

"What is this place?" asked his cousin, his voice quaking in fear.

Perrot pointed to the center of the chamber. "Stand here."

Gilles did as told, then Satan's voice rumbled through the chamber. "Who dares enter my dominion?"

And Gilles screamed.

Durant Residence

Paris, Kingdom of France

Thomas tossed a chunk of meat on the floor and Tanya attacked it, the mastiff's table manners on par with Enzo's, the only difference was she didn't eat at the table. Thomas had been raised to eat properly, to take one's time, to use one's utensils when appropriate, and Lady Joanne had been teaching them all the niceties of fine dining. Some of his most enjoyable times at the farm were watching her constant scolding of David and Jeremy's eating habits.

They had dragged little out of Christian earlier today, despite Mrs. Thibault's best efforts. It wasn't that the boy was withholding the information, it was that he simply didn't possess it. He knew his name and family name, which could help, since many people didn't have even that, but he had no idea of the name of the village he came from or where it was in relation to Paris. They could, however, narrow it down slightly. The boy was certain he had traveled in the carriage for three days and two nights from the cave to his new prison. He had also escaped during the night, and it was the same day that Thomas had found him, and since he had traveled on foot, it couldn't be far.

There were a few other pieces of information that could help, the existence of the cave one of them. Thomas knew nothing beyond his neighborhood and the route between here and the farm, nor did Enzo and Thibault. They needed somebody familiar with the area, and he could think of only one place to find such a person—the Templar fortress. Unfortunately, it was a place he dared not go. Some there knew him, but he wasn't a Templar. In an emergency involving the Order, he would of course be welcomed and any message he had to pass on received and acted upon. But this involved searching for the home of a child with a story so outrageous, there was little chance the Templars would take it seriously.

Enzo tore at a loaf of bread with his teeth. "You know, I was thinking, could Sir Denys de Montfort help us?"

Thomas' jaw dropped. "I can't believe I didn't think of him! If he could, I'm sure he'd be willing." He turned to the window to see it was pitch black outside and far too late to call upon the nobleman. "In the morning, we'll send him a message. He should have access to resources that might help us identify where Christian is from and where he was taken. There can't be too many estates in that area that are big enough to house an operation of that size. In the meantime, I suggest we all get a good night's sleep, for tomorrow will be a busy day, and even if it isn't, Sir Marcus and Simon are due to arrive tomorrow evening. I'm certain they'll have something to say on this matter."

He rose as did the others, and they cleared the table as Thomas prayed that something tomorrow would break in their favor so he could unburden himself of this unwanted responsibility.

He wasn't prepared to be a father to such a young child.

Charlotte's Residence

Outside Paris, Kingdom of France

His angel hadn't returned since she rushed out of the room, but the nurse had, his bandages changed only moments before, the task horrifically painful. "How does it look?"

"There's no sign of infection yet, but the doctor will be in later to check on you. Is there anything you need?"

"Just water."

"I'll bring water and wine. The wine should help numb the pain. I'll be back in a moment."

The nurse left the room and as he lay face down on the bed, it reminded him of the prostration he had been forced to do several times a day while chanting the oath they had been required to memorize, "Satan is my master, and I pledge my soul to him." The chant repeated in his head, other voices joining in as if those who served Satan were in the room, repeating it along with him. "Satan is my master, and I pledge my soul to him."

Tears flowed and he struggled not to sob, for if his body shook, the pain would be excruciating. The door opened and he squeezed his eyes shut, reaching up to wipe the tears away before they were noticed.

"I have your water and wine."

His heart leaped at his angel's voice. He sniffed. "Thank you, miss."

She placed the tray on a nearby table. "What would you like first?"

"Water, please."

She poured some into a cup then stepped over to the bed, perching on the edge. She leaned in, placing the cup to his lips, and he awkwardly drank it in, some of it dribbling out the corner of his mouth. She put the cup aside and stared at him. "What's this? You're crying?"

"No, I'm not."

She sighed. "There's no shame in tears. If there were, God would never have given us the ability to cry."

"I'm a man. We're not supposed to cry."

"Nonsense. The question is, why are you crying?"

He closed his eyes. She was his savior. He was tired of all the lies. He had to tell her the truth. The tears had nothing to do with the pain—pain he could handle. "I'm ashamed," he finally managed to whisper. A hand gently brushed through his hair, the caring touch harkening memories from when he was a child and his mother used to do the same thing. She had died when he was young and his father shortly after, surely from a broken heart. He and his siblings had been sent to live with an uncle, but the man was horrible to them, merely using them as labor. He had promptly run away, growing up on the streets of Paris, eventually recruited into one of the many gangs that ruled the slums.

"Shame is good. It means you recognize what you did is wrong."

He said nothing, instead losing himself in the distant memories as his angel continued to stroke his hair.

"I too am ashamed. I shouldn't have abandoned you like I did, but the shock of it all, it was too overwhelming. Do you forgive me?"

He opened his eyes. "There's nothing to forgive."

"Then you accept my apology?"

"Of course, though none was necessary."

She held the cup up to his lips again and he drank some more. "Would you like some of the wine now for the pain?"

His eyes widened slightly at the realization he was feeling no pain. He had been so lost in her ministrations he had forgotten all about it, though now that it was brought back to mind, his entire body ached once again. "Yes, please."

She rose, then a moment later a new cup with a fortified wine was placed to his lips, and he was far more careful drinking this, for not only was each sip a delight, he could already imagine the effects he would be enjoying shortly.

She withdrew the cup. "There, that's enough for now. The nurse was bringing you the swill we give the servants, but I replaced it with something that will have a far better effect. You should be feeling that soon." She set the cup aside then resumed stroking his hair. He closed his eyes, forgetting his troubles for a moment as the sweet elixir took effect, a warm glow spreading through his body, the edge taken off enough for him to almost forget what had been done to him and why.

"I have been asking some of the household staff what's going on at the barns, and they either don't know, or they're too scared to tell me. No one will speak of it."

"I suppose that's understandable."

"Yes. I suppose it is, though for a staff member to lie to one of the family is almost unheard of."

"How would you know, miss?"

She paused then giggled. "I suppose you're right, how *would* I know if I'd been lied to? But this is different. This time I know I'm being lied to. They all know something, though I suspect most know little. They've clearly been forbidden to tell me the truth, however. And there's only one person here who would have that power over them."

"Your father?"

"Yes. Obviously, he's involved. After all, this is his estate. And he must be involved willingly, for no one forces my father to do anything, not even the king."

"Satan is powerful, miss. I've seen it with my own eyes. He's forced the best of men to serve him. Terror is a strong motivator."

"Is that why you got involved? Fear?"

He sighed. "I wish it were as simple as that. I'll be honest with you, miss. I'm not a good man. I've lived on the street since I was a boy, picked many pockets, stolen many wares to survive. I've worked for bad people doing bad things. I've always known Hell would be my final destination unless I was somehow saved, and when I was brought to the cave and met Satan, it was fear that compelled me to pledge my allegiance, though there was a certain vested self-interest. I thought perhaps if I served him now, the eternal damnation I faced might be made a little easier."

The hand had withdrawn as he spoke the truth, and for a moment he regretted being so forthcoming, but he found she compelled the truth out of him. He didn't want to lie to her, he wanted her to know everything, he wanted someone to know the truth, the entire truth.

"At what age were you on the streets?"

He was about to shrug when he caught himself. "I'm not sure. Perhaps ten."

"Then you did what you had to do to survive. No child should ever be put in such a position." Her hand reached out, her tiny fingers running through his hair once again. "We're going to get you better and get you a real, honest job. How does that sound?"

He smiled slightly. "It sounds wonderful, miss, but it's all only a dream if I'm still forced to serve at the feet of Satan. He owns my soul until he frees me from my debt."

"And what debt is that?"

He shrugged. "I don't know. I assume I'm being punished for the sins I've committed during my life, and that when my punishment outweighs my crime, I'll be freed from this torment."

"That hardly seems fair. There are men who've done far worse, I'm sure, than anything you've done, and I've never heard of them being forced to serve Satan."

"You don't understand, miss, this is new. He's only recently broken through to our side using a cave outside a small village several days from here. He's recruiting and his numbers are growing rapidly. The work we're doing, we're preparing for something, something big."

"What work are you doing?"

"As more souls are condemned, the tribute being paid continues to grow. More and more items are being brought in. They're being repaired, cleaned, everything designed to increase their value, then they're being taken to markets in various cities then sold."

"How do you know all this?"

"Because I recognized some of the people coming to pick up the wares from my time in Paris in the gangs. A large amount of money is being accumulated and it grows every day. But there's more."

She inhaled sharply, her hand withdrawing its luxurious touch. "What?"

"Cloth is being woven by the children that are held here, all the same pattern, then seamstresses, some of them older children with experience, others adults whose souls have been damned as well, are making uniforms."

Her eyes narrowed. "Uniforms?"

"Yes, for soldiers. And just recently, weapons have begun to arrive.

Swords, daggers, chainmail, shields, helmets. Scores upon scores are stored in one of the new barns that was just completed."

She slumped. "What does it mean?"

"It means, miss, that Satan is building an army your father is destined to lead."

Thibault Residence
Paris, Kingdom of France

Thomas had sent a messenger requesting an audience with Sir Denys de Montfort the moment he had arrived at work. He sat at his desk, updating the books, while Master Christian entertained himself with Enzo, climbing up and down the man as if he were a tree. Mrs. Thibault was in her office with the door closed, her tolerance for the child's giggling expired. He understood it. She was never a mother, rarely exposed to children of this age, and this was, after all, a place of business.

The door opened downstairs and footfalls echoed as someone climbed the steps. He rose to greet them and was delighted to find it was one of Sir Denys' personal guard, decked out in the finest of garb.

"I have a message for Mr. Thomas Durant from my master, Sir Denys de Montfort."

Thomas bowed slightly. "I am Thomas Durant."

A folded paper sealed with wax was handed over and the messenger waited for a response. Thomas cracked the seal and unfolded it, the message indicating Sir Denys would be pleased to meet with him immediately.

Thomas' eyes bulged at the timing.

"I have a carriage waiting downstairs for you, sir, if you're able to make the appointed time."

Thomas raised his finger. "One moment." He walked over to Thibault's door and knocked gently.

"Yes, what is it?"

He opened the door. "A carriage has arrived from Sir Denys. He's agreed to meet me, however, it must be now. May I go?"

She flicked a hand. "Go, go, but leave Enzo here. I have some rather unpleasant characters due shortly and I don't want to be left alone with them."

"Of course not, ma'am, I'll be back as quickly as I can."

"And make sure you take that little imp with you."

"Of course, ma'am." Thomas closed the door and Christian looked up at him.

"What's an imp?"

Thomas exchanged a glance with the messenger. "It's just another word for young man."

"Oh."

The messenger smirked then led the way down the stairs. They stepped into the sunlight and the little boy gasped at the sight of the carriage, as fine as this neighborhood had ever seen, scores of people gathered around, curious as to why it was there. Thibault no doubt would have taken great delight at the spectacle. He glanced over his shoulder and smirked as he caught the woman in the window above, making certain the denizens that were her neighbors associated her with the ostentatious display of wealth.

Thomas and the boy climbed into the carriage and the door was closed. The messenger joined the coachman, and moments later they were underway. Christian had his face poking through the window, taking in all there was to see as the slum turned into increasingly respectful areas of the city. He was absolutely agog when the grand estates along the opposite side of the Seine, where nobility called home while in Paris, most with grand estates spread throughout the kingdom, came into view.

They reached Sir Denys' estate and the gates swung open, letting them up a long drive then into the courtyard. The carriage came to a halt and the door was opened by one of the staff. Thomas stepped down and helped Christian to the ground.

"Mr. Durant, it is a pleasure to see you again." Sir Denys stood at the top of the steps, his arms extended, a broad smile on his face. His new wife, the beautiful Helene, stood beside him with a beaming smile that would take any man's breath away.

"Who is your new friend?" asked Helene.

Thomas put a hand on the top of Christian's head. "This is Master Christian Roussel. It is of him I wish to speak to you."

Denys extended a hand toward the doors. "Then come in, come in. We'll have some food and you'll tell me all about it."

The boy was lost in awe at his surroundings, fascinated at the interior of a nobleman's house. It would have been unlike anything the boy had seen in his lifetime, nor was likely to ever see again. It was everything Thomas could do to get the boy to the table for the meal laid out. Christian finally settled down when he took notice of all the different breads, meats, and cheeses. Even Thomas was excited by what was on offer. Christian's hand darted out toward a bowl at the center of the table. "What's that?"

"Grapes."

His little eyes narrowed. "What are grapes?"

"Try one. Be careful though. There are seeds inside. Just take them and put them on the side of your plate," explained Helene.

Christian snatched one of the small purple orbs then took a bite, his eyes widening as a smile spread. "It's sweet!" Then his nose scrunched up. "And sour."

Everyone laughed and Denys leaned forward. "There are all types of grapes with different kinds of flavors. As you get used to the tartness, the sweetness will prevail."

Christian found a seed and spat it out onto his plate.

Thomas' jaw dropped. "Christian, don't spit at the table!"

The young boy stared at him, his mouth agape, revealing the masticated grape.

"Close your mouth."

Christian's mouth snapped shut.

"Use your fingers to get the seed out of your mouth and place it on the side of the plate. Do *not* spit it out."

Christian nodded and resumed his efforts as Thomas finished telling the story surrounding the young boy.

Denys folded his arms and leaned back, regarding Christian. "And you believe him?"

Thomas shrugged. "I believe he believes it. His reactions when relating the story were simply too emotional not to be real."

"A young boy's imaginings can be terrifying. A young boy's misunderstanding even more."

"You mean that it isn't Satan at all but something else?"

"Exactly. If Satan has indeed taken up residence in a cave not three days from the palace, I'm sure we would have had word of it by now, especially considering your boy here claims to have been missing for weeks if not months. The question is, what is really going on? If it is a satanic incursion into the kingdom, it must be dealt with."

"How? How does one fight Satan?"

Denys shook his head. "I'm not an expert in these matters, but there are those in the clergy who specialize in this. I would seek the Cardinal's counsel, however, that man is corrupt as one can get. The more likely scenario is that Satan has nothing to do with this, and that the boy misinterpreted something or was tricked. That is much easier to deal with."

"Who would deal with such a thing?"

"It depends where it's occurring. The King's Personal Guard would provide guidance, but whatever lord controls the lands where this is occurring would be responsible to raise a force to counter it, requesting assistance from surrounding lords should it be necessary. I think the easiest thing for us to do is to determine which estate he was being held on. That should be fairly easy. Do you remember exactly where you picked him up?"

"Yes, sir."

"Would you be able to identify it on a map?"

Thomas' eyes bulged, his experience with maps limited. "With some assistance, I believe so."

"Then we'll retire to my study and see what we find. If someone is in partnership with the Devil or pretending to be, they must be brought to justice."

Roussel Farm

Outside Gien, Kingdom of France

Perrot's cousin Gilles wept openly, his shoulders shaking with the horror of it all. The once confident man had soiled himself at the sound of Satan's voice, likely having never experienced anything remotely so terrifying. But it was the news that two of his sons had already been taken into the evil one's service and would only be returned if tribute were paid through goods or services, that had cleaved the man's soul hollow.

"How could you do this to my boys?"

Perrot didn't have an answer. None that was acceptable. "I'm so sorry, but I had no choice. I've run out of tribute to pay, and by offering your name and them taking your two sons, it's bought me three months reprieve, and the same is true for you if you provide names, especially names of people who have large numbers of children." His voice cracked. "You'll understand in time. There's no denying him. My neighbor Jeban, they killed his son when he couldn't provide tribute. I saw the body myself. You don't understand how evil Satan is. He's everything described by the priests. And who are we to fight him? We're mere mortals. Only God can fight evil like that."

"Has anybody tried? Has anybody gone to the priests to tell them what's happening?"

"Nobody dares."

"Do you still attend church?"

"No."

"Do any of you?"

"Not that I'm aware of. It's not something that's really spoken of. It just is."

"Then why hasn't the priest noticed that his flock has been shrinking? How long have you said this has been going on?"

"I'm not sure. Over a year."

Gilles rose, wiping his eyes dry and brushing off his knees. "Now that we speak of it, I have noticed attendance has been dwindling at my own church. How far has this spread?"

Perrot held up his hands. "I have no idea. All I know is some of the faces I recognize are not from the village, but from surrounding ones."

"I live a full day's ride away. If it's spread that far, hundreds could be involved. At least. What are we going to do?"

Perrot eyed him. "What do you mean what are we—"

"We have to stop this!"

Perrot sighed, his shoulder slumping. "That's what I thought at first as well. I quickly realized there was nothing I could do. This is Satan. He has the power to see and hear everything. If we stray, he would certainly know. We would be punished."

"But *is* he all-knowing? How can we be certain?"

Perrot shook his head. "We can't, and I'm not willing to risk the lives of my children. Even if there is the remotest of possibilities that it is true, just this conversation could be condemning their souls, and I want no part of it.

I'm sorry for what I did to you, but I had no choice. I'm fighting for the souls of my children and I suggest you do the same. Keep your mouth shut, do what they tell you to do, pay your tribute, and when you no longer can, you will do as I did no matter how horrifying you find the very notion at this moment."

Four men rode by on horseback, all dressed in the dark robes of their new master, a sight growing more common in the area as Satan's grip tightened. A shiver ran up his spine as the story of the four horsemen of the apocalypse came to mind. Was this indeed the end times? Was the final battle between good and evil about to occur? Was this cave outside the village he had grown up in the epicenter of that battle? If this were indeed where it would all begin, God's fury would be unleashed on his home.

And between Him and Satan, nothing would survive.

Good or evil.

En route to Paris, Kingdom of France

"Something occupies your thoughts. Care to share?"

Sir Marcus flinched at his sergeant's gruff voice. "What makes you say that?"

"Well, for one thing, you almost fell out of your saddle just now, and the other is that you've said almost nothing since we left the farm."

Marcus sighed. "My responsibilities continue to grow in areas in which I have no expertise. Give me an army of ten thousand men and I'll be completely comfortable leading it, but a dozen men, women, and children, plus God knows how many animals, and I'm at a loss as to how to handle things."

Simon regarded him. "You do realize you're doing a remarkable job, don't you? Every one of those children adores you and owes their lives to you. And those women all appreciate the sacrifices you've made on their behalf."

"Yes, I suppose that's all true, though if I were better equipped for these matters, perhaps they would all be better off than they are now." He held up a hand, halting Simon's protest. "Yes, I realize they are better off than

67

they would have been, but could things have been even better? I'm a man of war. All of us are. Working a farm and raising children was never to be part of our lives."

"Don't you believe this was always part of God's plan?"

"I suppose it was."

"You suppose? You're wounded in battle, and while you're recovering you receive a letter from your sister asking you to return home because she's ill just when you're no longer fit for battle—"

"I beg to differ there."

Simon chuckled. "At the *time*, you were no longer fit for battle. And don't you dare tell me that shoulder doesn't still bother you."

Marcus rotated the shoulder in question and winced slightly. "I suppose you're right."

"Then I'll continue. The timing was perfect. If you had been healthy, you wouldn't have returned. We arrived shortly after your sister's death, just in time to save your niece and nephew from the orphanage. We arrived just as young Pierre's parents were murdered and were able to provide him a haven. If your brother-in-law hadn't died when he did, Lady Joanne would have been his responsibility. But instead, when she sought refuge with her distant relative, she found you instead, the only man in these parts that could do anything to help her.

"Every one of those people owes their lives to you, and if God hadn't put you where He did, when He did, who knows what would have become of them all. Certainly, Lady Joanne and Beatrice would be dead, as would Madeleine and her niece and nephew. God put us on this earth to protect the innocent, and while our vow to the Order may have been to protect the pilgrims seeking answers in the Holy Land, we can still fulfill it here. If you were a different man, if you were a farmer and a father, most of those now under your protection would be dead. You, sir, are exactly who and what they needed, and God put you there. It's why the squires and I have been loyally by your side, despite our right to reassignment. You know me. If I felt we weren't doing God's work, then I would ask my leave."

His sergeant's words were exactly what he needed to hear, which was surprising considering the man was not known for his eloquence. "Wise words, my friend." He smirked. "I'm stunned they came from you."

Simon snickered. "Perhaps God put me here to provide you with counsel, and in His infinite wisdom knows when to put the words in my mouth that this old simple brain is unable to come up with on its own."

Marcus chuckled. "My friend, that old simple brain of yours deserves far more credit than you're willing to give it. And perhaps you're right, perhaps God did put both of us exactly where He needed me to be for the women and children, and you to be when my faith faltered."

"Perhaps so. But can I be honest with you?"

"Always."

"When I asked what was on your mind, I honestly thought you were going to say you missed Tanya, and that was why you were so glum."

Marcus tossed his head back, laughing hard with the realization that was indeed one of the reasons. The beast had grown on him and he found he now missed her company.

Simon hopped out of his saddle and picked up a stick from the side of the road and held it out. "If you miss her that much, perhaps we can play fetch."

Marcus roared, holding his stomach as his sergeant returned to his saddle. Marcus reached out and clasped his friend's shoulder. "Brother, I thank God every day that He put us together. You are the brother I always wanted, that every man wants, yet so few find. It is an honor to serve God with you at my side, even if it is to be spent on a farm, surrounded by women and children, rather than our brothers-in-arms battling Saracens. And don't worry, I would never ask you to play fetch with me."

Simon cocked an eye. "What about Jeremy?"

"Oh, him I'd order to in a heartbeat."

Charlotte's Residence

Outside Paris, Kingdom of France

Charlotte sat in her rocking chair, one of the house cats in her lap, purring away as she gently stroked her. She was troubled, deeply troubled. What Bouvet had told her was shocking if it were true. Satan was raising an army, for what purpose she could only imagine, but it was the fact her father appeared to be involved that was most troubling. She hadn't seen the man in almost two years, and even before she had left with her mother to attend school, the two of them had never been very close.

Her father was always working, always in Paris at the King's Court, and whenever at home, forever in a foul mood, cursing the king or some other nobleman for their stupidity or ignorance. She had always marveled at the things he dared say about the king, things she couldn't imagine him repeating in public.

Her mother, a cousin of the king, had always argued with him whenever he spoke ill of her relation. Over the past several years, most of their interactions had become heated. When they were in Bologna, it was the happiest she had seen her mother in a long time, and even while her mother

71

was dying, she had the sense her mother was relieved to be far from her father.

Her own relationship with her father had her uncertain as to what to do. She had questions that needed answers, and she could think of no one else but him that could answer them. Yet if she confronted him, and he were indeed involved in something nefarious, or worse was under the command of Satan, what answers could she expect?

She rose and the cat hopped from her lap. She peered out her window, her chest tight. She could see the cluster of structures from her window, though barely. A row of trees had been transplanted, already the height of a man, and within a few years would block any view from the house.

She gasped. This wasn't some short-term plan. Whatever was going on, was going on for the long term. Her father was definitely involved. The question was whether it was voluntary, or had the Devil indeed enslaved him, forcing him to do whatever it was he was doing? She had to find out, but how? She couldn't simply ask him, for any answer he gave would be a lie. She couldn't trust any of the staff—they were already lying to her, and she couldn't let them know of her suspicions.

How can one know when one's father's soul has been corrupted by the greatest evil of all time?

She returned to her chair and resumed her rocking. Who in her life did she trust who might help? She had friends among the other families in the area, but as she thought about it, she realized most of their fathers were friends with hers. There was a distinct possibility they were all involved in whatever he was.

She squeezed her eyes shut as her shoulders rolled inward and shook. She was all alone in this, perhaps fighting the Devil himself. "God, please help me. Please help my father."

And a smile spread as she realized who could help save her father's soul.

De Montfort Estate
Paris, Kingdom of France

Thomas stood as Sir Denys unrolled a large map, entire swaths of it marked in different colors and patterns of lines, the majority of it a light blue with Paris inscribed in large letters in the center. Denys weighed down the corners with small ornamental blocks, obviously meant for this purpose, then placed his splayed fingers in the center. "Now, obviously this is the city." He lifted his hand and swirled his finger around the rest of the map. "These are all the areas within several days' ride, each marked to indicate who owns the land or who has been granted dominion over it by the authority of the king. Now, you came in from Crécy-la-Chapelle, correct?"

"Yes, sir."

Denys traced his finger along a road then came to a stop, tapping it. "Here is Crécy-la-Chapelle. This is the road you would have come in on. How far into your journey was it that you discovered the boy?"

"Roughly halfway."

Denys' finger slid up the road and came to a halt. "So, around here?"

Thomas shrugged. "I believe so, but I can't be certain."

"Had you made it to Serris yet?"

Thomas' eyes widened slightly. "Yes, actually, we had just passed through, perhaps an hour before."

Denys repositioned his finger. "That would put you around here." He frowned and Thomas understood why. Half a dozen different colors and line-patterns surrounded the tip of Denys' finger. "There are a lot of possibilities here. These are the summer estates of some prominent families, none of whom I would call a friend."

Thomas regarded the nobleman. "May I ask why?"

Denys tapped his finger. "The king may be all-powerful, but he does have his rivals, and this group I would call a hotbed of discontent, constantly challenging his decisions, constantly criticizing him outside of the Court. If something nefarious was going on, it wouldn't surprise me if it were happening in this area. But that's political intrigue, not slave labor, not satanic worship. These are all decent people with different political beliefs. I know them all. I serve with them all in the Court, and I refuse to believe any of them would renounce their faith and serve the Devil."

"Perhaps they didn't have a choice?"

"Perhaps. And if they do indeed worship the Devil, that's the only way I could see this being possible. It's what the boy described that's happening on the estate that I simply can't reconcile. Holding children prisoner, forcing them to work, day in and day out. It simply makes no sense. These are all wealthy men, wealthy families. Why would they do such a thing?"

"Perhaps it's not for personal gain."

Denys regarded Thomas. "What do you mean?"

"I mean, if they are serving the Devil, then they could be doing it purely to be evil. Perhaps Satan thrives on pain and suffering, especially of children, so that's why they're doing it."

Denys stood straight, pulling at his beard as he thought for a moment.

"It's a terrifying notion that you posit, but it is as good an explanation as any."

"What do we do?"

Denys frowned as he folded his arms, staring at the map. "We can't directly challenge any of the families in this area. They're too powerful. What we need is proof. Right now, we only have the word of a child. He could be misinterpreting what he saw. He could be lying. What we need is proof, and the best proof is witnessed by one's own eyes."

Thomas tensed. "What are you suggesting?"

Denys jabbed his finger in the center of the suspect properties. "We need to find the barns that Master Christian referred to."

St. John's Church

Outside Paris, Kingdom of France

Charlotte exhaled heavily as she closed the doors to the church and pressed her back against them. Getting here wasn't easy as a woman, especially a woman of station. Women from families like hers didn't attend church outside of regular functions. She never missed a Sunday unless she was ill, but today was not Sunday and young daughters of powerful men like her father were not expected.

She stepped inside and breathed a sigh of relief to find it was empty. She was certain no one had seen her come in, and should God will it, no one beyond the priest would ever know she was here. The question was whether the priest would tell her father. She couldn't see it if he believed what she was about to tell him. But then again, she wasn't sure she believed it herself.

"Charlotte, is that you?"

Her heart leaped into her throat at the voice from her left, and she spun toward it as her hand darted to her chest. "Father François, you startled me."

The old man laughed. "And you startled me. I rarely have anyone bless me with their presence on this day, at this hour. How may I be of service?"

76

"I need advice, Father. I need to speak to somebody I can trust."

"You know you can speak to me of anything, child. Is this something you need to confess?"

She was about to say no when she caught herself. She had always been taught that anything said in the confessional could never be repeated. She wasn't certain whether priests, or more specifically Father François, adhered to that vow, but anything she told him outside of the confessional he could repeat without breaking any promise made to God. Though perhaps it *was* confessional worthy. She was, after all, questioning her father's integrity. Was that not a sin?

She nodded. "At least in part, Father."

Father François led her to the confessional and after the formalities, she began the most difficult discussion she had ever had. "As you know, Father, I've been away for a couple of years in Bologna, and that I've just now returned after my mother's death."

"Yes, my child, I prayed for her soul when I received word. Your mother was a good woman and I have no doubt she sits at our Lord's side in Heaven, looking down upon you and giving you strength to triumph over whatever it is that troubles you this day."

Charlotte smiled and inhaled deeply, drawing strength from his words and the thought of her mother smiling down on her. "Thank you, Father." She sighed. "Father, a lot has changed since I was gone, and something happened that has me scared and confused, and I don't know who I can speak of it to."

"You can't speak to your father?"

"No."

"And why is that?"

"I fear he may be involved. I fear…" Her voice cracked and tears flowed. "I fear he may have lost his soul to the Devil." She swore Father François had gasped, but she couldn't be certain over her own sobs.

"Explain to me why you think such a thing."

"Have you been to the estate lately, Father?" She could see François' head shake through the partition.

"Not recently. In fact, only once, when I received word of your mother, I paid my respects and we prayed together. That was the only time in over a year."

"But you used to be a regular guest!"

"True, but that was due more to your mother than your father. Though to be honest, invitations to most of the homes in this area are becoming fewer."

She tensed. Before she had left for Bologna, one never missed church, and each family in the area took it upon themselves to make certain the local priest always had a friendly table for dinner. "Are you saying you eat alone?"

"On most nights now, yes."

"Well, that is perhaps a good thing."

"Perhaps. Things are tense in the kingdom, and I believe many people fear inadvertently saying something that might reveal their position. And as you know, it is a sin to challenge the king. He holds his position by the grace of God."

She wanted to ask more but she was getting off track. "I'm sorry to hear that, Father, but when you were visiting, did you notice the new construction?"

"No, I did not."

"At the rear of the estate, we had several barns and now there are several more. I heard someone scream a horrible blood-curdling scream from there the day after I returned. I was concerned, so I went to investigate and I found a man who had suffered twenty lashes according to his friend. I had him brought to the house and I've had him tended to. He's told me a horrifying story about what's taking place."

"Remember, child, a punished man who does not accept responsibility for his crimes will often come up with the most outlandish of stories for anyone willing to listen."

She paused. The words were wise, though did they need to be said before the story was told? Was he attempting to discourage her from telling her story, or discredit it before it was even told? Was he indicating he wouldn't believe what she was going to say, or that he already knew? She was uncertain as to what to do.

"Tell me this story, child. What did this man say that has you so troubled?"

If she told him and he didn't believe her, or he already knew and didn't care, would he honor the sanctity of the confessional, or would he go to her father and tell him what she knew? She couldn't risk it. She forced a laugh. "You know, Father, you're right. This man would say anything to make himself appear innocent, to make me think he had been unjustly punished so that he could gain my sympathy. I provided him with a nurse and a doctor, as well as food and drink, because he's made me feel guilty, when it's all just nonsense." She made the sign of the cross. "Thank you, Father. I don't believe I need confession. You've restored my faith in my father and I will no longer listen to the lies of a guilty man." She rose and pushed through the curtain.

"My child, wait!"

But she ignored him and instead hurried out the doors and into the sunlight, more disturbed now than when she entered. If she couldn't talk to Father François nor her own father, who could she possibly seek help from?

She was alone in this.

Approaching the Summer Estates, Kingdom of France

They made quite the motley crew. It had been decided that heading to the country in Sir Denys' carriage might prove too conspicuous. Instead, Thomas had returned to his work and updated Mrs. Thibault, and it was decided that they would use her carriage. It was luxurious, bore no family coat of arms, and if spotted, couldn't be identified.

Her one condition was that she come with them.

He wasn't certain why, though he had no doubt it was for some selfish reason. Perhaps she was curious to see if Satan were indeed involved, and if he were, take the opportunity to introduce herself to her future overlord, for he couldn't believe a few recent good deeds could undo all the harm she had done for years. Whatever the reason, her being here meant Enzo was here. And that could only be a good thing, for Denys was traveling with them without his personal guard, which meant Enzo was their only defense.

Young Christian, of course, was with them, but they had left Tanya at home. She might be good in a fight, though if they found themselves in one, there would likely be no surviving it. They were here to gather intelligence, as Denys had described it, and a loud dog could prove problematic. They needed to determine if any of the boy's story was true, and the only way to do that was to find where he had been held prisoner. The boy had been in a panic as he made his escape, so details were few. All he could remember was running through the dark until he reached a road, then following a ditch, only leaving it to cross other roads. He recalled at least one time he had switched directions following another road.

As Denys had pressed him for more details, it quickly became evident the boy didn't know his left from his right, and the progress they thought they had been making in determining where he had come from was erased. The one thing of use, however, that Christian was certain of, was that he had escaped during the night and had been found by Tanya the next day—he hadn't spent another night hiding in the grass. It narrowed down their search area dramatically, and with all the estates accessible by road, they should cover them today.

Denys pointed ahead and to the right. "We're coming up on Lord Audibert's estate. He's quite influential in the Court, though he has been known to disagree with the king from time to time. He's certainly not in the king's good books, however he's too powerful to ignore and definitely too powerful to dismiss." He pointed at the large property surrounded by a fence made of stone. "Does this look familiar, Master Christian?"

The boy shrugged. "I don't know."

Thibault frowned at him and pointed at the substantial fence. "Do you remember having to climb that?"

The boy's eyes bulged. "No. No, I don't remember climbing *anything* like that."

"Did you squeeze through the bars of any fence?"

"No. No, I didn't."

"Well then, it can't be this one, can it?"

Christian shrugged again. "I suppose not."

"That's good." Denys crossed it off the map as they continued forward to the next property. The carriage kept a leisurely pace and didn't slow so as to not raise suspicions. The next property was smaller with a similar fence and it was dismissed for the same reason as the first. It was the third property that held potential.

Thomas excitedly pointed. "Look, no fence!" As they neared the property, putting the fence of the neighboring estate behind them, he realized he was mistaken. There was a gate and a long drive leading up to a massive estate, a fence surrounding it, though not the entire property.

"Why would they do that?" asked Enzo.

Denys was quick with an answer. "Expense. This is Lord Archambaud's property. It's massive. To fence in the grounds would cost a fortune and would serve little purpose out here. Do you recognize this, Master Christian?"

Christian stared out the window and shook his head. "No. But I never really saw the house, or at least I don't think I did. I just remember running."

Thomas peered out the window. "I don't see any barns."

"Neither do I." Thibault pointed. "But see how the ground rises and the home sits at the highest point? We don't know what lies beyond that."

"Then what do we do?" asked Enzo. "How are we to know?"

"Perhaps we can't be certain," replied Denys. "But for now, we're here to eliminate possibilities. This one, we'll have to keep on the list."

The rest of the afternoon remained uneventful and they eliminated all but three properties as possible locations for where Christian and the others had been held.

Thibault wasn't pleased. "Well, that was a waste of time."

Denys regarded her. "Actually, I think it was a great success. We now have three possibilities instead of over a dozen."

She dismissed his positive attitude with a bat of her hand. "Three possibilities, none of which prove the boy is telling the truth."

Christian stared at the floor, his hands clasping and unclasping in front of him, and Enzo placed a massive paw on his back, stroking it.

"We've also found nothing to contradict the story," added Denys. "And I, for one, believe that we have actually identified the location."

Thomas stared at him. "Which one?"

Denys tapped the map, indicating the largest estate. "Lord Archambaud's. It's one of only three without a fence, we couldn't see the rear of the property, and of the three, he's the biggest pain in the king's backside. He's very outspoken, and very powerful."

Thibault frowned. "But what does any of this even mean? What does holding a bunch of children captive and making them clean up trinkets have to do with a rivalry with the king?"

"If I had to hazard a guess, he's gathering funds to raise an army."

"That's one hell of an accusation."

Denys threw up his hands. "Frankly, Mrs. Thibault, I have no idea what's going on here. None of it makes sense. Children being kidnapped, forced to work, murdered if they disobey, forced to pray to Satan, told that if they didn't work their parents' souls would be lost forever. Does any of this sound rational to you? If it's all true, then something truly wicked is occurring in the kingdom, and it's our duty as good Christians to put an end to it."

Thibault grunted. "I don't think I've ever once been called a good Christian."

Thomas suppressed a smile and Enzo outright laughed.

"If something's going on," said Denys, "we need to determine what it is and whether it needs to be stopped. The first step is the easiest. Find where this boy was held. If that place exists and other children are still held there, then we must believe his entire story is true."

Thomas shivered. "You mean that Satan is indeed behind this?"

Denys frowned. "If we are to believe the boy, then yes."

Enclos du Temple, Templar Fortress
Paris, Kingdom of France

Marcus rode through the gates of the massive Templar Fortress, the impressive complex a display of the Order's wealth and power, wealth and power that rivaled that of any king including King Philip IV of France, who owed the Order a substantial amount of money after his campaigns in the north. Every time Marcus passed through these gates, he felt at peace, he felt at home, something he had only experienced in the Holy Land surrounded by his brothers, and was only beginning to feel at the farm. He wondered if he'd ever completely embrace his new home, as he did any Templar establishment, even if never visited before. In time, perhaps, yet this had been his life for so long, it was hard to imagine the simple, quiet life of a farmer ever bringing him the comfort and excitement brought by the sight of the members of the Order in full regalia on horseback, running drills, or simply going about their business.

"Now *this* I miss," said Simon as they stopped to take it all in.

Marcus agreed. "It is a sight to behold, is it not?"

Simon pointed as a stableboy rushed forward to clean up a recently deposited gift from one of the horses. "And see, look at that. The only shit in sight tended to by a boy rather than a man."

Marcus chuckled. "It really is an obsession with you, isn't it?"

Simon shrugged. "As it should be. What man in his right mind would want to shovel shit, day in and day out?"

Marcus urged his horse forward at a slow gait. They came to a stop at the entrance to the headquarters of the Templar Order in France. They both dismounted and a stableboy Marcus recognized, Quentin, rushed up to them. Marcus smiled at the child. "Master Quentin, it's good to see you are well."

"And you too, Sir Marcus, Sergeant Simon. How may I be of service today?"

"Two fresh horses and supplies for two days."

"Will you be staying at the fortress?"

"No, we'll be staying at Thomas Durant's overnight, then returning to Crécy-la-Chapelle tomorrow."

Simon grunted. "Unless we get lucky."

Quentin's eyes narrowed. "Lucky?"

Marcus gave Simon a look. "Ignore my sergeant. He's simply less than eager to return to the farm and shovel shit."

Young Quentin shrugged. "You get used to it after a while. Now, I don't even smell it."

Simon put an arm around the boy and faced Marcus. "Can we keep him?"

Marcus laughed. "Then who'd tend to his duties here?" He slapped Simon on the shoulder. "Perhaps you should do as young Master Quentin has done and embrace the job rather than protest it. In time, you too may learn to ignore the smell."

Simon grunted. "I doubt that's even possible for a man my age with such a discerning nose. It can pick out a Saracen from a Christian in the deserts of the Holy Land."

Marcus snorted. "While you *were* famous for making your guesses, you were wrong as often as you were right."

Simon's jaw dropped. "I challenge that claim!"

Marcus laughed. "We'll see what David and Jeremy have to say about it when we get home."

Simon spat. "Those two always take your side."

Marcus grinned. "That's because I'm always right." He headed for the doors before Simon could respond. He stepped inside to find the desk sergeant manning his post as Marcus had imagined he might himself, someday, when he was too old to wield a sword. He had always assumed he would die on the battlefield, but if he did manage to survive, he would have been honored to live out his days in some administrative position, worthy of the respect his service was due.

Now, it was more likely he'd die shoveling the shit that Simon hated. He just prayed when he took his final breath, it wasn't after he had collapsed in a pile of what he was shoveling.

"Sir Marcus, a word?"

Marcus turned to see Sir Matthew Norris, head of the Order in the Kingdom of France, beckoning him. Marcus headed toward the man with Simon on his heels. "Sir Matthew, it is good to see you are well."

"Likewise, Sir Marcus. Come with me. There's something we must discuss."

Marcus extended a hand toward Simon to ask if he could accompany them, but Matthew beat him to the punch. "Bring your sergeant. This will concern him as well."

They followed Matthew to his office and Simon closed the door as Matthew took a seat behind his desk. Marcus sat in front of him and Simon took up a position at the door.

"As I'm sure you're aware, we've suffered losses in the Holy Land, and I've been forced to send much of the garrison to reinforce our positions. It leaves me short on experienced leaders like yourself."

Marcus leaned forward with anticipation. "Sir, if you require my service, you have it."

Matthew smiled. "I never doubted it. We have an odd situation. We're not sure what's going on, but we've lost communication with one of our outposts two days from here, and the last two messengers we've sent have been refused passage by the locals. Now, we've had situations in the past where there's been some misunderstanding or a perceived offense that have riled up the locals, so I'm sure it's a simple matter. There's no point in sending another messenger, so a contingent must be sent to investigate. Would you care to lead it?"

Marcus smiled. "I'd be delighted. I assume my sergeant is to accompany me?"

"Yes, you will command the mission. Your sergeant will be the chief. You'll be leading ten men in addition to yourself and your sergeant, all I can spare at the moment, though it should be more than enough for anything you may encounter."

"And when do we depart?"

"As soon as possible."

"Very well." Marcus turned in his chair toward Simon. "Sergeant, make the preparations."

Simon bowed. "Yes, sir." He left the room and Marcus turned back to Matthew.

"If I may have an hour, I'd like to update Thomas Durant as he's expecting us to stay tonight at his residence."

"Of course." Matthew rose, as did Marcus. The fortress commander extended an arm and Marcus clasped it. "Good luck, Sir Marcus. Find out what's going on with our outpost, and either deal with the problem, or send back word if additional forces are required."

"You can count on us."

Roussel Residence

Outside Gien, Kingdom of France

Perrot sat at the dinner table, sullen. His cousin Gilles had already left, refusing to speak to him again, and he didn't blame him. What he had done to his poor cousin was unforgivable, but he had no choice. He was battling for the souls of his children, for his family, for himself. Satan held dominion here, the vast majority of the town already converted. Those who hadn't yet been were well aware that something evil had taken over and were hiding in their homes, some holding vigil in the church.

The satanic soldiers now freely roamed in their black robes, and he had heard tell that they had taken over the town of Montargis, the largest in the area, and a key trading location for anyone with goods to barter. When he had sold his cow there last week, underpriced, he had seen dark-robed figures around the town, but to hear that such a place with at least a thousand souls living there now belonged to Satan was terrifying.

His dominion was spreading like a plague, but what Perrot couldn't understand was why God wasn't taking action. Why was God letting this happen, letting this evil spread, allowing the kidnappings, the murders? He could only assume it was because they had sinned in some way and this was their punishment, but how far was this punishment to spread? Throughout the region? The kingdom? Christendom? The world? How far was enough, or was this indeed Armageddon, beginning here in his small village?

If these were the end times, then perhaps God wouldn't come to their rescue. Instead, He would sit back and see how people like him reacted and choose who deserved entry to Heaven and who merited eternal damnation. And with what he had done to his cousin, there was no doubt as to where he was destined to spend eternity.

He grasped at his temples, squeezing hard as he shut his eyes.

"What's wrong, Husband?"

He sighed, staring at his wife Marie. "I don't know what to do about what's going on, about what we're being forced to do."

She hissed. "It's forbidden to speak of it. He'll know."

He sat up straight, regarding his wife sitting across from him at the table. "Does it really matter?"

"What do you mean?"

"I mean, we're all condemned to Hell no matter what we say or do. The more I think about it, the more convinced I am there is no saving our souls, no matter how hard we work, no matter how much we sacrifice. This has been going on for over a year. Have you ever heard of a single person gaining their freedom? Look at our village. It is filling with men not from around here. How many farms now have camps on them? And when will we be asked to provide for this growing army?"

"Army?"

"If not an army, then what? Their men all dress the same, they all carry swords or lances. They're clearly an army, and they're *his* army. And things are getting worse every day. The longer we participate in this, the more condemned our souls become."

"What are you suggesting?" she whispered, her voice quavering, the terror this conversation was bringing her evident.

"We need to leave while we still can."

She gasped. "Leave? Leave our home, our farm, everything we have? Where would we go?"

"I don't know. As far away from here as possible. Far enough to where the evil hasn't spread."

"But how would we survive?"

He threw up his hands. "How can we survive here? The tribute grows more difficult to pay with every week that passes. God forgive me, but I just delivered my cousin into their hands, and they've already taken two of his sons. We can't go on like this. Even if there's no way to save our souls, what right do we have to condemn others? This has to stop. Surely you must agree?"

She burst into tears and covered her face with her hands. "Yes, I know, but I'm scared."

"I'm scared as well. But we have no choice. And if we're going to do this, we have to do it now."

She removed her hands from her face and stared at him, her eyes wide. "You mean leave now?"

"Yes, it has to be done under cover of night. We'll pack what we need for the journey in the cart, and take several of the chickens and one of the milking cows. The animals will provide for us, and if anyone stops us, we'll tell them we're heading to the market to sell the cow in order to pay tribute next week, and we wanted to get there early because the prices are always better in the morning as opposed to the end of the day."

"Do you think they'll believe it?"

He shrugged. "If they don't, then so be it. We're condemned already. At worst, our eternal damnation is hastened, but perhaps if we take this small action now, God will forgive us for what we've done." He rose and rounded the table, extending his hand to her. "Shall we risk it all and perhaps save our souls?"

She took his hand and rose, her eyes filled with tears, her face with fear, yet she drew a deep breath, struggling to fill herself with courage, then nodded. "I stand with you, Husband."

Approaching Durant Residence
Paris, Kingdom of France

Marcus rode through the slums of Paris, memories of the Holy Land springing to life. Paris was quite different from Acre, but it had its similarities. The smells and sounds were unique in their own ways, but it was the bustle of activity that he reveled in. For decades he had lived in tight quarters with his brothers, within cities teeming with residents and pilgrims. The laughter, the arguments, the bartering, the shouts of passion and pain.

It was life, it was humanity, it was God's creation in all its glory and all its shame.

He missed it.

Life on the farm was too simple, too good. He missed the range of human activity that a city like this provided. It had him wondering if there was some way he could bring those on the farm into the city, but it wasn't an option. The farm was what made everything possible. They grew food that fed everyone and could be used to barter for whatever else was necessary in the city. The only way to survive was to work, and as Templars, they couldn't.

Unfortunately, if he were to continue to honor the vow he made to his late sister, the farm was the only option. The special dispensation granted by Sir Matthew allowing them to remain members of the Templar Order had made things far more tolerable than if they had been forced to leave the brotherhood entirely.

He was looking forward to commanding the mission to investigate what had happened with their outpost. While he expected little to no action, it would still be a thrill to command a dozen men on a mission that would likely last a week including travel. It was unfortunate the farm couldn't spare David and Jeremy, for they would certainly relish the opportunity to participate.

He spotted Thomas' home just ahead and his eyes narrowed slightly at the sight of a carriage in front. A conveyance such as this was rare in these parts, and rarer still at a humble home such as the Durant family's. The coachman stood tending to the horses, though he bore no family coat of arms, nor did the carriage. It was odd. From experience, most who could afford such a luxury were eager to display their family coat of arms. This carriage either belonged to a nobleman hoping to travel incognito, or someone with no family name that had attained their wealth through perhaps nefarious means.

He smirked as a thought occurred to him, and he tested his theory. "Is Mrs. Thibault inside?"

The coachman confirmed his suspicions. "Yes, sir."

"Thank you." Marcus tied up his horse then rapped on the door. It opened a moment later, the massive bulk of Enzo blocking any view of who else was inside.

"Sir Marcus, we weren't expecting you so early." Enzo stepped aside and Marcus entered, finding Thibault sitting at the table with Thomas and a young boy, but more surprisingly, Sir Denys, who rose to greet him.

Tanya bolted into the room from the back of the house and Marcus greeted her then ordered her to sit. He bowed. "Sir Denys, an unexpected pleasure."

Denys returned a respectful bow, chuckling at Tanya's display. "For I as well. I had hoped to see you before I took my leave of these good people. I didn't expect to be so fortunate, however."

Thomas indicated a chair. "Can I get you anything?"

Marcus took a seat. "No, I only have a few moments. I'm just here to tell you that Simon and I have been assigned a mission and will be leaving shortly, perhaps for a week."

Denys returned to his seat. "A mission within the kingdom? Am I allowed to inquire as to its nature?"

Marcus grunted. "Nothing exciting, I'm sure. We've lost contact with one of our outposts a couple of days out of the city, and two messengers that were sent out to investigate have been turned away by locals. I'm leading a small contingent to find out what's happened." He scratched Tanya behind the ears.

"Does this happen often?" asked Thomas.

"On occasion. Usually, it involves some sort of misunderstanding that's easily resolved. I suspect that the moment we show up, the few troublemakers will disband, a discussion with the local leaders will take place, and things will quickly return to normal. It's four days travel there and back, and I suspect we'll be there a day or two at most, but don't be surprised if we're not back for a couple of weeks. If you need to reach me, go to the fortress and they'll send a message through the network."

"And where is this outpost?"

"A town called Montargis."

Denys shook his head. "I don't believe I've ever heard of it."

Marcus grunted. "Well, I can guarantee you I've never heard of it."

"Well, I've heard of it," said Thibault. "It's a small town, nothing remarkable, surrounded by farming communities. Most of the crops and livestock for the area go through there."

"Is it known for its criminal activity?"

She shook her head. "Not particularly, though all trading hubs do have their scoundrels since money is involved."

"That's unfortunate," said Denys. "Perhaps one of your fellow knights took exception to something he saw and this provoked a reaction."

Marcus nodded. "That's what I suspect. A small show of force should be enough to handle it. I suspect no swords will be drawn." He waved a hand at Thibault and Denys. "I'm sorry, but I have to ask, what brings the two of you here together?"

Thibault cackled. "We're hunting Satan."

Marcus' eyebrows shot up. "Excuse me?"

Thomas shifted in his chair. "Perhaps I should explain."

The explanation was fantastic, almost ridiculous, but the fact everyone in this room, all people he respected to varying degrees, appeared to believe the boy's story, or at least part of it, lent it some credibility. "So, you've found these three properties that might be the location of this child's prison. What do you now intend to do about it?"

Denys frowned. "I'm not certain. If I had an ally in the area, I would take advantage, but unfortunately I don't. This entire cluster of nobles are part of a circle I have never been welcomed into nor wished to be."

Marcus tapped the map that had been brought out. "You said this is the most likely one?"

"Yes."

"And it had no fence surrounding the entire property?"

"No. Master Christian said he escaped the barn and never had to climb a fence."

Marcus regarded the boy sitting in Enzo's lap, his eyes wide with the hope that the Templar Knight would believe him.

"Well, obviously you have to confirm the boy's story. If children are indeed being kidnapped, held prisoner, and forced to work, that's a crime that cannot go unpunished. But if those involved get suspicious because you begin asking questions, they could move the children or merely kill them, as they apparently have no compunctions about murdering a young child."

"Then what do you suggest?" asked Denys.

"Someone needs to go in at night on a reconnaissance mission, and none of you are trained for such a thing. Sir Denys, I have no doubt you could accomplish it, however, if you were caught, it would compromise your position in the Court. And Enzo, you're simply too big. They'd spot you from a mile away."

Thomas held up his hand. "Don't look at me, you know I'm not your man."

Marcus laughed. "With proper training, you could be, but there's no time for that. I'll have a message sent to David and Jeremy. They're trained for this, and should be able to determine quite quickly whether the boy's story is true."

"But what about Satan?" asked Thomas. "What if what the boy says is true?"

"Then God will protect us."

Thibault frowned. "God never protected this boy."

Marcus put a hand on Thomas' shoulder. "If that were true, then He never would have delivered him into Thomas' hands."

De Rancourt Family Farm

Crécy-la-Chapelle, Kingdom of France

"I have a message for the Squire David of the Templar Order!"

David's eyebrows rose as everyone at the newly enlarged table twisted toward the door. He rose, as did Jeremy, then opened the door and peered into the dusk to see a Templar messenger dismounting.

"Are you the Squire David?"

David bowed slightly. "I am."

"I have a message from Sir Marcus de Rancourt."

David stepped forward and took the folded paper from the messenger. He cracked the Templar wax seal and unfolded the page, squinting at the message in the dim light. His reading and writing skills had improved dramatically with Lady Joanne insisting everyone on the farm master what she claimed were essential skills. He was quickly realizing they indeed were.

"What's it say?" asked Jeremy.

"Something is afoot outside of Paris, and we're needed for a reconnaissance mission. Thomas has all the details, but we're to leave in time to execute the mission tomorrow night."

Jeremy grinned. "Finally, some excitement. Does it say what it involves?"

"No, which suggests to me it's of a sensitive nature and Sir Marcus didn't want to risk it being intercepted. Thomas has all the details."

Jeremy turned toward the fields. "What about the farm?"

"We'll let Isabelle know. She and her father can arrange volunteers from the village while we're gone."

"How long do you think we'll be away?"

"Yes. How long will you be abandoning us for?"

David flinched at Lady Joanne's voice, turning to see her standing in the door, her hands on her hips.

"Well?"

He shrugged. "A few days at least." He held up the page. "There are few details here. Thomas is to provide them, but we're needed tomorrow night. If that's all, we could be back the following day, but if there's more involved, it could be longer. As soon as I know, I'll send a messenger with details." He turned to Jeremy. "Go let Isabelle and her father know what's going on."

Jeremy's eyes darted toward the open door. "But I haven't finished eating."

David gave him a look. "Hunger can wait."

Jeremy groaned. "Fine, I'll let them know. But if anyone touches my plate, I'll take their hand just like the Saracens would."

David chuckled and dismissed the messenger. He returned inside and closed the door before taking his seat after Joanne returned to hers. He handed her the message from Marcus, as there was nothing in it she shouldn't see. She read it then handed it back.

"You failed to mention that he's on a mission himself that could have him away for over a week, when he was due to return tomorrow."

"Yes, milady, I'm sorry. In the excitement of the moment, I forgot to relate all the details. But I'm certain Mr. Leblanc will be able to arrange all

100

the help you need on the farm while we're away. And the crops are already planted, so it should mostly be menial work that the children can assist with." He frowned. "I just wish Tanya were here."

"As much as I hate to say it, I too wish she were here," said Beatrice, never a fan of the massive creature though clearly appreciating the security she provided as a deterrent and a sentry.

"When we reach Paris tomorrow and find out what's going on, we might be able to make arrangements to have Thomas return her here."

Joanne put an end to things with the curt wave of her hand. "Nonsense. We women will take care of everything as we usually do. This is a peaceful place, now that the village has accepted us, and we will be safe. I'll have Isabelle bring one of her dogs over tomorrow to provide us with some warning should someone enter the property at night, but other than that, we'll be fine. Don't worry about us, just send us a message when you know what's going on."

David smiled. "I have no doubt you will be able to manage things far better than Jeremy and me, and that you're correct. You're perfectly safe. If you need us, if there is any emergency, you know where to go to flag down a Templar messenger. He will bring the message to the fortress and they'll know where we are, though I'm sure that won't become necessary."

Joanne agreed. "I'm sure it won't." She reached out and squeezed David's hand. "You two just be careful. Whatever this is, for some reason it sounds dangerous to me. First, Sir Marcus and Simon are sent away on an unexpected mission, and now you two are called upon to investigate something that has Sir Marcus concerned enough that he would have you leave your posts here guarding the children. I have a bad feeling. There's something strange in the air. I don't know what it is, I can't put my finger on it, but I just have a bad sense about everything these days."

David tensed. Joanne was an intelligent, rational woman, not known for hyperbole, and if she was concerned, he should be as well.

En Route to Montargis, Kingdom of France

Marcus led the column of a dozen knights, sergeants, and squires, with spare horses as well as pack horses. He had briefly filled in Sir Matthew on what Thomas and the others had told him, since he had assigned David and Jeremy to a reconnaissance mission and they were technically Templar resources. Mathew had expressed skepticism, of course, though supported the mission and asked that he be updated should anything of concern be found. If a nobleman were indeed involved, the chances of the king taking action were slim.

Fortunately, the Templar Order was not bound by the laws of kings, only those of the Pope and God Himself. And children kidnapped and held as slaves, murdered for no apparent reason, went against all laws. If Satan were indeed involved, it was their sworn duty to fight him at all costs, and expel him from this realm.

He wished he were the one investigating, not David and Jeremy. He had relayed to Simon the story he had been told, and "Bullshit!" was the immediate reply.

Marcus chuckled. "How can you be so certain?"

"The boy is obviously lying. You should hear some of the tales that come from Jacques and Pierre. Little boys lie to cover up their sins, and the bigger the sin, the bigger the lie. This boy must have done something truly horrible to concoct such a story."

Marcus had come to the same conclusion before the story was finished. It was the reaction of the boy and those who had spent time with him that had him believing at least some of it was true. "You might not be so quick to jump to conclusions if you had met the boy and seen the others. For Sir Denys to give up his time, and especially Mrs. Thibault, they must have found at least some of the boy's story believable. If it were merely Thomas and Enzo, I too would likely dismiss it out of hand, but Sir Denys and Mrs. Thibault are aware of how the world works."

"But Satan? You really believe Satan is behind this?"

"Perhaps in not such a literal way. But remember, Satan is behind all evil, and if children are being kidnapped, forced into slavery and killed, then I can't imagine anything more evil."

Simon chewed his cheek. "It definitely should be looked into. Let's hope those two children don't screw this up."

Marcus regarded him. "Children?"

"David and Jeremy."

Marcus laughed. "Those two children are far older than you were when we met."

"I know, and remember how stupid I was?"

Marcus snorted. "No, I suppose you weren't the sharpest tool in the shed." He became serious as they turned onto the road that would take them south and toward their ultimate destination. "The frustrating part of this is we're passing right by the estates in question."

Simon turned in his saddle. "Is there time for us to take a look?"

Marcus firmly dismissed the idea. "Absolutely not. We have our orders.

104

David and Jeremy will receive the message this evening if they haven't already, and will be in position tomorrow night to see what's going on. If they find anything, they're to inform Sir Matthew and he will take appropriate action. When we finish this mission, whatever is transpiring at those estates will hopefully have already been dealt with."

"And if it is Satan?"

"Then we'll fight him too, and with God on our side, we'll win."

Durant Residence
Paris, Kingdom of France

Thomas wasn't certain what had changed, but tonight, he didn't feel safe, even though Tanya was downstairs as well as Enzo. He had a sense the kingdom itself wasn't safe. As the events of the past two days progressed, things became more real. David and Jeremy would be arriving tomorrow afternoon, then they would all be heading to investigate the identified estates for what at best could be a child slavery setup, or worse, a satanic outpost not a day's ride from where the king held reign in the name of God.

Things were becoming too real, and while he wanted to refuse to believe Satan was involved, the longer he lay here in the dark, struggling to fall asleep, the more convinced he became that the dark one was indeed involved, and if he were, how could they possibly hope to prevail? They could all die tomorrow night, and though they were on the side of good, he had no idea if Satan was powerful enough to steal their souls and punish them in Hell for eternity as retribution for interfering in his business. Or would God have the power to intervene and save them from the fallen angel's revenge?

He shuddered then sat up. He climbed out of bed and lit a candle, savoring the comfort the light brought. He sat at the writing desk that had once been his father's, then began to pen a letter to Isabelle, one she would only ever see should he fall to Satan's blade tomorrow night.

Approaching Montargis, Kingdom of France

Perrot dared only bring four days' worth of provisions. Normally, a journey to Montargis would only merit two days', but he would give the excuse that they might stay longer should the prices be too low. Every argument he crafted in his head was based upon tribute, since the only people who would pay them any mind would be the black-robed soldiers. No one else should care about them, and should Satan's growing legion interfere, surely the explanation of increased tribute to their master would get him past any challenge.

They had left the village without incident, which wasn't necessarily a success since they lived on a farm, and the path he had chosen to head directly for Paris meant they didn't have to pass through the small cluster of buildings. But now they were approaching Montargis, an apparent stronghold for Satan's legion. He had no intention of passing through it, instead planning to take the road that went around the town, allowing those who had no business within it to avoid the hustle and bustle it was renowned for during daylight hours.

Dawn was breaking and they were passing the occasional other traveler, and it was clear to him who had and hadn't lost their souls to Satan, for those who had never smiled, and those who hadn't exchanged greetings with aplomb. His two daughters were still asleep in the back, and he had instructed his wife to remain silent unless asked a specific question by anyone they might encounter, and to be merely civil with her pleasantries. Forcing smiles would do them no good. They weren't attempting to trick those who hadn't been enslaved. They had to draw as little attention as they could from the enslavers, and smiles were a sure sign that one's soul hadn't yet been taken.

Marie gasped and he glanced at her. "What is it?"

She jerked her chin forward. "Look."

He raised his head, which he had been keeping low so as to avoid eye contact with anyone. Two men in black robes rode toward them on horseback. "Remember, say nothing unless they ask you a question. We're going to the town to sell the cow so we can pay next week's tribute. You and the children came with me to visit our cousin."

One of the men raised a hand, indicating for them to stop, and Perrot gulped as he pulled back on the reins. He grabbed the brake and hauled up on it.

"Remove your hood," ordered one of the legion, and Perrot complied. "I recognize you. You have a farm just outside of Gien."

"Yes, sir. I do. And I believe I recognize your voice. I am happy to be greeted by one of my master's servants familiar with me."

The man seemed satisfied with the words exchanged so far. "What are you doing here at this hour?"

Perrot motioned to the town at their right. "I've come to sell a cow at the market in order to pay tribute next week."

"At this hour? You must have been traveling all night."

"We were, but I wanted to get to the market early. The prices at the auctions in the morning are always better than the afternoon, and I wanted to get as much as possible so I could pay the most in tribute to our master."

"I'm certain he appreciates your efforts." The man indicated Marie. "And why does your wife travel with you?"

"After we sell the cow, we intend to visit my cousin. He recently pledged his soul to our master, and we wish to aid in the transition."

The other one spoke up, noting the obvious. "If you're here to sell the cow, why are you bypassing the town? You should have turned back there."

Perrot was prepared for this. "No, I have a friend at the north side of the town who always allows me to clean up my livestock before the auction. I didn't want to pass through the town as people were beginning to set up. It would merely delay us."

Both men regarded him for a moment then the one apparently in charge waved his arm. "Move along."

Perrot bowed his head. "Thank you, sir. Satan is my master, and I pledge my soul to him."

His wife echoed the words, as did the two soldiers. Perrot released the brake and flicked the reins. The horse whinnied and they were under way once again. They slowly passed their two challengers, and Perrot dared not look back. The turn he would need to take to head into town was within sight, and if the men now behind them didn't continue on their way soon, he would be forced to make the turn.

Marie began to look back and he hissed at her. "No!"

He continued at a slow pace, giving the men as much time as possible to continue on their journey. As they neared the turn, he risked a shoulder check that could be excused as looking for other riders coming up behind him before he made the turn, and he breathed a sigh of relief when he found the two men were gone. He flicked his reins, passing the turn and Satan's stronghold on Earth, then rehearsed for any new encounters they might have in the light of day, in the heart of darkness.

Charlotte's Residence
Outside Paris, Kingdom of France

Charlotte sat in her room, once again rocking in her chair, deep in thought. Her visit with Father François yesterday had her feeling more isolated than ever. She was alone in this. She couldn't speak with anyone within the household, nor anyone outside it. Her only ally lay in a room down the hall, recovering from wounds so grievous he'd be of no help for weeks, if ever.

A thought occurred to her. If her father were indeed responsible for what had happened to this poor man, how might he react to him being within the household? She would have to make a point of mentioning at dinner that the man had barely spoken a word, and didn't seem to remember what had happened to him. It might buy Bouvet enough time to continue his recovery under proper care, for if her father were involved, and he thought for a moment Bouvet was revealing his secrets, he could put the man to death, or at a minimum, relegate him back to the filthy bed she had found him in.

A horse neighing drew her attention and she got out of her chair and headed for her open window. She cocked an ear and caught voices from the other side of the house. She scurried out of her bedroom, across the hall, and through her late mother's dressing room. She rushed to the window, peered outside, and gasped at the sight of Father François clasping her father's hand in front of the priest's carriage. For a man who had only been here once in over a year, the fact he was here now only a day after she had paid him a visit couldn't be mere coincidence. He was here to betray her, and she thanked God she had had the wisdom to stop herself from revealing everything.

She gasped. She *had* revealed something critical—that Bouvet had spoken and revealed disturbing truths about her father. If Father François related this, then Bouvet was doomed.

Father François glanced up and Charlotte jerked back from the window, her heart hammering. Had he seen her spying on them? She couldn't be certain, but she didn't dare look. All she knew was that Bouvet was in serious danger and she had to do something about it. What, she had no clue. She hurried back toward her room then stopped in the hallway, making a beeline for where Bouvet was convalescing. She entered the room and found Dr. Pigache with him.

Pigache turned and smiled. "Ah, fortuitous timing. I was just coming to see you. I'm sorry I was late today, but Lady Couve required my services this morning." He indicated Bouvet. "He continues to improve and there's no sign of infection still, so we'll continue with his care as we've been doing."

"That's good news, Doctor."

"I'll come back tomorrow to check on him, hopefully in the morning unless something else comes up." Pigache lowered his voice. "Have you been able to determine what happened to him?"

Weakness washed through her body and she was certain she paled. There was no way she could tell this man the truth. He was friends with her father. "Only bits and pieces," she finally managed, her mind racing as she concocted what she prayed was a believable fiction. "I think he got in an argument with some others and they did this to him. He doesn't seem willing to talk about it."

"That would make sense. He'd be afraid of retribution if you got them in trouble. I'll talk to your father about this. I'm certain he'll want to deal with it personally. His staff did this and that can't be allowed to stand."

The very idea had her knees shaking. "Please, don't mention this to father. He has enough on his mind as it is."

Pigache paused. "You want me to lie to your father?"

"No, no, that's not what I mean. I mean, simply don't trouble him with it. Let's get this man back to health so he can return to work without fear of retaliation. Then when the time is right, I'll bring it up with father so he can deal with it. Like I said, he has enough on his mind with everything going on."

Pigache regarded her. "And just what is going on?"

It was an interesting question that could mean many things. She decided to test him slightly, and simply waved a hand in the general direction of the barns. "You know, the new construction and everything."

Pigache pursed his lips. "No, I'm not aware of any of that."

She shrugged. "Perhaps I've spoken out of turn. I think it's best we leave Father's business to him to share."

"Agreed. You're turning into a very wise young woman."

She smiled. "Thank you, Doctor." She had the distinct impression the man had no idea what was happening on her father's estate, which had to mean he wasn't involved. Father François had immediately challenged her story before she had told it, which to her meant he knew what was going on. And the very fact he was now downstairs conversing with her father was proof of that. She couldn't take Pigache into her confidence, not yet, but she could dare a question. "Can he be moved?"

Pigache's eyes shot wide. "Whoa, why would you move him?"

"If it became necessary. For example, if I were concerned of retaliation against him."

"You mean to another room?"

"No, to another estate."

Pigache sighed. "Ideally, he should not be moved, not even to another room. Those wounds need time to heal, and it's far, far too early. Perhaps in a week you could risk it."

"But if we had to risk it today, for example?"

Pigache glanced over at Bouvet. "He might not survive the journey, but if he did, he would need immediate medical care as he has now." He stepped closer. "Have you found out something? When we spoke yesterday, you expressed none of these concerns."

She wasn't certain how to respond, but she had to tread carefully. "I've just had time to think about it, and I'm concerned with those who did this to him being so close. They could easily sneak into the house and finish the job."

Pigache folded his arms, staring at her for a moment. "That is a legitimate concern, and if that *is* your concern, moving him to a nearby estate might not provide much, if any, protection if they find out where he's been taken."

"Then where could I take him?"

Pigache sighed. "The only place far enough that would have proper care would be Paris."

"Paris? How can I possibly get him there?"

"The only hope of him surviving is if it's by carriage, but it's several hours journey on rough roads. It could be agonizing for him. It could be fatal."

Bouvet spoke, startling Charlotte, who had assumed he had been asleep the entire time. "I'd rather take the chance than die here helpless in bed."

"Then it's settled," said Pigache. "We'll move him together in my carriage. If anyone asks, I'll say he needs more personal care than I can provide here, but we won't mention that we're taking him to Paris."

"Doctor, why would you take such a risk?"

Pigache glanced toward the window and the barns. "Because, Milady, something is going on here."

"What?"

"I don't know, but the very fact that your father hasn't once asked me about what happened to this man makes me think he's fully aware already, and perhaps even sanctioned it."

She shivered at his words, for they must be correct. "You get him ready to move. I have to hear what Father François is saying to my father." She hurried from the room and returned to her own, then lay on the floor.

"Your daughter knows more than she should."

She nearly fainted from the words as she pressed her ear against the polished wood, listening to the conversation in her father's library below. She had discovered years ago as a child that she could hear almost every word spoken, and had used this knowledge to eavesdrop on many discussions and arguments between her father and mother.

"It would appear so." Her father cursed. "The punishment should have been lashes followed by death, not just lashes. I had hoped the spectacle would strike fear into the hearts of the others so they would be more vigilant. From now on, all failures will result in death so this never happens again."

Tears flowed freely as Charlotte struggled not to sob, for if she could hear them, they could hear her. Her father was involved, and to listen to him speak of taking lives so cavalierly, he must certainly be working for the Devil, for no God-fearing man would casually execute men for failing to do their duty, a duty that involved imprisoning children used as slave labor. It was unfathomable. And the fact Father François knew as well was simply stunning. How could a man of the cloth be involved in such a thing? It was terrifying.

"So, what are we going to do about your daughter?"

Her father growled. "She's not supposed to be here. One of the reasons I sent her and her mother away was so that this could be taken care of quietly. By the time they were supposed to return, it would have gone far enough that there would be no need to hide it."

"She obviously must be spoken to."

"Yes," replied her father. There was a pause. "I'll speak to her tonight. I'll post guards around the property and she won't be allowed to leave. And speaking of guards, that fool must be taken from my house and executed in front of the others for having betrayed his oath and discussed our master's business with those who haven't yet sworn their allegiance to him."

She almost cried out at the words. The fantastic story was true. Her father was a servant of the Devil, of Satan. Everything Bouvet had said was true, and it sickened her. She grabbed at her stomach as it flipped and she battled the urge to vomit. This was her worst nightmare coming true. Yet it wasn't. Never in her worst could she have imagined her father a servant of the Devil, kidnapping and killing in the evil one's name. Her father had essentially said she would be held prisoner in her own home so she couldn't interfere. But what if Satan demanded her life as well? Would her father obey that command? Was his soul that far gone that he would kill his own daughter? Any other father, she might have had doubts, but with hers, she had none.

He would definitely kill her.

There was a tap at the door and she nearly soiled herself. She scrambled to her feet and opened it to find Pigache standing there.

"We're ready to go," he whispered.

"Good, I have to get out of this place." Her voice cracked. "And I'm never coming back."

Durant Residence
Paris, Kingdom of France

It felt like the longest day in Thomas' life, everyone, including Mrs. Thibault, simply waiting for the arrival of David and Jeremy. Little work had been done, even Tanya sensing the nervous tension as she lay on the hearth rather than nose around the house. The two squires should be arriving shortly unless they had run into some delay along the way. The workday was behind them, and now everyone was gathered at Thomas' home, including Thibault and Sir Denys, who had arrived a few moments ago.

"We'll use your carriage once again, Mrs. Thibault, if you don't mind," said Denys.

"If I minded, I wouldn't have brought it."

Denys chuckled at the woman's curt response. Everyone was on edge, and it was clear to Thomas that with the possible exception of Denys, everyone now feared they were going up not just against a nobleman, but against a nobleman in the service of Satan.

Noises outside had everyone's ears perking and Enzo rose, lumbering toward the door. Someone knocked.

"Thomas, it's David and Jeremy."

Relieved sighs escaped all around the room and Enzo opened the door. Tanya bounded from her perch to greet the familiar arrivals, and David laughed as she leaped up, putting two paws on his shoulders and licking his face. He gave her a scratch and a firm pat, then pushed her down. Jeremy was the next to be assaulted by love from the dog.

Thibault looked on with disdain, her nose turned up at the dog's massive tongue lapping away. "That's exactly why I'll never allow a dog within my home. Cats are much more practical. They keep mice at bay, provide you company when you need it, and are more than happy to ignore you when you want them to."

Enzo grunted. "I've never seen a cat scare off a man."

She smirked. "Then you haven't met some of my cats."

David plunked himself in a free chair then Jeremy did the same as he ordered Tanya to sit. The dog ignored him, instead heading for the hearth once again.

"How was your journey?" asked Thomas.

David shrugged. "Uneventful. Sorry we're late, but we stopped at the fortress to inform Sir Matthew of our arrival and see if there were any messages from Sir Marcus."

"And were there?"

"No, not yet. Sir Matthew has indicated he wants to be informed as to what we find tonight, which means he knows more about why we're here than we do. Sir Marcus indicated in his message that you would fill us in."

Thibault snickered. "Oh, you're not going to believe this one, I assure you."

David eyed her. "Why? What's going on?"

Thomas brought them up to date, introducing young Christian, explaining how he had found him, the boy's story, why he brought in Denys, and the results of yesterday's exploration. And he was quite certain both squires thought it all ridiculous.

Jeremy stared at Thomas. "You're not serious, are you?"

Thomas returned the stare. "Completely."

Denys leaned forward. "We wouldn't all be here if we didn't believe at least some of the boy's story."

Jeremy rolled his eyes. "Satan? Demons? It's all rather fantastic, isn't it?"

Denys held up a hand. "Set that part aside for a moment. If there is indeed an estate where children are being held prisoner, kidnapped from their homes and forced to labor for hours on end, is that not worth investigating?"

David conceded the point with his own raised hand. "You're right, of course. If this is indeed occurring, it needs to be stopped. So, I assume the mission is to investigate these three estates you identified as possibilities?"

"Yes." Denys tapped on the largest estate. "And this is the first one we'll check. I know the man who owns it and I don't like him at all. He strikes me as the type, more than any of the others in this area, who would use children in such a way. He is not known as a family man despite having a daughter. This is where we'll start, gentlemen, and I highly recommend we get under way now so that most of the distance is covered before night falls."

Charlotte's Residence

Outside Paris, Kingdom of France

Charlotte's arms and shoulders screamed in pain as she carried the front end of the stretcher down the stairs with Dr. Pigache at the far heavier end. Pigache had made certain that Bouvet had taken several large swigs of the fortified wine, then had explained how essential it was he remained as quiet as possible, no matter how bad the pain became. The poor man was biting down on a round stick Pigache had provided, and judging from the groans and whimpers behind her, he was in agony, though managing to remain relatively quiet.

They had so far avoided anyone in the household, and she was fairly certain her father was still conversing with Father François in the library. There was something else amiss that she hadn't noticed until now—there were far fewer household staff than before. That could be a simple fact of her mother and her not being there for the past two years, meaning far fewer people were necessary, though she feared something far more sinister. The staff were good people. Had they protested? Had they fought back and been killed? Or had they been recruited out of fear like Bouvet had been? Why they were no longer employed in the household would be something she could concern herself with later. For now, she was grateful as they used the staff stairs to avoid the risk of running into her father.

They reached the ground floor and a door leading to the side of the estate. "I have to put him down," she whispered. "I'm afraid I'm going to drop him. He's just too heavy for me."

"Move forward as far as you can."

She did as ordered.

"All right, on two. One, two."

She kneeled, letting go of the poles as her knuckles touched the ground. She stood, the relief instantaneous, the release blissful. She flexed her hands and stretched her muscles as Pigache opened the door to the side of the house then peered about.

"It looks clear," he said. "Can you manage?"

"I'll have to."

"Good girl. You're doing fantastic. We'll turn things around this time, though. Hopefully that'll make things a little easier on you. I'll lead the way." He turned around and picked up his end. Bouvet grinned at her as she now faced him.

"The view has much improved, miss."

She smiled, giving him a look. "You're drunk."

"Yes, I am. And thankfully feeling little pain."

"Good. Let's keep it that way. And let's keep quiet."

They stepped through the door and outside. "Back up a bit," said Pigache, and she did. He balanced one of the poles on his hip then reached out and closed the door before quickly grabbing hold of the stretcher once more. "Let's make this quick."

They hurried toward the front of the house and the gravel courtyard where his carriage sat. Her head spun from left to right, keeping an eye out for anybody, occasionally glancing up at the windows, praying no one saw them, at least not until they reached the carriage.

She gulped.

"Father François' coachman," she hissed. "On our left."

Pigache's head spun toward the man. He cursed. "Just keep going. Ignore him."

But he was too close to believably ignore. He was leaning against the wall of the estate, eating a roll and drinking a cup of something no doubt provided by the kitchen staff. She jerked her head at him. "Come over here and give me a hand with this. He's too heavy for me."

The coachman's eyes widened and Pigache played along. "Well, don't just stand there, man. The mistress of the household gave you an order."

The coachman hurriedly placed the roll and cup on a window ledge then rushed toward them, taking over Charlotte's end of the stretcher. "What's wrong with him?"

"Construction accident," said Pigache. "I have to get him to my practice if we have any hope of saving his life."

The coachman glanced at Charlotte. "Why are you carrying him, Milady? Surely your staff could have."

She wasn't accustomed to thinking on her feet, though perhaps the truth was the best way to go. "With my mother and I away, father reduced the staff. I offered to help so as not to interfere with the household duties. Unfortunately, I overestimated my strength."

They reached the doctor's carriage, his own coachman hopping down and opening the rear hatch. "Let's get him in the back." The stretcher was pushed through the opening then the hatch shut. The side door was opened to reveal Bouvet inside with barely enough room for someone to attend to him.

"What goes on there?" shouted someone, and her heart almost stopped as she recognized the voice of the head butler, Rogier, a long-time loyal servant to her father.

"Just ignore him. Get in the back."

She did then the door was closed behind her as the carriage rocked, a whip flicked, and the horses whinnied. They jerked forward and Bouvet groaned as she kept her head down, not wanting to be seen by the butler.

"I said, what goes on there?" Rogier was close now as the carriage continued to gain speed.

"I'm transporting my patient. He needs help I can't provide here," replied Pigache.

"Have you received permission from my lord to do so?"

The carriage continued forward. "He's a patient placed under my care by your lord. No permission is necessary."

"I'm not certain that my lord would agree!" shouted Rogier as they drove past him.

"I shall come by tomorrow and explain," shouted Pigache as the carriage turned slightly and they headed down the laneway leading to the road in front of the estate and possible freedom. Unfortunately, they hadn't escaped unseen, which meant her father could order his men to pursue.

This wasn't over.

There was little doubt that her father's butler would report the incident. The question was, what would her father do about it? Would he believe the fiction told by Pigache, or would he give pursuit? If he didn't want to raise suspicions as to what was happening on the estate, he might just let them go. Violently taking back a worker who had been tortured on one's property was definitely not a way to keep a low profile. The problem was Bouvet knew the truth, and if he were to survive and repeat it, her father's operation could become known regardless.

The door opened and she gasped as Pigache climbed in from above. He hauled the door closed and sat. "How's our patient doing?"

"As good as can be expected, but each jolt is agonizing to him."

"There's not much we can do about that since the butler saw us leave. I fear your father will send men to pursue us."

"Then what can we do? There's no way a carriage can outrun men on horseback."

"No, there isn't. There's only one thing I can think of to do, but it's risky."

Her heart raced even faster as her hands clenched and perspiration ran down her spine. "What did you have in mind?"

"We need to obtain another carriage."

This caught her off guard. "Why?"

"Trickery is the only thing that will get us out of this."

"Where are we going to find another carriage?"

"At the home of my patron." He indicated Bouvet. "My concern is him. It will involve moving him again."

"I don't see that we have a choice. If we are indeed being pursued, we have little time, and if caught, I fear he'll be killed regardless."

Pigache frowned. "Just what did you overhear in your father's library?"

"The worst any daughter could imagine, confirmation of everything Bouvet has told me, including that Satan is behind all this."

Pigache's eyes flared. "Then we must do everything we can to get him to Paris before it's too late."

En Route to Paris, Kingdom of France

The switch had been swift and successful, Dr. Pigache having informed his patron that he needed a carriage so he could head to Paris for a consultation. Apparently, no questions had been asked, and the carriage granted. The only difficulty had been the coachman provided. Pigache had made it off the estate, then rendezvoused with them farther down the road where a difficult conversation took place.

"I don't understand, sir, what's happening?" asked Pigache's patron's coachman.

"This patient needs to get to Paris urgently, and your master's carriage will provide a much more comfortable ride for him than my utilitarian one that was never designed for comfort over great distances."

"But my master said you required a ride to Paris for a consultation."

"And I do. I'll be taking *my* carriage to Paris."

The man's eyes narrowed. "You're not accompanying your patient?"

"No, my nurse will be. If anything were to happen along the way, there's nothing that can be done for him regardless. Only the care of a hospital will save him." He handed the man a piece of paper. "It's essential you get to this address as quickly as possible. Stop for nothing. Just get there. Every moment counts in saving this man's life."

"I suppose it's all right," the man finally said after weighing the situation. "I was asked to bring you to Paris, and that's still my destination."

"And I will meet up with you there and explain any confusion to your master when we return tomorrow."

The man bowed. "Thank you, sir. That would be appreciated."

The switch had been made and both carriages were under way within moments, but in that precious time, they had lost any advantage. She peered out the rear window through a sliver in the curtains. Four men on horseback, wearing long, dark robes, charged toward them, and she had no doubt they were part of Satan's army, sent by her father to bring them back. She ducked and double-checked that all the curtains had been closed. They were as they had been the previous ten times she had checked them.

Bouvet had passed out from the pain of the last transfer, and she just prayed he didn't cry out when the horsemen came within earshot. The galloping hooves became overwhelming, and when combined with her pulse pounding in her ears, she found herself begging God for relief.

The horses sped past them as the coachman slowed, and she breathed a relieved sigh as the sounds of their pursuers left them behind. She sat upright as her carriage gained speed and clasped her hands in front of her face, squeezing her eyes shut as she prayed for Pigache, who was just ahead of them and would no doubt be overtaken at any moment.

"Milady, it appears those men on horseback are accosting Dr. Pigache. What should I do?"

"Just pass as if you didn't know who it was. Say nothing. Ask no questions. Just keep going."

"Yes, Milady."

She could tell from his voice that he was confused and she decided some further reassurance was necessary. She leaned out the window. "If you interfere, you'll surely share any fate Dr. Pigache faces."

"Yes, Milady, understood." The man's voice quavered, but there was more certainty there this time.

She again checked the curtains, then ducked as they slowed. Her chest ached at the shouts ahead, then she became queasy at the sound of swords drawn.

"What is the meaning of this?" demanded Pigache. "You have no right to interfere!"

"Where is your patient, Doctor? Where is the Lord's daughter, Charlotte?"

"They aren't with me, you fools! Look for yourselves! I dropped them off at my practice. Now I'm headed to Paris for a consult."

The voices faded and she strained to hear whether the doctor's story was believed. Somebody cried out, a horrendous, blood-curdling scream, and she pushed to her knees and took a risk, opening up a slight sliver in the curtains so she could peer out behind them. She stifled a scream at the sight of a sword being pulled from Pigache's stomach. The man collapsed to the ground, gripping at the wound, and she too collapsed on the seat, hugging herself as she sobbed at the death of a good man and the final confirmation she needed to know that her father was truly evil and must be stopped before it was too late.

And Satan's dominion spread to the capital.

En route to the Summer Estates, Kingdom of France

Sir Denys sat back in his seat as they passed a carriage heading in the opposite direction toward Paris. "This is an odd time for Lord Barbet to be heading for Paris."

Thomas squinted. "Why does that name sound familiar?"

"Because one of the estates we looked at yesterday belongs to him."

"One of the three?" asked Thibault.

"No, his estate had a fence surrounding its entirety so we ruled it out."

"Do you think it means anything?" asked Thomas. "I mean, traveling at this time of day, someone in his position?"

"I doubt it. And besides, we don't know who's in it. It could be empty for all we know, heading into Paris to pick him or someone else up. And carriages are lent all the time."

Jeremy poked his head out the window. "How much farther do you figure?"

"We're almost there. When we reach the area, we'll have to act quickly. A carriage on the side of the road could be noticed. Just everybody stick to the story we rehearsed."

"Ma'am, something ahead transpires!"

Thibault cocked an ear toward her coachman. "What?"

"There's a carriage to the side of the road. I believe two men are dead on the ground."

Denys poked his head out the window to see for himself. "Do you see anyone else?"

"Four men on horseback just fled as we rounded the bend."

"What do you see?" Thibault asked Denys.

"As your coachman described, a carriage with two men on the ground. Let's stop and check it out."

"Yes, sir," replied the coachman.

They came to a halt. David and Jeremy exited either side of the carriage first, their bows at the ready. "It's safe to come out," announced David.

Denys and Enzo climbed out next and Thibault held out her arms to Christian. "You stay with me, boy. There's nothing you want to see out there."

He sat in her lap and Thomas climbed down, his heart thumping. He cocked an ear and thought he could hear the pounding of hooves in the distance, though it was difficult to say for certain whether it was imagined over the noise of the creaking carriage, the neighing horses, and the others examining the scene. He was, however, certain whatever he was hearing was heading away from him.

Enzo glanced at the bodies then positioned himself on the road, a dagger in one hand, a hammer in the other. Thomas joined Denys as he kneeled beside the bodies. He pointed at one of them. "This appears to be the coachman, and I think this is a doctor. I think I've seen him around the Court on occasion. I don't recall his name. I wish I could remember who I had seen him with." He turned his head toward Thomas. "I wonder if there's some connection with Lord Barbet's carriage that we saw pass us earlier."

THE TEMPLAR DETECTIVE AND THE SATANIC WHISPER

"What? Do you think Lord Barbet killed them?"

"I'd be stunned if it were true, though with what we're dealing with, I suppose anything is possible. It's certainly an accusation I wouldn't want to make without proof." He rose. "We should leave here immediately. We don't want to be seen with these bodies."

Thomas stared at the dead men. "We're just going to leave them here?"

"We have no choice. No one can know what we're doing tonight, which means no one can know we were here. Someone will come along eventually and arrange a proper burial."

Denys opened the carriage door. "Let's go. Quickly."

Thomas climbed in, followed by Enzo, the squires, then finally Denys. The carriage got underway once again, everyone subdued. Could this merely be a coincidence? Two men murdered in the area where a powerful nobleman might have turned to Satan? Had this doctor discovered something that they didn't want revealed? It was late in the evening. It was the road to Paris. Why would the men be out at this hour heading into the city unless it was an emergency, and if it were, where was the patient?

Connected or not, the discovery had him far more tense than when they began this journey.

En route to Paris, Kingdom of France

Charlotte sat, her tears now mostly under control, though every once in a while the image of Dr. Pigache being murdered by her father's men would overwhelm her, renewing her cries. She divided her time between checking on Bouvet and peering through the rear window, watching for any sign of pursuit. Pigache's swift death meant he couldn't reveal the fact she and Bouvet had switched carriages, but she couldn't remember if she had seen his coachman alive. If he were, he might tell them what had occurred. Once they realized the carriage that had passed them was the one they were actually searching for, they would soon be in pursuit and would catch up to them in short order.

They had to reach Paris, and they had to reach the hospital if Bouvet were to have any hope of surviving. But would they be safe there? Her father had proved he was a murderer. Would his men follow them into the hospital and kill them there? There would be nobody to stop them, and that assumed they reached the hospital at all. She was aware of its location on the opposite side of the Seine from where they now were, in the more affluent part of Paris. They could waste an hour getting to it, an hour they might not have.

132

"Milady, someone approaches from behind at a gallop!"

Her chest tightened as she moved the curtain slightly aside, peering out into the dusk. She could see someone approaching fast. He was alone, and as she squinted, she was certain he wasn't wearing the dark robes of the men that had slaughtered Pigache.

Yet that meant nothing.

"Make room for him to pass!"

"Yes, Milady."

The coachman pulled back slightly on the reins and their speed dropped, allowing their pursuer to close the gap all the more quickly. And as he approached, the large cross of the Templar Order on his tunic became visible, and she sagged in her seat with relief. He raced past, and as he did, a thought occurred to her, a thought that changed their plans entirely.

Approaching Lord Archambaud's Estate

Outside Paris, Kingdom of France

David sprinted through the ditch along the side of the road that ran in front of the estates. The homes were massive, unlike anything he had ever seen, even larger than the ones in Paris. Most of those were temporary residences, where the noblemen spent their time while conducting business in the capital. These estates were their homes where they spent the majority of their time when not at their ancestral lands, and where their families lived for much of the year. These were their show pieces. This was how they displayed their wealth and power to their fellow noblemen.

But none of that mattered now. He had a specific estate to reach unnoticed, and it was just ahead if he remembered the map correctly. He dropped to his belly as they reached the laneway leading up to another estate. Jeremy joined him as they both scanned the area for any evidence of guards or sentries. The large gate was closed, and while there was a guard post, it appeared unmanned.

David tapped Jeremy on the shoulder then indicated for him to cross the laneway to the ditch on the other side. Jeremy jumped up and darted across the lane before dropping out of sight. David listened for any evidence his friend had been spotted, but heard nothing. He rose and raced toward Jeremy's position when he heard a hiss.

"Down!"

David hit the ground, his entire body flat, struggling to hear what had prompted Jeremy's warning. Whistling. But from where? It sounded close, but the whistling continued uninterrupted, which had to mean he hadn't been spotted.

Jeremy rose slightly and beckoned him forward. David crawled on his belly toward his friend as the whistling continued to grow louder. He couldn't stop. If the guard were indeed returning to his post, then he would certainly spot him should he remain prone in the middle of the laneway. David continued to crawl forward then winced as his bow scraped on the gravel.

The whistling stopped.

He carefully removed the bow and gripped it by one end, handing it toward Jeremy. Jeremy reached out and grabbed it. The whistling resumed and David exhaled the breath he hadn't realized he was holding. He scrambled the last few paces then rolled into the ditch. He cocked an ear, listening for the whistle, then heard it.

But they were still too close to the guard's post. He rose to a crouch and hurried along the ditch with Jeremy, praying the noise they made was drowned out by the whistling of a guard either too disinterested in doing his job properly, or so scared he used the whistling to cover up the sounds of any danger that might lurk in the darkness.

When he felt they had put a good distance between them and the guard, he stopped. Jeremy handed back his bow as they both listened for any sign they had been heard, but found none, the whistling continuing, though faint.

David pointed just ahead where the fence ended. "That should be it. We have to be extremely careful from this point on. No talking unless absolutely necessary. Keep your eyes wide and your ears open. If they do indeed have some criminal operation going on here, it's bound to be well-guarded."

Jeremy disagreed, as he had during the planning stages. "I still think we'll find it lightly guarded. After all, the boy did escape, and they have to be out here in the middle of nowhere for a reason."

There was no time to debate. "I hope you're right, but just in case, we must be careful. At the first sign of any opposition, we fall back. We don't engage unless absolutely necessary. Understood?"

"Understood."

"Then let's go." David rose and continued forward, reaching the end of the fence, revealing the massive estate of Lord Archambaud. The home itself sat well back from the road, atop a slight hill, surrounded by a fence. What was beyond that fence was of no concern—the boy had indicated that he hadn't climbed any. Denys and Thomas had reported that they couldn't see anything from the road, so if the operation existed, it was taking place beyond the hill. Their safest bet was to pass along the fence they had just been following that now separated the two properties.

It was a cloudy night with only a half moon, which should provide them with sufficient cover. His only concern were sentries hiding in prepared positions designed to protect against exactly the type of incursion they had planned. But they had no choice: They had to press on, they needed answers. While he didn't believe they were about to run into Satan, if children were indeed being kidnapped and forced into labor, murdered if they didn't obey, that was certainly the work of Satan, for he had a part in all evil that took place on God's earth.

And it was up to people like him and Jeremy, who had sworn an oath to protect the innocent, to act as the Good Lord's soldiers.

The Summer Estates

Outside Paris, Kingdom of France

Enzo stood outside with the coachman as the rest of them waited impatiently inside. Sir Denys couldn't risk being seen, for there could be no possible explanation for him being here in these parts at this time of night. Should they be challenged, Mrs. Thibault was their first line of defense. She assured them she had concocted a sufficiently scandalous story to tell should anyone insist on an explanation for her being there. Denys had demanded to know what the story was, but she refused.

"It's a story that Master Christian's ears shouldn't hear until he understands the ways of a man and a woman."

Denys had been apparently satisfied or revolted enough not to demand any further explanation. A small part of Thomas was dying to know what the story was, and it sickened him slightly that a dark corner of him wanted them to be discovered so the story would be revealed.

Christian had fallen asleep in Thibault's lap after the excitement of David and Jeremy's departure was finished and he had been given some bread as a snack. Thomas prayed the boy remained asleep until the squires' return. A

137

squirming, impatient child was the last thing they needed, and the thought had him wondering if he were fit to be a father. Children squirmed, children were impatient, and it was often at the most inconvenient of times. Yet he cut himself some slack. This wasn't his child, and he didn't have the years of parenting that would go along with someone of Christian's age.

He had to admit, however, the notion of bringing a child into a world so dark held no appeal. Yet when he looked at Mrs. Thibault sitting across from him, gently stroking Christian's hair, a desperately lonely woman who had no one but him and Enzo in her life, he could say without a doubt he didn't want to end up like her. He wanted to marry Isabelle, have a brood of children, then raise them together, grow old together, and leave a new generation behind that would fight whatever evil a new day might bring.

But that all assumed this wasn't an incursion by Satan and the beginning of a battle that might doom them all.

Enclos du Temple, Templar Fortress
Paris, Kingdom of France

The carriage pulled up to the gates of the massive fortress, the gamble Charlotte had thought of earlier about to be tested. They had made it to Paris, which surprised her. It had to mean that the coachman had died either before Dr. Pigache, or had refused to betray them, displaying bravery far beyond anything she could imagine of herself.

"State your business."

"Please speak with my lady," replied the coachman, and she opened the door, a Templar standing there, several more in the background.

The man bowed. "Milady, what business do you have here?"

She pointed at Bouvet. "I have a gravely wounded man who requires medical attention."

The Templar frowned. "Is he a member of our order?"

She lied. "I cannot say for certain, but he is a Christian, and I fear he won't survive to make it to the nearest hospital. I understand you have medical facilities here, your own doctors, your own nurses. Please, have one of your doctors look at him and then he can assess whether this man can be safely moved."

Bouvet groaned, and she couldn't be certain if it was for effect or genuine.

The Templar held out a hand, indicating he wanted to look for himself. "May I?"

"Of course." She stepped out of the way and the Templar peered inside, gasping at the blood-soaked bandages on Bouvet's back.

He stepped back down and yelled, "Open the gate and send for the doctor!"

She breathed a sigh of relief as the gates swung open and one of the Templars climbed up on the carriage, taking the reins. She sat back down as they cleared the gates, and when they closed behind her, her entire body relaxed, for this was the first time she had felt safe since this ordeal began.

Lord Archambaud's Estate

Outside Paris, Kingdom of France

David scurried another twenty paces then froze, listening for any evidence he had been detected, and again he heard nothing but the sounds of the countryside. He indicated for Jeremy to proceed, and his friend rushed up to his position and continued forward another twenty paces. They repeated this along the neighboring fence, and soon crested the hill. David dropped to his stomach and crawled forward until he had a clear sight of what lay below at the rear of the estate, and his stomach twisted as it exactly matched the description given by young Christian.

A cluster of large barns fenced in at the corner of the property.

Jeremy crawled up beside him and cursed. "I can't believe the boy was telling us the truth. Could Satan actually be at play here?"

David shook his head. "I don't know, but if one part of his story is true, then why not all of it? We still need to be sure. All I'm seeing are barns. For all we know they're filled with livestock. Christian could have been a stableboy here and ran away, concocting a story so we wouldn't send him back."

Jeremy pointed. "Far right. Two men."

David squinted, searching for what Jeremy had spotted. He found them walking along the fence line of the compound. Both had swords swinging from their hips, and it was enough to confirm something nefarious was occurring here. Men with swords did not guard livestock. "I have to get closer. I need to see what's in those barns." He turned to Jeremy. "You stay here. If something happens, get back to the others and tell them what you saw, then get back to the fortress so they can send help."

Jeremy frowned. "It'd be safer if we both went."

"Yes, it would be, but if we're both caught, the others won't know why, and one of them might be foolish enough to come looking for us and get themselves caught. No, it's better if I go alone. That way you can get help. Just try to make sure you're not seen when you make your escape. We don't want them to send out riders looking for you. They could discover the carriage."

Jeremy sighed. "Fine. You're right, of course." He indicated the guards. "If they're walking the perimeter, they should have their backs to you for long enough to get the job done. Go."

David didn't hesitate. He instead leaped to his feet and sprinted along the gradual decline toward the compound, his eyes glued to the two guards' backs while occasionally allowing his eyes to flick to either side in case others made an unexpected appearance. He reached the fence and came to a halt, crouching low.

And listened.

Snoring. Lots of snoring. If he closed his eyes, he could imagine he was back at any number of Templar barracks he had slumbered in during his years of service. He examined the fence not mentioned by Christian. It clearly wasn't meant for security, instead more of a demarcation line separating the estate from the compound. The boy could easily crawl underneath it with room to spare, which was why he had probably forgotten it. It was another minor point of the boy's story confirmed—he had climbed no fences.

David lay flat and squeezed under the fence, thanking God for his slender frame and squire's clothing. Neither Marcus nor Simon could have circumvented the fence as he just had. He had lost sight of the guards but had a good sense of where they ought to be. He darted toward the nearest barn, pressing against the wood, noting that it was new construction, perhaps only months old. Heavy snoring could be heard as he pressed his ear against the wall. These were men, not children. Children didn't snore like that. If he attempted entry to confirm his suspicions, he could be facing a score or more of armed, possibly trained men—or simply tired laborers sleeping off a hard day's work.

He still had little evidence that the boy's story was true.

He darted across to the next barn nearest him then pressed his ear against the wood. This time he heard some light snoring at a higher pitch. His heart nearly stopped at a child's whimper. This could be what he was seeking. This could be the proof he needed. He scurried around to the front of the barn facing opposite the fence line the guards would be patrolling. His heart was hammering now, for he was certain he was about to prove Christian's story true, which meant the guards would kill him if he were caught.

He reached the side door and found it secured merely with a pin. He removed it then gingerly opened the door, praying the hinges didn't betray him. He stepped inside then closed the door behind him when it squeaked. He froze. Somebody whispered then another, and the whispers definitely weren't those of men. He cringed as he let go of the door. It stayed in position. He had only moments. If the guards reached this side of the fence line, they would see the door ajar.

He surveyed his surroundings. A single torch at either end was lit, casting a gentle glow over the area. Stalls lined either side, just as they would in any other barn, their gates all closed. He peered over the nearest, and wasn't certain as to what he was looking at. There was a wooden box divided into four parts with a hinged door blocking him from seeing what was inside. Something moved. He leaned closer and gasped at the tiny set of eyes peering up at him. A painful lump formed in his throat as another set of eyes appeared.

This was it. This was exactly what Christian had described. His story was true. Yet there was still one part that needed to be confirmed, and he asked the only question he could think to confirm it. "Who is your master here?"

All eyes dipped toward the ground, and one boy whispered the most chilling thing David had ever heard from the mouth of a child.

"Satan is my master, and I pledge my soul to him."

David held a finger to his lips. "I was never here." He scurried back to the door before the children could betray him either innocently or intentionally. The door squeaked painfully loud as he swung it open and again as he closed it. He stuck the pin in place, then sprinted for the fence, grabbing the top board and vaulting over it. He could hear footfalls pounding and he hit the dirt, pressing himself into the tall grass.

The footfalls came to a stop. "I know I heard something," said one of the guards.

"I heard it as well. It sounded like hinges squeaking."

"Check all the doors of the children's quarters."

David twisted to get a look behind him and saw the men split up, heading toward the barns on the left of the camp, including the one he had just been inside. If any of the children who had seen him were truly indoctrinated or fearful enough of punishment, he could be betrayed at any moment. He waited for them both to round the rear of the barns and out of sight, then he rose, sprinting toward the neighbor's fence and the safety of the shadows it provided. He dove to the ground as he reached it, and pressed into the grass, struggling to control his breathing, then flinched at rustling behind him.

"It's me, Jeremy."

David breathed a relieved sigh as his friend came up beside him.

"What did you find?"

"Everything Master Christian said we would. Let's get out of here before we're found out." David rose to a crouch then rushed along the fence line, back toward the road. He kept his head twisted to the side to listen for any signs of trouble at the compound, but it was impossible to know for sure over their footfalls and his pulse pounding in his ears.

There wasn't much farther to go to the road. It would take time for the guards to inspect all the doors, and their attention shouldn't be on the neighbor's fence line, but on the compound itself. They had to take a chance. They couldn't risk the guards questioning the children, for judging by the terror in those innocent eyes, there was no way any one of them would dare not reveal his secret.

Somebody shouted behind them. David hit the ground just paces away from the corner of the fence and Jeremy landed beside him. David rolled onto his back and pushed up on his elbows, staring behind them, and breathed a sigh of relief as he realized they had long since crested the hill and were out of sight of anyone on the compound.

"Let's go!" He rolled to his feet and raced the rest of the way, darting to his left and putting the fence between him and any line of sight from the estate.

But they still weren't safe. Somebody had noticed something. It was too early for the children to have been interrogated, unless pure luck had them choosing the stall he had peered into. More likely, they had spotted his footprints in the dirt, heading to and from the fence line. It meant they could be sending out search parties to find out who had violated their perimeter.

Whatever the reason for the alarm being raised, they had no time to waste, and David shifted from the ditch to the road, sprinting as hard as he could toward the carriage that waited not far from them. A horse whinnied behind them and Jeremy shoved him into the ditch. He tumbled to a halt as Jeremy landed atop him, then they both scrambled to hide in the grass as at least two riders approached from the distance.

Any doubts as to what was happening and how desperate those responsible were to keep this a secret were now gone. They had the information they needed, but they had to survive to share it. He readied his bow and drew an arrow from the quiver as Jeremy did the same, his eyes wide.

"Are we doing this?"

"Only if it becomes necessary. Right now, they have suspicions. If we kill any of them, they have proof. If it looks like we'll be discovered then we fight to the death. One of us has to survive to tell what we saw."

"Then it must be you," said Jeremy. "It was your eyes that witnessed whatever it is they did." He grinned. "But if given a choice, I'd rather we both survive to see the dawn."

The Summer Estates

Outside Paris, Kingdom of France

"Something is happening," said Enzo as he poked his head inside the carriage. "Two men approach on horseback, and they're in a hurry."

Sir Denys cursed. "Something must have gone wrong. They must have been discovered."

"What should I do, ma'am?" asked Enzo.

"Exactly as we discussed." Thibault handed the sleeping Christian over to Denys. "Cover your face and say nothing, no matter what."

He nodded, pulling the hood of his cape over his head and slinking into the far corner of the carriage. Christian spread out along the seat beside him, stirring momentarily then falling back to sleep.

The horses came to a halt. "State your business here!" shouted someone.

The coachman responded. "My mistress' business is no concern of yours."

Swords drawing set the tone she had expected all along. She gathered herself, preparing for the confrontation ahead. It wouldn't be the first time she had given this performance, but it was certainly the first time it wasn't true, and that it was being told to those who served Satan. For a brief moment, it had her wondering whether the Devil might intervene.

"I demand to speak to your mistress."

Enzo opened the carriage door as he had been instructed, and she stepped out onto the road, glaring at the two men on horseback wearing black robes. Previous experience suggested a non-stop verbal assault was usually quite effective with men such as these who would have rarely encountered it from a woman dressed as she was. "What is the meaning of this?"

"What is your business here?"

"It is my business and none of yours, I can assure you." She dismissed them with a wave of her hand. "Now get out of here. I have no time to waste on the likes of you."

A sword was directed at her chest. "You will tell us your business or face the consequences."

Enzo stepped forward but she extended an arm, stopping him. "You obviously have no idea who I am, and that's to be expected. However, ask yourself this before my man here tears off your arms and beats your friend to death with them. Look at my carriage, look at how I'm dressed, listen to how I speak, and look at the hour. If I did not have business here, would I be here? And look who lives here. The kingdom's most powerful men, men who have needs, men whose pleasures and desires I cater to. Now, if you want me to tell you my business, I will. I will name the member of nobility I am here providing a service for, and then when I inform him that I was forced, at the point of a blade, to betray the quite vile perversions I provide him, I have no doubt he will hunt you down to preserve his secret. So, I'll give you one more opportunity to either ask your question again, guaranteeing your death before morning in a most horrible way, I'm certain, or to move on, for whatever business you think you have here, you certainly don't."

Both men glanced at the two properties the carriage was parked in front of, both powerful lords, and if Denys were to be believed, allies of Lord Archambaud, the man very likely the master of these two fools.

The blade lowered. "Have you seen anyone come by here in the past little while?"

"No, only the two of you."

"Very well." The man sheathed his sword as did his partner. "I suggest you conclude your business here, ma'am, as quickly as possible lest you be challenged by someone without as much concern for discretion." He bowed slightly as did his companion, then they both galloped away.

Thibault made certain they were indeed gone before climbing back into the carriage. Denys removed his hood, marveling at her with a smile and wide eyes.

"Very impressive. I'm not certain even I would show such bravery when faced with similar circumstances."

She batted her hand. "It was nothing, though they are correct. We need to leave here as soon as possible. When those two report back to Lord Archambaud and tell them what I said, I'm quite certain he will have no compunctions about forcing me to reveal who my so-called client is."

"Someone approaches, ma'am," reported Enzo.

"On horseback or foot?"

"On foot, ma'am."

She leaned out of the carriage, preparing to deliver her speech once again, when she breathed a relieved sigh at the sight of the two squires racing toward them. She beckoned at them. "Get in, get in. We need to get out of here now."

Jeremy then David climbed in followed by Enzo, the entire carriage shaking violently with his weight. The coachman climbed up into position,

Enzo closed the door, and the reins flicked, the carriage underway a moment later. Everyone remained silent as the coachman executed the difficult turn, and once they were underway, leaving the estates behind, she asked the question she had no doubt the others were desperate to hear the answer to.

"What did you find?"

David glanced at Christian, now awake. "Everything he described."

Enclos du Temple, Templar Fortress
Paris, Kingdom of France

Charlotte watched as two Templars carried Bouvet inside. Her coachman addressed her, fear in his eyes. "Milady, I'm not sure what I'm supposed to do. You saw what I saw. Those men murdered Dr. Pigache. We only escaped because they were brave enough to not reveal the truth. But somebody's going to figure it out. What are we going to do?"

And that was the question, wasn't it? Someone would eventually figure out how they had escaped, and even if they didn't, her father was fully aware she was involved. She could never go home. In fact, she had no idea where she would go, and had no means to support herself regardless. She finally answered. "I can see only two possibilities. One is that you return home and tell your master exactly what happened, every detail. Keep nothing secret. If they ask you why you didn't turn around when you realized something was wrong, answer honestly, that after witnessing ruffians murdering Dr. Pigache, you felt it unwise to turn around and head back in the direction of the murderers. Just tell them you kept heading for Paris, where you felt it was safest, and then I told you to go to the fortress, which you agreed with, as it was safer than the hospital we were supposed to go to. You left me and the patient here, then immediately returned home to report what happened to your master. Your second option is to never return home, and to lose yourself in the city."

He didn't appear to like either option. "Who were those men?"

"Do you really want to know?"

He eyed her. "You know?"

"I do. Or at least I know whose orders they were operating under."

He frowned and lowered his voice as he leaned in closer. "It's your father, isn't it?"

"How did you know?"

"It's all the talk among the staff of the households in the area. Something big is going on."

She tensed. "Do you know what?"

"No. And the bits I've heard are simply too fantastic to be true."

"Don't be so sure."

"Surely it can't be true!"

"Without you telling me what you've heard, there's no way for me to say for certain."

He regarded her then rapidly spilled everything he knew. "There's been a lot of new construction on many of the properties in the area to create workshops for children and to train men for war. You've been away for some time, Milady, so you haven't been witness to the goings-on, but for months now men have been passing through the area, some on horseback, some in carts, all wearing the same robes as those men we encountered tonight. I've seen it myself several times, but always dismissed the speculation as nonsense until now."

"Is your master involved?"

"No, I don't believe so, though I believe he's under pressure to join whatever is occurring. I overheard a heated argument between him and your father several months ago, and since then, I haven't been asked to bring my master to your father's estate, which as I'm sure you remember was a regular occurrence before you left."

Her palms were pressed together in front of her mouth, her wrists bending to-and-fro as her fingertips tapped her lips. This was a terrifying development. It meant that more were involved. It meant this was far bigger than she had imagined.

And it meant neither of them could ever go home.

Templar Commandery
Montereau, Kingdom of France

It had been a late start to their journey, and Marcus had been pleased with how much distance they had traveled. His contingent was well rested, though he and Simon were weary as they had been in the saddle longer than the others. He had decided to push through after dark to take advantage of their progress. It had them reaching one of their commanderies in the middle of the night, where everyone could sleep in a proper bed with a full belly, rather than on the side of a road on the ground, under a tent with rations.

His decision to press on to gain the proper night's sleep, was proving to be wiser than expected.

"Sir Marcus de Rancourt, I'd like you to meet one of our messengers, Remy."

A young man bowed deeply to the Templar Knight. "It's an honor to meet you, sir."

"Likewise." Marcus gave Sir Antley, the knight in charge of this commandery, a puzzled look.

"Remy was one of the messengers turned away by the townsfolk. I thought you might like to speak with him."

Marcus' eyebrows rose slightly at the explanation. "Indeed, I would. What can you tell me?"

"Not much that's helpful, I'm afraid, sir. I was delivering messages to the outpost in Montargis, as I do every day. When I reached the outskirts of town, there was a roadblock set up. They appeared to be allowing everyone through, however, when I rode up, they said no Templars were allowed to pass, and ordered me to turn around."

"Did you challenge them?"

"Yes, sir, I did, but they didn't seem to care about my right as a Templar to pass. When it became clear I would be unable to continue, I decided it was best to turn around, for there were half a dozen of them, all with swords."

Simon, who had entered the room a few moments ago, asked, "Did any of them draw on you?"

"No, though most were prepared to draw."

Marcus folded his arms as he regarded the young man. "So, you had reason to fear for your life?"

"I believe so. All I know is, I won't be returning there, not without an escort or until things have been settled."

"And did they give you any indication as to why Templars were being excluded? Was there some disagreement between the outpost and the locals?"

"No. Nothing at all was said by way of explanation, merely Templars are not allowed."

"And other than this roadblock, you saw nothing else unusual?"

Remy shifted from one foot to the other, scratching the back of his neck as if uncertain as to what to say. Marcus gave the man a moment to collect his thoughts, but Simon was having none of that.

"Out with it, man! No matter how trivial, it could be important."

Remy's cheeks flushed but he finally spoke. "Well, I feel silly for mentioning it, but well, none of them were smiling."

Marcus' eyes narrowed. "What do you mean? The men who confronted you?"

"No. Well, yes them too, but I mean, everybody. Normally, you see a mix of emotions. Some people are happy, some are angry, some simply have no expression at all. But here, everybody on foot, on horseback, in a carriage, *everyone* I saw on the roads into the town appeared depressed. Oh, and did I mention the men in black robes?"

Marcus shook his head. "No, you didn't."

"Well, there were these riders in black robes with hoods that covered their faces. They were all armed, riding along in pairs."

"Did you interact with any of them?"

"No. However, I'm quite certain a pair of them followed me to and from the roadblock. It wasn't until I was at least an hour away from the town that they turned around."

Simon chewed his cheek. "And the men manning the roadblock, were they wearing these black robes?"

"No. They appeared to be locals. I recognized a couple of them. I don't know them by name. The unpleasant sort. Men you just assumed were up to no good if you saw them on the street."

"So, perhaps this is a local gang issue, as we suspected," said Marcus, addressing Sir Antley. "Perhaps someone at our outpost intervened in their affairs. It wouldn't be the first time such a thing has happened. This could simply be a matter of showing the flag in force and reestablishing order."

Remy cleared his throat. "I should mention that I saw dozens of these men in black robes. If they are indeed involved, you could be facing superior numbers."

Marcus inhaled deeply as he reassessed the situation. Local ruffians didn't concern him. Their numbers would have to be significant to pose a challenge. Most men like that were poorly equipped, poorly trained, and once a few fell to the sword, easily scattered. Even if they faced forty or fifty, he wasn't worried. It was these men in the black robes that had him questioning what to do. Wearing matching robes meant they were all part of the same organization. The fact they were boldly displaying themselves in public meant they felt secure, and if Remy had seen dozens outside of the town, how many were inside?

And who were they? The criminal element he had encountered throughout his lifetime rarely were foolish enough to wear anything that would publicly identify them as on the wrong side of the law. Who were these men, emboldened enough by their numbers to reveal themselves in public?

"Why black?" asked Simon.

Marcus regarded him. "What?"

"Why black robes? Why robes at all? Why not just a cape or a tunic? If you're trying to mark yourselves as a member of some group or some army, black robes seem a bit excessive."

Antley scratched his beard. "Robes would tend to suggest a religious order, wouldn't they?"

Marcus agreed. "That's a definite possibility. But if that's the case, then we're dealing with something entirely different here. The criminal element rarely finds God, and if you were a religious order, why would you turn away Templars?"

"Perhaps it's one of our rival orders. Teutons? Hospitallers?"

Marcus pointed a finger at him. "Now, that's a definite possibility. It could be one of our rivals, or perhaps a new order that seeks to challenge us." He frowned. "This changes things. We could be facing significant numbers. Well-trained significant numbers."

"What are we going to do?" asked Simon. "We're a dozen men, including squires. We don't have sufficient numbers to challenge possibly scores of trained men, especially if they're from a different order. Many of them could be knights, well-equipped and battle-tested."

Marcus pursed his lips. "You're right. To challenge that roadblock with our small contingent could be suicide. We need to know more about what we're up against. We need a new plan."

Enclos du Temple, Templar Fortress
Paris, Kingdom of France

David stood in front of Sir Matthew's desk, his heart pounding, his palms sweating. He was a mere squire, and despite having been in the man's presence before, this was the most senior Templar in the kingdom, and it always made him nervous. Their return home late in the night had been slow but uneventful as he described to everyone else what he had seen in as much detail as possible, so should they need to tell the story to someone else, they could deliver more than generalities.

At the crack of dawn, he and Jeremy had woken and readied themselves to meet with the Templar commander. They arrived at the fortress early and partook of the facilities, bathing themselves and getting fresh uniforms for the meeting rather than arriving just in time with the stink of last night's efforts still on their person.

Matthew finally looked up from the stack of messages he had been reading. "I take it you completed your reconnaissance mission?"

"Yes, sir," replied David.

"And was it a success?"

David shifted uncomfortably. "I suppose that's a matter of perspective, sir. We accomplished our goals, confirming the boy's story."

Matthew paused as the implications of David's words sank in. "So, children are being held prisoner there?"

"Yes, sir. In quite inhumane conditions. I saw entire barns that I believe to be filled with children. Four to a stall, all locked in small boxes. They appeared terrified, and when I asked them who their master was, one of the children replied, 'Satan is my master, and I pledge my soul to him.'"

Matthew made the sign of the cross then leaned back. "And the estate in question belongs to Lord Archambaud?"

"Yes, sir, if Sir Denys isn't mistaken."

"I'm certain he isn't. Now, you said the guards within the compound were wearing black robes with hoods, as were the two men on horseback who confronted your companions?"

"Yes, sir."

Matthew held up one of the messages in front of him. "This came this morning from Sir Marcus. He reached our commandery in Montereau late last night and was able to interview one of the messengers that had been refused entry into the town of Montargis. Apparently, those manning a roadblock appeared to be local ruffians, but throughout the area, the messenger saw horsemen wearing robes much as you described. Sir Marcus and Sergeant Simon will be attempting to sneak into the town today to assess the enemy's numbers."

David exchanged a worried glance with Jeremy. "Are you saying these two things are related?"

"It would be quite the coincidence if they weren't, don't you think?"

"What are we going to do? If Satan is indeed involved, then his influence has spread almost all the way to the capital."

Matthew regarded him. "Why do you believe the source isn't Lord

Archambaud's estate?"

"Because of what the boy said. He said he first heard Satan's voice in a cave near his village where he grew up. Then he was taken on a journey that lasted several days before he was imprisoned at Lord Archambaud's estate. That has to mean the source of Satan's powers is near this boy's home."

"Then I would suggest to you that the boy's home is near the town of Montargis, where according to Sir Marcus, men on horseback wearing black robes ride in the light of day with impunity." He rose. "But there's more that you need to hear. We had unexpected visitors last night. You need to hear their story."

Templar Commandery

Montereau, Kingdom of France

Marcus lay in bed, his rank meaning he was separated from Simon and the other sergeants and squires. The other three knights on this mission, none of whom he had met before, were still fast asleep. Only he and Simon had remained awake to meet with Sir Antley and the messenger.

He had penned several letters and they had been immediately dispatched. One had been to Lady Joanne, to indicate he might be longer than expected, another to David and Jeremy at Thomas' home indicating the same, and to keep their eyes out for any suspicious things in the area including men wearing black robes. He hadn't said anything to Antley or the messenger about the story Christian had told them. He couldn't be certain there was any connection, but the boy was certain he had been taken on a carriage ride of several days from his home, and their destination by carriage could take that length of time.

It was the black robes that had him considering a connection. Black certainly connoted darkness, evil, Satan himself. Could this be a religious cult they were dealing with that had nothing to do with God, but instead with Satan? Could they be riding around with impunity because the evil one provided them with protection? And if that were the case, was Christian's story true? Marcus couldn't believe it, yet he had seen many things in his lifetime. He had seen evil at work, and had seen the glory of God with his own eyes.

He never doubted that God existed, never doubted the word of the Bible, and absolutely believed Satan existed and was constantly attempting to undermine God's good work. But the evil he had seen had always been subtle, hidden in the dark corners of the cities, in the brutality of the battlefield, never parading around on horseback in plain sight, wearing a uniform that clearly identified them.

Something was definitely going on here, and if this were indeed the work of Satan, if the Devil himself had an army in the Kingdom of France, his squires, along with anyone else involved in the endeavors back in the capital, including Thomas, could be in danger. The reconnaissance mission should hopefully be over with, so the risk to them now should be minimal.

He had also sent a message to the fortress informing Sir Matthew of what was going on and to prepare to send a significant number of reinforcements. Unfortunately, as Sir Mathew had already indicated, the Order was undermanned and wouldn't be able to muster a significant response. But if what he feared could indeed be true, this was a threat to everyone in the kingdom, in fact, everyone in Christendom, and assistance might be required from those who purported to rule this land in the name of God.

The Templar Order could not be alone in this fight.

Enclos du Temple, Templar Fortress
Paris, Kingdom of France

Charlotte sat at Bouvet's bedside, gently stroking his hair as the nurses tended to his dressings. The guards had attempted to persuade her to leave the fortress and head to the nunnery under Templar protection, but she had refused to abandon Bouvet's side. The Templar hospital was mostly manned by nuns rotated in and out during the day to the nunnery, though the doctors were, of course, male. The doctor who did the initial assessment had been grave in his delivery.

"If he makes it through the next twenty-four hours, then he stands a chance. But the trauma of the journey here may have already killed him.

"The journey may have, but my father would have."

"What do you mean?"

"My father, Lord Archambaud, is a murderer, and is working in partnership with Satan himself."

This had led to a meeting with the commander of the fortress a short while ago, where she laid bare everything she knew, holding nothing back, her father dead to her now, there no longer a need to protect the family honor. Sir Matthew had listened, asking the occasional question, then left, though not before giving her permission to remain in the male-dominated fortress. What was odd was that he didn't seem surprised by much of what she had told him. It was as if she were merely confirming what he already knew.

Bouvet was mercifully asleep, or perhaps more accurately passed out from the pain, and hadn't been able to corroborate any of her story, though she hoped he would in time. For now, her only concern for him was surviving the next twenty-four hours.

Matthew stepped through the doors, accompanied by two other men in brown tunics that she recognized as squires of the Templar Order. Both appeared shocked at seeing a woman dressed as she was in their fortress.

"Lady Charlotte Archambaud, I'd like you to meet two of our order's squires, David and Jeremy."

Both of the new arrivals bowed when David's jaw dropped. "Did you say Lady Archambaud as in Lord Archambaud?"

"He's my father."

The two squires exchanged excited glances before David turned to Sir Matthew. "What's going on here?"

"Lady Charlotte showed up in the middle of the night with this man, badly wounded." Matthew gestured at Bouvet.

David stepped closer to the wounded man and winced. "What happened to him?"

"Twenty lashes for allowing a boy to escape," explained Charlotte.

"A boy? Do you know the name of this boy?"

"No."

Jeremy jutted his chin toward Bouvet. "Does he?"

"No," responded Bouvet, startling Charlotte as she thought him still asleep. "But I know where he's from. Generally. I was one of the people who transported him to the estate."

"Where *is* he from?" asked David, clearly excited about learning more of a boy he couldn't possibly have met.

"From a village, half a day's ride south of Montargis."

Both squires spun toward Matthew at the mention of the town's name, and the man gave a slight nod. "Now you see why I wanted you to meet them."

Charlotte eyed them. "Why? What's going on here?"

David looked to Matthew for permission and the man gave it with a nod. David turned to her. "Milady, last night we conducted a reconnaissance mission of your father's estate to confirm the story of a small boy who escaped from there recently. We found a compound at the rear of the estate, out of sight from the road, where children were being held in cages, claiming that Satan was their master."

She gasped and bit down on the knuckle of her forefinger. "So then it's true. My father *is* involved." Her heart ached. She had already known he was, yet to hear it confirmed by Templars that there were indeed children held at her home as prisoners was heartbreaking. She sniffed. "I spoke to the coachman who brought me here last night, and he said it's his understanding that this could be happening on many of the estates in the area."

Jeremy cursed and immediately apologized. "Then this could be far bigger than we thought."

Matthew agreed. "And when you couple that with the report I received from Sir Marcus this morning, it would certainly seem we have a much larger problem here than a runaway boy or child slave labor."

"Don't forget Satan," muttered Jeremy.

"No, we obviously can't ignore that factor. David, you said the child at the prison told you Satan was his master. The young boy that escaped said the same thing, as has our wounded guest. And while I have no doubt that he is involved as where there is evil, he lurks, the question is, why is it so brazen? I can't recall in my entire lifetime encountering an evil man who claimed he was working on behalf of Satan. He was simply an evil man. But here they all seem to know they are working directly for him. That means either they've been tricked into believing this, which I find difficult to believe, or they have indeed been directly pulled into this by Satan himself."

Charlotte indicated Bouvet. "He assures me he heard Satan's voice."

"As does young master Christian," said David. "He swears he heard the Devil's voice speak to him in a cave."

Charlotte indicated Bouvet. "Exactly. He too said it was in a cave."

"Do we know where this cave was?" asked Matthew.

"Outside the boy's village," replied Bouvet, his voice barely a whisper.

She looked down at him with a smile, hiding her fear that he wouldn't make it through the day, but the conversation taking place right here, right now, told her they had made the right decision. What was happening was bigger than one man's life, and if anyone could bring an end to it, it was the Templar Order. She turned to Matthew. "If we are indeed dealing with Satan, how can we possibly stop him? He's too powerful."

Matthew shook his head. "No, he's not. Not in the face of God. What I've heard so far is that men and children have heard his voice then sworn allegiance out of fear. Show them that there's nothing to fear and that allegiance will waver then collapse. But more importantly, with God on our side, he will give us the strength we will need to combat the forces of evil, including the dark one himself."

"Then you will take on this fight?"

"As we are sworn to do." He turned to David. "Tell Sir Denys that I wish to meet with him as soon as possible to see what participation we can expect from his peers in the Court and the king himself. Once we hear back from Sir Marcus this evening, we should have a better idea of what we're facing. I'll have messengers sent out to bring all resources within the kingdom to the fortress. The immediate concern should be to rid the threat posed to the capital and free those children, then march in force to Montargis to put down this satanic incursion. But like I said to Sir Marcus, we're severely weakened here. We will need the cooperation of others, otherwise all hope is lost."

Templar Commandery
Montereau, Kingdom of France

Marcus and Simon stood in front of Sir Antley. "Well, I'm no expert, but I do believe the two of you appear to be reasonably successful businessmen who could believably own horses and have business in Montargis."

Marcus stared down at himself, unaccustomed to wearing such clothing. It was uncomfortable, though anyone who did wear this type of dress on a regular basis would likely say his armor was unbearable. Their outfits had been pieced together from donations made to the Order for the poor. The elite, while well-intentioned, sometimes didn't understand how inappropriate certain donations were. Clothes such as these were useless to the working man.

But they were perfect for today's purposes.

Simon grabbed his balls and adjusted them. "I feel ridiculous."

Marcus grinned at him. "And you look ridiculous, but let that not deter us." He turned to his second-in-command of the unit he led. "Do you know your orders?"

"Yes, sir, we are to sit on our asses and wait while you two have all the fun."

Marcus laughed. "I'm happy to hear you were listening. We should be back by nightfall." He held the heavy purse in his hand. Templars were never to carry more than four *deniers* on their person unless under exceptional circumstances, and this was a substantial amount of gold. "I still feel uncomfortable with this. Like I'm betraying the Order."

Antley, who had provided the handsome sum to both of them from the Templar treasury he was master of, shrugged. "You must look the part, gentlemen, and successful businessmen do not travel with eight deniers between them." He pointed at the purse in Marcus' hand. "I do expect a full accounting of any expenditures."

Simon grinned, holding up his own heavy purse. "Don't worry, wine and women only."

Antley gave him a look and Simon glanced at Marcus.

"And here I thought you were the only one without a sense of humor."

Antley frowned. "I think your sergeant has spent a little too much time on that farm of yours. Perhaps another tour in the Holy Land fighting the Saracens might be in order."

Simon shrugged. "As long as I don't have to shovel shit, I'm good with that."

Antley laughed. "Then a demotion to stableboy!"

Marcus slapped Simon on the shoulder. "What say you to that, Sergeant? Would you like to report to David and Jeremy?"

Simon regarded both men then spat. "I'd rather join the Saracens."

Marcus roared with laughter, as did Antley and the others. Marcus headed for the door. "Let's get going. I want to be in and out of that town as quickly as possible."

Thibault Residence

Paris, Kingdom of France

Thomas sat at his desk, counting the morning's collections he and Enzo had gathered from those who hadn't voluntarily brought their weekly payments to Mrs. Thibault directly. It was the worst part of the job, for he had to demand the money while Enzo growled and made faces behind him. He was the one who suffered their fears, who heard their pleas for more time. In the past, Enzo would be the one who would go out alone to make the collections, but too often that resulted in broken thumbs or other maimed body parts that prevented the debtor from earning a living. Thomas had pointed this out to Thibault, and she had agreed, rewarding him with the punishment of being the intermediary between a debtor's body and Enzo's fists. It didn't limit the excuses, but sometimes it allowed him to provide advice that hadn't occurred to the debtor.

Sometimes it was simple advice, like today. "My chimney broke, so I can't run my second oven and I don't have the money to fix the chimney." His solution? Thibault would lend the money to fix the chimney, add it to the overall debt, and the delinquent debtor could continue his payments rather than face Enzo's wrath. Thomas had arranged to get the baker back up and running at full capacity, thus earning his employer more money. He hated putting someone further into debt, but their debt would quickly spiral out of control if the chimney remained unrepaired. And the cost of the chimney repair was minor compared to the cost of the second oven financed through Thibault.

People like Lady Joanne's chambermaid Beatrice didn't understand what life was like here. The world ran on money. Those who had it, had everything, those who didn't, had nothing. Something trivial to the rich, like a chimney repair, could mean the difference between feeding one's family, or continuing to make a living. And for those not good with money, who couldn't see past the immediate numbers, they made foolish decisions like the baker had until provided sound advice by someone like Thomas, who was becoming quite adept in his new role. Every time he helped someone, like he had today, he felt slightly better about his job.

The door opened downstairs and somebody hurried up the steps, muttering and cursing. Thomas rose and placed himself between the stairs and Christian, who was playing on the floor in the corner. The curses grew louder as whoever it was approached.

"Enzo, get out here!" shouted Thomas.

The door to Thibault's office burst open and Enzo stepped out. As soon as the man arrived, a dagger was produced.

"Where is she? I'm going to kill her! I swear, I'm going to kill her!"

Enzo's fist darted out, caving in the front of the man's face, sending him tumbling down the stairs, a sickening crack heard as his neck broke at the bottom of the steps, ending the verbal tirade.

Thibault appeared a moment later. "What the devil is going on out here?"

"It was Mr. Curie," said Thomas. Curie was one of their problem debtors who had fallen into arrears on his loan, and instead of dealing with it, had turned to the drink.

"How the hell did he get past the guards?"

That was a good question. How had he? There was no way the men outside guarding the door would have ever allowed Curie up the stairs in the state he was. Thibault had several criteria that must be met before anyone was allowed up. They had to be sober, calm, and unarmed.

And Curie was none of those.

Thibault pointed down the stairs. "Go check on them. See what the hell is going on."

"Yes, ma'am." Enzo lumbered down the stairs, stepping over Curie's body, then opened the door. "They're not here, ma'am."

Thibault and Thomas exchanged puzzled glances. "What do you mean, they're not there?"

"They're not here."

"Check with the sentries. Find out where the hell they went."

"Yes, ma'am." The door closed below and Thibault pursed her lips. "That makes no sense for two men to abandon their posts, especially that post. I don't think it's ever happened in all my years."

"Perhaps they were lured away."

"If they were, it was certainly coincidence. Curie doesn't have the brains to pull something like that off."

The door opened downstairs and Thomas' heart leaped into his throat before Enzo entered followed by one of their sentries usually stationed across the street on a rooftop.

"So, what have you found out?" called Thibault down the stairs.

The sentry, Coustant, replied. "A man approached them just a short while ago. He talked to them for a few moments then they left together. I assumed they would come back right away, but when they didn't, I came down the back stairs of my post to report it to you. But when I reached the street, I saw Curie entering. I didn't have time to stop him, and I wasn't sure what to do. Then Enzo appeared and now here I am."

Thibault cursed then pointed at Christian, his eyes wide. "Cover your ears boy, there are adults talking." He slapped his hands over his ears and she pointed at Coustant. "Go get another of the sentries and have him man the door. Then put the word out. Get some of our off-duty men and rework the guard schedule. I want all posts fully manned all the time. Anyone else who isn't assigned to a duty right now, I want them out looking for those two morons who abandoned their post and put my life at risk."

"Yes, ma'am. I'll see to it." Coustant rushed out the door.

"Who was manning the door?"

"Estienne and Symon," replied Enzo.

Thibault's eyes widened. "Estienne's been with me for over a decade. I can't believe he would abandon his post."

"I'm sure he had good reason, ma'am," replied Enzo. "We need to find out who the man was that came to the door."

Thibault laughed. "Good luck with that!" She frowned. "I hope nothing has happened to them. They're too good to have been lured away for no reason. Whatever that man said to them had them thinking it was more important to go with him than to protect me."

Thomas folded his arms as he leaned against the wall. "Then they must have thought there was some threat against you and went to investigate."

The door opened downstairs and Coustant leaned in. "Mr. Porchier to see you, ma'am."

Everyone's eyebrows rose except for Christian's.

"Porchier? Why would he be coming to see me? Send him up!" Thibault turned to Enzo. "Keep your eyes open. You know how I don't trust this one."

"Yes, ma'am."

Thibault returned to her office to take up position at her elevated desk while Enzo remained at the top of the stairs. Thomas stepped back toward his desk but didn't take his seat. Porchier was the worst type. He was in the same business as Thibault, but Thomas had the distinct impression the man preferred when his debts went unpaid. He was his own Enzo, delivering the beatings, breaking the hands, punching in the noses. He thrived on human pain and misery, and in the brief time Thomas had worked here, the man had never set foot in Thibault's office.

Porchier appeared at the top of the stairs. He glanced at Thomas with disdain, then acknowledged Thibault's enforcer. "Enzo, have you gotten even uglier since I last saw you?"

Enzo didn't take the bait, instead extending an arm toward Thibault's office. "She'll see you now."

Porchier grunted. "As if she has a choice."

Enzo growled, his chest expanding. "She always has a choice."

Porchier took an involuntary step back and forced an uncertain laugh. "Yes, I suppose she does. But since she's chosen to see me now, would you get out of my way? I have a schedule to keep."

Enzo stepped back and Porchier entered Thibault's office. Enzo followed him in, but left the door open, no doubt so he could hear if there were more unexpected visitors coming up the stairs.

"Porchier, what an unexpected…pleasure isn't the word I'm looking for."

Porchier chuckled. "No, it's not the word I would use either, but enough with the pleasantries. I came to ask if you had experienced the same problems I have, but the fact I had to step over a body at the bottom of your steps tells me perhaps you have."

"And just what problem is that?"

"Have any of your men been disappearing lately?"

175

Thomas' eyebrow shot up.

"Why?"

"Just answer the question."

There was a pause before Thibault replied. "I had two just leave a few moments ago with no explanation, though for all I know they could be back in a couple of moments."

"Did a man approach them?"

"As a matter of fact, yes."

"Then they won't be back."

"What do you mean?"

"I mean, I lost two this morning, four yesterday, and I was talking to Macy last night. He said he's lost six in the past two weeks and has heard tell of others disappearing over the past several months."

"Why is this the first I'm hearing of this?"

He shrugged. "Perhaps you don't pay enough attention to the goings on."

"Thanks for the critique. For you to come to me with this tells me you have concerns. What are they?"

"I would think they'd be rather obvious, wouldn't you? We're all being affected. Our men are being poached out from under us with no explanation."

"What do you think is happening?"

Porchier sighed and Thomas heard him drop into the chair in front of Thibault's desk. "The only thing I can think of is that there's a new player, and he's recruiting, making them offers they can't refuse."

Thibault disagreed. "That can't be it. At least the offer part."

"What makes you say that?"

"One of my sentries saw the entire thing. A man walked up to my two guards, spoke to them for a few moments, and then they left together willingly. One of them has been with me for over ten years. No offer would tempt him to leave without at least first talking to me. They were tricked into leaving their posts. And besides, if so many men were being recruited by a new player, where did the men go? Between you, me, and Macy, we cover most of the city. Surely they would've been seen by someone."

"What are you suggesting?"

"I'm suggesting they're either dead or have left the city."

"But who would kill them?"

"A vigil…" Enzo stumbled over the word.

"Vigilante," called Thomas, helping out his friend.

"Aye, a vigilante."

"Thomas, enough of the eavesdropping. Just get in here," snapped Thibault.

Thomas' cheeks flushed but he obeyed the order.

"My bookkeeper," was all she said by way of introduction, directing him to the corner of the room where Enzo usually stood vigil. She resumed the conversation. "Yes, I suppose a vigilante is a possibility, though I find that highly unlikely. I think it's more likely that it is a new player, but where our people are being taken to is the question."

Thomas' mind drifted. Christian had mentioned there were guards where he had been kept. Those guards had to have come from somewhere, and they couldn't be good people. Could they have been recruited from the streets of Paris, from the souls already condemned to Hell for the criminal lives they already led?

He opened his mouth to suggest the possibility when Thibault gave him a look, then said, "It's very curious and indeed affects us all. I have my men out searching for the two that abandoned their posts. It just happened, so there's a chance we might find them, which means we might get an explanation as to what this man said to lure them away. If I hear anything,

I'll let you know."

Porchier rose. "Good. I'll do the same. The others have agreed to as well. Like you said, this affects us all. If there's a new player, we need to know who it is and take them out before they become a problem."

Thibault frowned. "If they've already recruited so many of our own people, they already are a problem."

Approaching Montargis, Kingdom of France

They were less than an hour from the commandery before they spotted their first riders wearing the black robes. Marcus had acknowledged them with a courtesy not returned. Simon hadn't been too impressed.

"I should slice their throats for their insolence."

Marcus chuckled. "You forget I'm not a knight. Today, I'm a trader. Do you acknowledge every peasant on the road?"

"Even in disguise, we're hardly peasants."

"True, but if these men believe they are serving Satan, then certainly they believe they're above us."

Simon spat. "No one who serves Satan is above anything."

The next hour of their journey had been spent discussing contingencies should things go wrong. Unfortunately, all their escape plans involved fighting their way out of the area. If they were fully equipped with their armor and warhorses, he saw little problem in making an escape. But dressed as they were, with horses exposed to any blade or arrow, one or both of them could fall quickly. They had to go about their business, do nothing suspicious, and hopefully exit unscathed. It was essential whatever intelligence they gathered make it back to the commandery and ultimately, Sir Matthew.

As they approached the trading hub of Montargis, the men Simon had taken to calling "Satan's Soldiers" grew in number, yet none of them paid them any mind.

Simon gestured ahead. "That looks like the roadblock."

Marcus peered down the road and saw a cluster of people on foot, horseback, and in carriages, backed up a short distance, exactly as the messenger had described. Everyone was being waved through from the looks of it, and he had a suspicion that only those who might pose a challenge were turned away, such as members of various religious orders like the Templars, clergy, or representatives of the king.

There was one difference, however, from what the messenger had described—those manning the roadblock no longer appeared to be mere troublemakers from the town, but instead were all Satan's Soldiers.

It appeared their grip on Montargis was now complete.

Marcus turned to Simon as they approached the roadblock. "Now, remember, we are traders. We are not Templars, I am not a knight, you are not a sergeant, and we are due no respect by any man. If you take offense, you kill us."

"Fine. As long as later I'm allowed to act on my offense."

Marcus chuckled. "My friend, I have a sense there will be plenty of opportunity for that in the coming days."

They added themselves to the queue waiting to clear the roadblock, and Marcus listened for any clues as to what was being asked, if anything, so he might prepare an answer to some unexpected query. Nobody was being turned away, and he had to wonder if other orders in the region were already aware of the problem. No Templars would be coming here until this was resolved, and perhaps the same was true of other organizations. No questions were asked, and he got the sense this was merely a screening routine where one's clothing was the only thing inspected.

They were waved through without incident, not a single word spoken. Marcus said nothing as they continued into the town. It was tempting to turn off the main road that passed through the center of the town and take another route with fewer people, however, that would have made them more conspicuous—everyone was heading toward the center of town.

The mission was now underway, as it had been since they spotted the first of Satan's Soldiers on horseback, the mental tally of how many they faced ratcheting up rapidly. Every single black-robed man had a sword, some had bows and arrows, a few had lances, but the vast majority, whether on foot or on horseback, seemed ready to fight with the sword only. Yet none appeared prepared for a true fight. A single, properly equipped Templar could take on a score of these men.

For the moment, their strength was in their numbers. He had already counted well over one hundred, and was approaching two hundred when they reached the center of town. He had to question where they were garrisoned. This number of men would require significant resources. He had to assume they were spread out in smaller groups throughout the area, perhaps billeting on farms they had taken over, and that had him wondering how much of the force was actually in the town, and how much lay outside, waiting to be called into battle should it become necessary. Whatever the case might be, it was clear they had full control.

He spotted a few locals that weren't vendors, though not a single child was within sight. His chest tightened at the thought that perhaps they had been taken as the young boy that had escaped claimed.

They passed through the town center, the haggling as noisy as any market, whatever fears that might be here forgotten once money exchanged hands. An auction off to the right appeared in full swing, those in black robes not participating, instead merely making their presence known as they passed through the market.

But as he continued, he noticed behind every vendor, behind every auctioneer, was someone in a black robe in the background, no doubt there to take their cut. And he finally realized what was going on here. This was a massive fundraising operation.

The question was, for what?

He suppressed a gasp as they rounded the bend, the Templar outpost just ahead. The flag of the Order that should be flying proudly in front was gone. That could mean only two things—it had been taken by outside forces and no one was left to replace it, or the post had been abandoned in an orderly fashion and the flag taken with his brothers, so any approaching would know the outpost was no more.

Sir Antley had given them several letters of credit that they could use as an excuse to enter the outpost should it be open, but there were half a dozen of Satan's Soldiers milling about, no doubt keeping an eye on things. The question was, were they watching for anyone attempting to make entry to do business with the Order, or were they watching for anyone to come out?

Other than the flag being removed, there was no evidence of a fight here, no evidence of bloodshed. Could there be members of the Order hiding inside? This was a supply post. They would have enough food and drink to last for months, depending on their numbers. He had to know, but there was no way they could approach without being confronted.

They continued past, nodding pleasantly at the black-robed soldiers who continued to ignore them, then down the main road where he spotted a blacksmith toiling away. Marcus guided his horse toward the man's shop and dismounted.

The man looked up. "How may I be of service, gentlemen?"

"We're just here for a few hours. We'd like the horses fed and watered."

"I can take care of that for you. Payment up front, though."

"Of course." Marcus dropped a generous amount in the man's hand and the blacksmith's eyebrows shot up.

"This is too much."

"I want a little bit of information as well."

The man stepped back, fear evident. "I'm a loyal servant to our master. Are you not?"

Marcus played along. "Aren't we all? But we're not from around here." He patted his pocket. "I have letters of credit. The Templars owe me money. I was coming here to collect, but I noticed that their flag isn't flying. What can you tell me?"

The man eyed him suspiciously. "If you had truly given your soul to our master, then you wouldn't need to ask that question." The man surreptitiously moved his tunic aside, revealing a wooden cross before quickly hiding it.

Marcus smiled slightly. "I think you and I serve the same master, and it's not the master who controls this town."

The man slipped the payment into his pocket. "I'll take care of the horses for you," he said, his voice slightly raised compared to a moment ago.

Marcus didn't look, but could already hear two riders behind them, no doubt Satan's Soldiers.

"I'll check their shoes for you as well. We wouldn't want you throwing one on your journey back home."

"That would be appreciated."

The riders continued past and out of earshot.

"There's little time." The man lowered his voice. "If they see you here when they come back, they'll know something is amiss. You have to get word out. We need help. Satan has taken over this town and our Templar friends are dead. It was one of the first actions Satan's men took when they arrived. They conducted the raid at night. Your men didn't stand a chance. There were simply too many. They cleaned everything up and took down the flag. They've taken down any Christian symbols. Even the church bells no longer ring."

"Do you know what they're up to?"

"No, but they take a twenty percent cut of everything, and their numbers continue to grow."

"Where are they keeping them?"

"They come and go, but word is they've taken over most of the farms and villages in the area, and have set up camps on each farm, forcing the families to feed them with a share of their crops."

"What's their ultimate goal?"

"I have no idea, but I assume it's to spread evil throughout the kingdom."

"Do you know if the back of the outpost is watched?"

"No, it isn't. I walk past there every day and it isn't. There is an entrance there if you want to go inside, but you would be foolish to do so. If you're caught, they'll kill you." The man eyed them. "You're not traders with letters of credit, are you? You're Templars."

Marcus smiled but didn't answer. "We'll take our leave of you now, but be prepared for us to leave quickly. Make sure the horses are never in a state where we can't get on them immediately."

"You can count on me, knight of the Templar Order."

North of Montargis, Kingdom of France

Perrot rode in silence, exhausted, his eyes barely open. They hadn't stopped traveling since they had left the farm, and they didn't dare stop. His aim was to be at least one day's ride past the last of the men in black before they stopped, and they hadn't yet reached that goal, two men on horseback spotted this morning.

As they continued to put distance between themselves and the evil behind them, the question now was where to go? He had no family that he was aware of in Paris or the surrounding area, nor did his wife. They could find a church and throw themselves on the mercy of its parishioners, yet that was a short-term solution. They were escaping an evil that the kingdom clearly wasn't aware of, for he had seen no evidence of any army marching to counter Satan's incursion.

And until Satan was fought back into his realm, his army defeated, there would be no returning home.

Yet if this was the end times, perhaps none of that mattered. But he refused to believe it. His understanding of Revelations had the final war taking place nowhere near the Kingdom of France, so why would Satan be marshaling his forces here? No, this was not the Armageddon prophesized in the Bible. This was the Devil's attempt to seize control long before those events were to occur, to enslave the world to do his bidding.

The world had to know.

He turned to his wife. "We have to go to the king."

Her eyes widened. "The king? Have you gone mad? The king will never listen to us. We'll never be granted an audience."

"No, of course not. But if we tell someone at the palace what we know, maybe they'll bring the information to him so he can act and save the kingdom before it's too late."

"They'll think you're a fool. They're liable to lock you up."

"Then what would you have us do?"

"I think we go to a church like we planned, speak with the priest, and seek his advice. A man of the cloth is more likely to be concerned about what we have to say than a nobleman. Once we tell the church what we know, we've fulfilled our obligation to our fellow man. Then we must figure out how we're going to survive."

He frowned. "If we can't convince them to take action, then perhaps there's no reason to worry about survival."

His wife gave him a horrified look. "You're not suggesting what I think you're suggesting."

His eyes narrowed. "What do you think I'm suggesting?"

"That we commit the ultimate sin?"

He gasped. "Of course not! I would never suggest such a thing. I merely meant that life might not be worth living should Satan hold dominion over the kingdom. We would likely die in the struggle that would follow."

His wife glanced back at the children asleep in the back. "We have to do something. If not for us, then for them."

His chest ached with her words, for she was right. This wasn't a fight to save his soul or that of his wife. This was a battle to save the souls of their children, of all the children of the kingdom. If Satan had been as successful as he feared so far, it was because of his generation and the sinful lives they led. The children were innocent and they deserved a chance to grow up, to fall in love, to marry, to have children of their own in a world where a loving God watched over them rather than a hateful demon.

They had to somehow get what they knew into the proper hands, and an insignificant priest at a simple random church was not that person.

His wife pointed ahead. "Look."

He raised his head and spotted two Templars on horseback, their cross proudly declaring their commitment to God and their Lord Jesus Christ, on display for all to see. These would be the type of men that would be fighting the battle ahead.

As the two knights rode past them, he wondered what they would do if they knew what he knew, and it gave him an idea. "We should tell the Templars."

His wife twisted around to see the two that had passed them. "You mean them?"

"No, we go to the fortress in Paris. They might listen to us. You're right, going to the palace would be a waste of time. The nobility won't listen to us. We're insects in their minds. Even if we got someone to listen to us, they probably wouldn't repeat it to anyone else for fear they would be thought the fool. And going to a church and telling some priest what we know likely will receive a politer response, but be no more effective. But Templars? I've heard they show equal respect to everyone, no matter their station. If we go to the fortress and tell them what we know, I'm certain they'd at least send someone to investigate, and they would know how to marshal a response."

His wife's head slowly bobbed. "I think you might be right. But why wait?"

He stared at her, puzzled. "What do you mean?"

She grinned and pointed ahead. "Is that not a Templar flag?"

He squinted at the sight ahead, a large building with a Templar flag flapping in the gentle breeze, the men milling about in white, black, and brown tunics signifying their rank.

And for the first time in at least a year, he felt safe, and in the presence of God.

Montargis, Kingdom of France

Marcus stood watch as Simon put a shoulder into the door. The lock splintered and Marcus winced at the noise. Simon stepped swiftly inside and Marcus followed, closing the door behind him, but not before giving the street that ran behind the outpost one last look. Nobody appeared to have noticed, and he had the sense that if anyone had, they were too scared to say anything.

He turned to see they were in a supply room, stripped bare, no doubt by Satan's Soldiers. Blood was on the floor but no bodies were in sight. Whoever had conducted the massacre had cleaned up after themselves—the stench of rotting corpses would only draw unwanted attention. They slowly searched the small outpost, finding it indeed abandoned as the blacksmith had said it was. When this was all over, they would attempt to locate the bodies so they could be given a proper Templar burial.

Simon stood at the front, out of the line of sight of the shuttered windows. "Well, I think we've answered the question as to what has happened to our outpost."

Marcus agreed, a frown creasing his face. "Judging from the amount of blood, I doubt any prisoners were taken. They came in here, killed everyone, took the bodies to hide their crime, and took the supplies to feed their army. We have our answer. Now we need to deliver what we know."

A shadow moved in front of one of the windows and Marcus pressed a finger to his lips.

"I thought I heard something," said a voice from outside.

"I didn't hear anything. Are you sure?"

"If I was sure, I'd be busting down the door. Go get the commander. He can decide."

"Where is he?"

"I think he's at the auction, monitoring the tribute." Footfalls indicated one of the men had left while the other paced the wooden walkway in front. Marcus gingerly stepped toward the rear hallway leading to the storage rooms and sleeping quarters, and Simon followed. A board creaked and Marcus' head spun to see Simon wincing.

The pacing out front stopped. "Whoever's in there, come out in the name of your master!"

Marcus muttered a curse then continued forward. Simon raised his foot, causing the floorboard to creak yet again. The order on the other side of the wall repeated in an even more urgent tone. They had been discovered, so there was no point in worrying about creaking floorboards now.

Marcus marched past the rooms then stopped, stepping into one that hadn't been completely pilfered. He grabbed a set of armor for a horse and handed it to Simon, then took one for his own steed. They had Templar markings all over them, which was likely why they had been left behind.

"Let's go."

They headed for the rear exit as someone pounded on the front door. Marcus couldn't imagine it being locked, so he had to assume it was a coward attempting to put on a show that he was taking action. Marcus yanked open the rear door and stepped out onto the road, finding it still deserted. He ran as fast as he could with the heavy load toward the blacksmith as Simon growled and cursed behind him.

"You do realize that without our own armor, our horses may need to report what we've discovered?"

"Then we'll brief them on the way."

Simon grunted. "Have I ever told you your sense of humor stinks?"

"On many occasions, my friend." Marcus spotted the blacksmith just ahead. He whistled and the man raised his head, pausing his brushing of Simon's horse. His eyes bulged and he threw the brush aside, grabbing Simon's saddle and tossing it back in place before dropping to his knees and tightening the straps. Marcus dropped the armor onto the ground beside his horse as the blacksmith helped Simon fit the other set of armor into place.

"Trouble?"

"You could say that. We were unfortunately discovered," said Simon. "We managed to find armor to protect the animals, but not the humans."

The blacksmith turned to Marcus. "Can you two handle this for a moment?"

"Yes."

The man disappeared into his shop as they finished fitting the armor on Simon's horse, then turned their attention to Marcus'. The blacksmith reemerged, hauling a heavy load that he dropped on the ground before disappearing back inside.

Simon gave Marcus a look. "That looks like Templar chainmail."

"Back to work."

They quickly finished fitting the armor on Marcus' horse as the blacksmith, full of surprises, reemerged, this time with two swords. He pointed at the pile. "Your order commissioned me to make repairs and to fashion them two new swords. I figure since you're members of the Order, you might as well collect, as I was paid in advance."

Marcus smiled and stepped over to the pile of chainmail. "Keep an eye out."

The blacksmith nodded as Simon helped Marcus into the heavy chainmail, then Marcus did the same.

"Two men on horseback," hissed their surprise supplier.

Marcus continued working then slapped Simon on the back. "You're good to go." They mounted their horses and slung their swords. Marcus turned to the blacksmith. "If anyone asks, we stole the chainmail and swords from you at knifepoint."

"Don't you worry, I'll make up the most horrific of stories that will make them think you were one of them." He pointed to their right. "Go that way then take your first right. It will take you to the road that bypasses the town. Take another right and you'll be headed for the checkpoint."

Marcus nodded. "Thank you, and good luck to you, sir."

"And to you, Templar."

Marcus urged his horse forward, emerging from the stables and into the daylight, and within sight of half a dozen of Satan's Soldiers. But that made no difference now. Their horses' armor clearly marked them as Templar, and there would have been no avoiding being spotted immediately. Marcus turned to the right, blasting past the startled enemy, then turned right again, heading toward the road the blacksmith had spoken of. They reached a full gallop, charging past startled travelers, though encountering no resistance yet.

He glanced over his shoulder as they approached the road, and he spotted half a dozen riders behind them giving chase. They weren't a concern as long as they remained behind them and none were skilled archers.

A haunting horn pierced the air and Marcus cursed as he turned onto the road. Someone had raised the alarm, which meant those ahead would be expecting them. But that was why he had grabbed the armor. A well-trained warhorse like those they were riding, when properly equipped, could charge through man or beast without fear.

Half a dozen black-robed riders ahead turned at the alarm that repeated behind them.

"I'd pay all this useless gold we have on us for a pair of good archers," said Simon.

"As would I, my friend." Marcus drew his sword and Simon did the same. They headed directly for all six men now making a line across the road. Marcus picked out the weakest man, the inexperienced enemy's blade dipping repeatedly as he struggled to hold the heavy weight out in front of him. Marcus aimed his sword directly at him, adjusting his steed's bearing so it would take him just right of the man who was no threat. It was the man farther to the right, who held his sword well, that was a potential concern.

They continued to bear down on the group as Marcus urged his horse forward, the beast not hesitating to obey his direction. His weak opponent broke, urging his horse out of the way so as not to be hit, leaving a gap large enough for Marcus and Simon to wedge through.

Marcus urged his horse slightly more to the left, causing the opposing horse to panic and rear up on its hind legs, tossing its rider before bolting, leaving a wide gap. Marcus charged through, his blade slicing open the enemy on his right as Simon followed.

The alarm continued to sound behind them. The roadblock was within sight, the road they were on merging with the main road just ahead. Their enemies and the innocent turned toward the ruckus and people dove into the ditch, desperate to get out of the way, those with carts and carriages urging their horses forward, hoping to make it past where the roads merged before the Templars and their pursuers were upon them.

Satan's Soldiers scrambled, unprepared for this eventuality. Some drew their swords, others raced for their horses, but more stood about, uncertain as to what to do. Marcus leaned in his saddle as he took the turn at full speed. He chanced a shoulder check and saw Simon directly behind him and at least a dozen riders in pursuit. They charged through the roadblock never meant to defend the line, but instead merely create a chokepoint.

They cleared the roadblock and Marcus leaned forward, urging his horse onward rather than engaging with targets of opportunity. The horn continued to sound behind them and the enemy that lay ahead continued to take notice, but none dared confront them as they were coming upon them too quickly, posing far too fearsome a sight for men with mere swords and black robes.

Marcus kept the pace, quite certain their horses, Templar trained, were in far better condition than those of their pursuers. He did another shoulder check, confirming Simon was still with him, and noticed the enemy pursuers now numbered only half a dozen.

"Archer on your left!" shouted Simon.

Marcus cursed and leaned far to his right, using the armored horse's body as a shield. An arrow whipped past and someone cried out, an innocent traveler taking the hit from the top of their cart. Marcus could see Simon executing the same maneuver as a second arrow flew. He spotted it graze off the armor of Simon's horse and clatter to the ground. He twisted his head forward, searching for any archers on the other side that they were both now fully exposed to, but saw no one. The enemy had likely posted a lone sentry meant to take out anyone attempting escape, obviously not expecting armored Templars to be the escapees.

Marcus righted himself and checked again for their pursuers, now numbering only two, already backing off. As the distance grew, he eased up, allowing his horse to slow as the alarm faded in the distance along with the hooves pounding behind them.

Simon came up beside him. "It would appear we made it."

Marcus grunted. "Don't be overconfident. We're still within their territory." As if to confirm his point, they blasted past two of Satan's robed warriors. Marcus slowed a little more. They were far enough away now that anyone they encountered couldn't know who was involved in the incident in town. All they were doing was drawing attention to themselves. Their pursuers were gone, any bravado they might have had lost with their numbers.

He brought them to a canter and they soon blended into the thinning travelers, though two Templars on warhorses didn't exactly blend. But as the distance grew, the numbers of Satan's Soldiers thinned and no longer presented a challenge. It would appear their mission would be a success, though the news they brought was heartbreaking. He had no idea how many men were assigned to the outpost. It could be as few as half a dozen, but they were all dead, the outpost looted, the Templar Order humiliated in the town of Montargis at the hands of Satan and his minions.

Action would need to be taken, but it would be a large undertaking. They were facing hundreds in the town alone, and only God knew how many were on the surrounding farms. The question was, were the commanders of this force putting it on display in the town so that those who traveled through it would spread the word of how powerful they were, or were they hiding their numbers so that when a response came, they could surprise and overwhelm their challengers?

It was a piece of intelligence he hadn't expected to have to collect, and unfortunately, there had been no opportunity, nor would there be, to find out. They would have to assume the worst, and that meant a force far larger than the Templars could muster alone would be required.

Enclos du Temple, Templar Fortress
Paris, Kingdom of France

David stood against the back wall of Sir Matthew Norris' office, one squire from each of the orders represented allowed in the room to cater to any of their master's needs. He was there to serve a dual purpose—that of servant to Matthew, and to brief everyone on what he had seen firsthand, a task he had just completed.

Matthew was summarizing everything they had found to date when there was a knock at the door. David rushed forward and opened it. A messenger handed him a sealed letter for Matthew from Marcus. David took the message and passed it to his commander, who snapped the seal and unfolded the paper, his eyes flaring.

"Gentlemen, this is the report I've been waiting for. Earlier today, two of our order made entry into the town of Montargis and discovered all at our outpost had been murdered, and the outpost looted. Sir Marcus de Rancourt counted over two-hundred hostiles in and around the town, with reports that more were billeting at farms in the area. A roadblock is manned, not by hooligans as was earlier described, but now by what Sir Marcus refers to as Satan's Soldiers."

The commander of the Hospitaller Order guffawed. "Satan's Soldiers? I've heard no evidence that Satan is involved."

Matthew agreed. "You are correct. Of course, all we have for the moment is the word of a small boy and a man of questionable repute. However, there is no denying that there is a force involved here that is significant in number and appears to be growing. And if they have brazenly attacked and murdered everyone at a Templar outpost, then they are a threat to us all. According to the guard we have in our hospital, the area around the town of Montargis is the epicenter of whatever is going on. However, we have a more immediate concern only a few hours' ride from here, and that is this compound, and possibly others, where children are being held as slave labor."

The head of the Order of Saint Lazarus nodded. "I agree. It is our Christian duty as knights to act in defense of the defenseless. I am prepared to commit all of my order's resources to this one effort."

The Hospitaller commander regarded his counterpart then agreed. "Very well. The Hospitallers will commit our resources as well."

Matthew smiled. "As will the Templar Order. I have sent a messenger to the king, informing him of the situation, but unfortunately, as is typical, we have received no response."

The Hospitaller chuckled. "That's because you continue to piss him off. Forgive the man the money he owes you. It might just save your order an unpleasant future in the kingdom."

Matthew smirked. "What money?"

All three knights roared with laughter, the secret that King Philip owed the Templar Order an ungodly sum the worst kept secret in the kingdom.

"When can you be prepared?" asked Matthew.

The Hospitaller answered immediately. "Two hours?"

The Lazarist gave a firm nod. "Two hours sounds right."

Matthew rounded his desk, shaking both men's hands. "Then in two hours, our three orders shall do God's work to free these children from the hell they suffer on this earth."

Templar Commandery
Montereau, Kingdom of France

Marcus sat with Sir Antley and several other knights. He had dispatched a message to Sir Matthew when they arrived at the commandery. The Templar messenger network, spread throughout Christendom, would have already had the message delivered. While Paris might be two days' ride from here with horse and cart, it was only hours for the network.

The intelligence had been delivered, and it was up to Matthew to act upon it. With his message, he had also dispatched one to Denys, informing him of what they had discovered, and to warn the Court. The king and his noblemen would need to raise an army swiftly and march on Montargis without delay. He prayed that the warning coming from Denys rather than the Templar Order would have more effect on the king. Unfortunately, Denys wasn't the most respected member of the Court, but he was a very intelligent and resourceful man.

"How many men do you think headquarters can muster?" asked Antley.

Marcus frowned. "From what I saw, not even one hundred knights and sergeants. We might be able to scrounge up another fifty if we're lucky, perhaps one hundred from surrounding commanderies and outposts, two or three men here and there. I know the messages have gone out and the men are on their way, and if I knew we were only facing what I saw, then I would be confident we would be victorious. But there could be hundreds of the enemy scattered throughout the area. We need a large enough force to sweep through the entire region, eliminate all the enemy, then find and converge upon this cavern that is purportedly Satan's gateway into our realm."

"And what do we do there?"

Marcus frowned. "I have no idea. Never before in my life have I directly confronted Satan, though I have slayed countless numbers of those who did his work."

"God will show us the way," said one of the other knights and Marcus agreed.

"You are right, of course. Put me in front of the beast, and if my soul is pure, God will guide my blade and send the evil that threatens this earth back from whence it came."

Palais de la Cité

Paris, Kingdom of France

Sir Denys read the message from Sir Marcus, forwarded from his estate, confirming his worst fears. Moments ago, he had received another message from Sir Matthew, informing him that the Templars, Hospitallers, and Lazarists, would be performing their Christian duty and moving on Lord Archambaud's estate tonight, then sweeping the area in search of any other operations involving imprisoned children.

Things were moving fast, and judging from what Sir Marcus had written, the size of the opposing force numbered in the hundreds. And while a kingdom could marshal tens of thousands of soldiers over time, gathering even several hundred on short notice could prove difficult. He had already committed his own personal guard, but that was only a couple of dozen men. They needed an edict from the king declaring it compulsory that anyone with a private guard commit their troops.

He spotted the king's aide, Sir William, and flagged him down.

"Sir Denys, it's good to see you. Congratulations on your recent nuptials."

Denys bowed slightly. "Thank you. It's unfortunate you couldn't attend. It was a most pleasant affair."

William smiled. "Unfortunately, the affairs of the king kept me busy."

Bullshit. You've never had any respect for me, and wouldn't be caught dead setting foot in my home.

"The kingdom must always come first, and that is why I must speak with the king immediately. It is a matter of quite some urgency."

William grimaced. "I'm afraid his majesty is far too busy today. Perhaps sometime next week."

"I'm afraid it can't wait. I must see him immediately." He shook the two messages. "The Templars, the Hospitallers, and the Lazarists are already moving on this, as well as my personal guard. Scores, perhaps even hundreds of children's lives are at stake, as well as potentially the security of the very kingdom itself."

William's eyes narrowed slightly, no doubt accustomed to hearing hyperbole from those seeking an audience with the king. However, the mention of three of the greatest knightly orders within the kingdom, normally rivals, working together, appeared to catch his attention. "And just what are they moving on?"

Denys lowered his voice and the hammer that he was convinced would get him his audience. "Lord Archambaud's estate."

William's eyes shot wide, a slight smile sneaking into the corners of his mouth at the mention of his master's greatest rival. "Lord Archambaud, you say?"

"All evidence suggests he's behind this. I and my allies are moving this afternoon and would like to do so with the blessing and authority of the king."

William regarded him for a moment. "Come with me."

Enclos du Temple, Templar Fortress
Paris, Kingdom of France

Charlotte wailed in anguish at the nurse's pronouncement. Bouvet was dead. "I'm afraid he was just too weak, Milady. I'm so sorry."

The priest who had taken Bouvet's final confession and performed the last rites, took her hand. "If there's anything I can do, my child, you just let me know."

She stared the man directly in the eyes. "Pray for all of us, Father, for I fear he is but one of many yet to die."

The priest, who obviously wasn't aware of what was going on, peered at her with puzzled eyes. "To what do you refer, my child?"

"Nothing I wish to speak about at this moment." She withdrew her hands and ran her fingers through Bouvet's hair one last time before the nurse covered his face with a sheet. She turned to the priest. "You will make certain he receives a proper Christian burial?"

"Absolutely, my child. I will see to it personally."

"Thank you. If there are any expenses, you let me know. I'll make certain my family covers them."

203

The priest bowed slightly then left, leaving Charlotte to grieve. This was only the third time she'd experienced death in her life, the first being her mother, the second Dr. Pigache, but for some reason this was striking her harder. Her mother had died over a period of months, her death expected in the end, and while she suffered, there was no cruelty in her death. Pigache's had been sudden and at a distance. But this was different. This man, while not innocent, was also a victim, and as far as she was concerned, had been murdered by her father in the most brutal of fashions.

Whipped to death as an example to the others to not let kidnapped children used as slave labor in the name of Satan to escape.

It was an act of pure evil, ordered by her father. He had to pay, he had to be brought to justice, but there was one thing she had learned as a member of a very powerful family—justice was rare when it came to nobility.

The nurse who had dealt with Bouvet in his final moments returned. "Milady, we must begin the preparations. It's best you leave now."

Charlotte sniffed. "Yes, of course." Her shoulders slumped. "I have nowhere to go."

"Oh, you poor dear. You're welcome to stay at the nunnery until you can figure things out. I'll arrange transport if you like."

"Yes, please do so." Life in a nunnery. It was certainly not what she had expected out of life as the daughter of a prominent member of society. She had expected to marry well and live a life of luxury, but that was no longer to be. She had gone against her father, and if God still held any sway in this land, her father would be put to a swift death in the coming days. The family's wealth would go to the next male heir, and as she had no brother, it meant her uncle, who was very close with her father. For all she knew, he could be involved in this as well, but even if he wasn't, if he found out her part in his brother's death, he would likely make her life a living hell.

She headed for the door to the outside. She couldn't be in here anymore. She stepped out into the courtyard of the massive fortress and was surprised at what she saw. Scores of men were readying for war, supplies being loaded into wagons by squires and laborers as horses were readied by stableboys. Dozens of knights in their armor sparred with each other as they loosened up for what was to come.

The gates were open, Templars of varying ranks rushing in, then she saw something that almost had her heart stop with fear. A dozen Hospitallers entered on horseback, and amazingly rode into the courtyard unchallenged. She had to know what was going on. She spotted Sir Matthew and made her way toward him, much of the courtyard stopping what they were doing and staring at the lone woman. It made her self-conscious, but she didn't let that stop her.

Matthew noticed her and excused himself from the men he was speaking to. He quickly closed the distance. "Milady, I just heard the news about Mr. Bouvet. You have my condolences."

"Thank you, Sir Matthew." She gestured at the activity surrounding them. "May I ask what is happening?" Her eyes bulged as a group of Lazarists entered the fortress, also unchallenged.

"We're preparing to free the children. As we're uncertain of the size of the force we're facing, the Templars, Hospitallers, and Lazarists have agreed to set aside their differences and perform their Christian duty to protect the innocent."

"And what of the king? Will he not be contributing?"

Matthew frowned. "Unfortunately, we have heard nothing from him concerning the matter, and we have no time to waste waiting for him while children suffer and perhaps die."

"Will you be going to my father's estate?"

"Yes, Milady, his is the first we intend to liberate. We will then make a sweep of all the estates in the area."

"And my father, what will you do to him?"

"If he resists, he risks being killed. If he surrenders, he will be brought before the King's Court to face whatever judgment the king sees fit."

"I must come with you."

Matthew's eyebrows rose. "I'm not sure that's wise, Milady. It could be very dangerous."

"I won't get involved in the fighting, I'll stay well back, but I must see my father, even if it is for the last time, and even if he is dead."

Matthew regarded her for a moment and she was certain he was going to refuse her request, but instead he gave a curt nod. "Very well. You'll stay with the rear force, then be sent for when things are secure."

She curtsied. "Thank you."

Matthew pointed to the hospital. "Please wait either inside or by the door. There's far too much activity here, and it's only going to get worse. We'll be leaving in about an hour." He quickly ran his eyes over her disheveled, bloodstained clothing. "If you would like, I can see if the nuns can arrange fresh clothing for you."

"No. If I do get a chance to speak to my father before he dies, I want him to see what I've been through thanks to him."

Matthew smiled slightly. "I understand completely, Milady, and may I say, you are as remarkable a young woman as I have ever met. The courage you have shown matches that of any knight under my command."

A painful lump formed in her throat at the words she didn't deserve. She was terrified. She wasn't courageous. She had merely acted in self-preservation.

He smiled at her. "I see you doubt my words, but let me say this. Courage doesn't mean a lack of fear. Courage means confronting the challenges that lie ahead, including the enemy desperate to defeat you. Despite the fear in your heart, you, Milady, took action despite it, and while in the end Mr. Bouvet died, your bravery very well could end up saving the lives of potentially hundreds of children. You should be proud of what you've done. You will be in the Templars' prayers tonight."

A tear ran down her cheek and she quickly brushed it away. There was no crying in a Templar fortress. "Thank you for your kind words. Now, I will leave you to your business and stay out of your way. And I can assure you, you will all be in my prayers from this moment on, until the final sword is sheathed and the last arrow is returned to its quiver."

Matthew bowed deeply, placing a hand over his heart. "You humble me, Milady."

Palais de la Cité
Paris, Kingdom of France

Sir Denys bowed deeply in front of King Philip IV. The monarch sat behind his desk, his scowl slightly less pronounced than usual when it was Denys gracing his presence. Philip the Fair, a name no doubt chosen by himself as it had nothing to do with weighty matters such as justice, instead having everything to do with his appearance, was a vain man who thought himself handsome. Denys supposed he was. He was by no means hideous, though Denys had been told by many a woman over the years that he was far fairer than the king, which was perhaps why the king did not enjoy his presence.

Philip indicated his aide. "I've been told an interesting story." He held up the two messages. "And these dispatches lend credibility to that story. But I want to hear the words from your own lips while I look into your eyes, for it is a story that is difficult to believe, made even more so by its source."

"I assure you the child is most earnest in his claims."

Philip dismissed Denys' words with an angry flick of his wrist. "I'm not referring to the boy, I'm referring to you."

Denys suppressed his frown, instead bowing slightly. "I do acknowledge that my past behavior has been suspect at times, however as I'm sure you're aware, I am a reformed man. I have married and taken on the responsibility for the late Lord François de Montglat's family."

"Yes, I have heard this and I will be following your reformation closely." Philip tapped the dispatches now sitting on his desk. "This is a serious matter. Most serious. I too have received word that the Templars, Hospitallers, and Lazarists are marching in short order on the estates in question. They have requested my blessing and authority for their operation."

Denys tensed. "Will you grant it?"

"Normally, I wouldn't. You know how I feel about religious orders, especially the Templars who seem to think they can act with impunity in my kingdom. And I would certainly never grant it under your word alone." Philip leaned back, folding his arms. "However, my understanding is that Lord Archambaud's own daughter has condemned him. I've met her, of course, as she is my cousin, and for her to betray her father, who as you know is no friend to my family, tells me something is going on here that must be looked into." Philip regarded him. "What would you do if you were in my position?"

Denys chose his words carefully. "As you said, it must be looked into, but it is a delicate matter, as Lord Archambaud is very powerful and has many allies in the Court. Challenging him directly could be risky, and could cause you many headaches down the road. But if you leave it to the religious orders to do the dirty work, then the risk to you is minimized. And if you grant them your blessing and authority, should there be something to find, everything will be legitimate, and Lord Archambaud's allies will quickly fall to the wayside as they won't dare be caught up in a scandal involving the kidnapping and forced labor of children, nor the possible establishment of an army to challenge your rule."

"And if I don't give them my blessing?"

"Then if something is found, the credit will go to the religious orders for having acted on their own. Your Majesty, if you grant them your blessing and authority and there's nothing to find, the embarrassment lies with them, and you can always claim you acted because children were involved. The Templars did find something last night. There were children being held prisoner. If they act quickly enough, they will find the operation. There's no way they can move out in less than a day."

Philip sighed and leaned forward, rereading the dispatches before handing them back to Denys. "The operation shall be led by the Templar Order and conducted with my blessing and under my authority."

Denys bowed. "Thank you, Your Majesty."

Philip stabbed a finger at him. "If this in any way comes back to torment me, it'll be your head."

Templar Commandery
Montereau, Kingdom of France

"Sir Marcus, you must hear this."

Marcus rose as Sir Antley entered the room, followed by a terrified man in threadbare clothes. He smiled pleasantly at the nervous man as Antley extended a hand toward their guest.

"Sir Marcus de Rancourt, I'd like you to meet Perrot. He and his family arrived earlier today to inform us of the goings on around his farm south of Montargis."

Marcus' eyebrows rose. "Interesting. Why did you decide to come here, sir?"

Perrot stared at the floor, his entire body shaking. "Please don't call me 'sir.' I'm not worthy of such an honor."

Marcus smiled and directed the man to a chair then sat across from him. "Why don't you tell me why you came here?"

"It wasn't our intention, I assure you. We merely had to escape the evil that has befallen my home."

Marcus played dumb. "Evil?"

The man glanced around the room, as if checking for eavesdroppers. "Satan has invaded God's creation through a cave not far from my farm."

Marcus suppressed his excitement, though exchanged a glance with Antley who hid nothing from his position behind Perrot. "So, you took your family and fled. What was your destination?"

"We wanted to get as far away as we could from those who wore the black robes. Have you seen them?"

"Yes, I have."

"We were thinking Paris. Our plan had been to tell a man of the cloth what we know, but then when we saw this place with the flag of your order on display, we realized you were the best people to inform. You could take action, whereas the church perhaps couldn't."

"Well, you were right to come to us, and you brought us a critical piece of information that could change everything."

Perrot's eyes widened. "What?"

"The exact location of the cave. Do you have it?"

"I know exactly where it is."

"Could you show us on a map?"

Perrot scrunched his nose. "I don't think I've ever seen a map. It's easy to describe, though finding the entrance is tricky."

Marcus leaned back in his chair and scratched at his beard. "Would you be willing to show us?"

Perrot's eyes shot wide as his jaw dropped, all color draining from his face. "Do you realize how difficult it was to escape? And you would have me go back?"

"Your family would stay here, of course, or if you'd prefer, we'd send them to the fortress in Paris with an escort. You would come with several others to locate the cave. Once we see where it is, you're free to leave."

"And where would I go? There's no place safe within a day's ride of my village."

Marcus regarded the man. "You claim Satan has taken your village?"

"Yes."

"And that Satan is in this cave?"

"Yes."

"And that his evil is spreading?"

"Yes."

"Then if we have any hope of stopping this spread, of freeing your village, then we must know where this cave is. And if it is difficult to find, we need your help. You're the only person we've encountered so far that knows where it is. We have to find it so that we can put a stop to this."

Perrot eyed him. "How can you possibly put an end to this? You are mere mortals. This is Satan. He's too powerful for you to stop."

Marcus stared into the man's eyes, filled with fear. There was no doubt he believed what he was saying, just as had Christian and his apparent former guard now recovering at the fortress, according to the latest dispatch. There was something in that cave that had anyone exposed to it convinced they were dealing with Satan. While he still had his doubts, he was no longer convinced this was a hoax. Too many were involved. He had counted over two hundred men alone. A hoax that big would be challenged, people would lose their fear and leave, spreading word of what was happening. But this had been going on for some time, the evil spreading yet the secret maintained. It meant whatever had converted these people into servants of the Devil was so terrifying, so convincing, it was no ordinary hoax.

Or it wasn't a hoax at all.

Perrot's eyes filled with tears and he wiped them dry as he sniffed. "If I die helping you, what will become of my family?"

Antley stepped back into Perrot's line of sight. "I give you my word that should you fall, the Templar Order will see that your family is taken care of."

"And what of my sons? They've taken them. I have no idea where they are."

"We are conducting an operation later today where we hope to free perhaps hundreds of children. There is a chance your sons might be among them. What are their names?"

"The eldest is Renaut. He was only recently taken, but my youngest, Christian, has been gone for months."

Marcus cocked an eyebrow. "Christian? Your son's name wouldn't happen to be Christian Roussel, would it?"

Perrot gasped. "Yes! How could you possibly know that?"

Marcus smiled and reached out, slapping the man on the shoulder. "Because, Mr. Roussel, I have met your son and he is alive and well and staying with a very good friend of mine while this situation is resolved."

Perrot burst into tears. "Oh, thank the Good Lord. How did your friend come by him?"

"Your son escaped his captors and my friend discovered him on the road to Paris. Now, with one son safe and perhaps the second shortly, will you help us?"

Perrot again wiped at the tears. "For God to have forgiven my transgressions by saving my youngest son's soul, I am forever in His debt and I am dutybound to do whatever it takes to repay that debt. I shall show you where the cave is and stand by your side, no matter the consequences."

Thibault Residence

Paris, Kingdom of France

The door downstairs opened and Thomas' heart raced a little, still not fully recovered from the earlier incident. The body had been taken away, but the missing guards hadn't been found. Thibault was concerned. They all were.

"A Templar messenger for Mr. Durant!"

"Send him up!" responded Thomas as he rose from his desk. He breathed a relieved sigh as a messenger in his Templar markings entered and swiftly climbed the stairs.

"I have a message for Mr. Thomas Durant from Sir Matthew Norris."

"I'm Thomas Durant."

The message was handed over. Thomas broke the seal and unfolded the page, his eyes bulging as he read it.

An operation to liberate the estates will be underway shortly. I invite you and any involved to take shelter at the Templar fortress until this matter is resolved.

Thomas gulped.

"Is there a reply?" asked the messenger.

"Yes. Tell Sir Matthew that we will be arriving as quickly as possible."

215

"Very well." The messenger bowed then rushed down the stairs as Thomas entered Thibault's office.

"What have you got there?" she asked.

He handed her the message and she read it. "Interesting. I wonder if his invitation covered the likes of me."

Thomas couldn't be certain, though he had to assume it did. "I see no restrictions in the message. It's anyone I believe needs protection."

Thibault regarded him. "Do you believe I need protection, lad?"

"I fear we all might until this is over."

She sighed. "I suppose it is better to be safe than sorry. May I assume you are inviting me to go with you?"

"Of course. I believe you, Enzo, and Christian should all come with me immediately. When we get to the fortress, we'll send a message to Sir Denys to let him know where we are. If David and Jeremy are still there, we'll let them know."

"Very well. Enzo, have my carriage brought around. I'll pack a bag, then we'll go to your home, Thomas, so you and Enzo can gather some belongings, then we'll head to the fortress." She rose and sighed. "I'll be glad when this is all over. Satan is really becoming a thorn in my side."

En route to the Summer Estates, Kingdom of France

David and Jeremy rode near the head of the column. Sir Matthew was just ahead with the senior commanders of the three orders united in this crusade. As David was the only one who had been inside the compound, he was tasked with briefing all those who would be leading units into battle. His voice was growing hoarse with each repetition, but it was worth it. The more familiar everyone was with what they would be facing, the more chances their mission would be successful with as few casualties as possible.

He just wished he was with his master, Sir Marcus, at the commandery. An even bigger battle was coming, one that would require far more men than they had with them today. Matthew had let him read the dispatches, and they were troubling. They were facing hundreds, and perhaps far more, and the more he learned of what was going on, the more he became convinced that Satan was indeed involved.

If they were to march on the town of Montargis in the coming days, it would be the biggest battle outside of war the kingdom had seen in years, and it might likely be the greatest battle he and Jeremy, along with the others, might ever hope to be involved with in their new lives. But more importantly, if this were to be the final battle between good and evil on God's earth, he was determined to be a part of it, even if it meant certain death.

En Route to the Summer Estates, Kingdom of France

Sir Denys rode hard with his personal guard. They should have no problem catching up to the small army of three religious orders as they would be as fast as their slowest member, which included supply wagons. He had the written consent of the king for the operation and it was essential he caught up to Sir Matthew. They would be dealing with nobility, some of whom were the enemy like Lord Archambaud, but others who might resist simply because they didn't recognize the authority of those challenging them.

The papers he carried could save lives on both sides, but he also wanted to be part of this. He had committed a lot of sins in his youth, and thanks to the example set by men like Sir Marcus, he was determined to make good by being the best man he could be, to not only restore his family's honor, but to make his new wife proud of her new family name.

His marshal, Guillaume, pointed ahead. "I believe that's the rear of the column, sir."

Denys rose slightly in his saddle, spotting several men on horseback, one Templar, one Hospitaller, and one Lazarist. There was no doubt they had indeed reached the rear of the column. He eased up slightly so as not to alarm the rear guard, who had already taken notice of his small force's arrival. The three knights turned to challenge them, and Denys raised a hand, bringing his guard to a halt.

"I am Sir Denys de Montfort. I have urgent business with Sir Matthew Norris."

The Templar responded. "Yes, Sir Denys. We've been expecting your arrival. Your men are welcome to join us at the rear of the column and we'll integrate them before the fight. Sir Matthew has instructed me to tell you to proceed to the front where he will receive you."

"Thank you."

Denys turned to Guillaume. "I'll leave the men under your command until we reach our final destination."

"Yes, sir."

The three knights moved aside, letting Denys pass. He did a shoulder check to see that his men were indeed allowed to join the column, then put them out of his mind as he weaved his way to the front. It was an impressive display, at least two hundred men, mostly sergeants and squires, though several score were knights.

He spotted Sir Matthew ahead, riding with a Hospitaller and a Lazarist, no doubt the commanders of their respective orders. It was heartening to see such unity. "Sir Matthew!" he called out, and the man turned in the saddle.

Matthew smiled and beckoned him forward. "Sir Denys, I was hoping you would reach us in time."

Denys urged his horse forward as room was made for him at the front of the column.

"Sir Denys de Montfort, may I introduce Sir John de Villaret, Chief Hospitaller for the Kingdom of France, and Sir Nicolas de Pins, Chief Lazarist for the Kingdom of France."

Pleasantries were exchanged before Denys handed over the papers from the king. "It took some convincing, but our mission now has the blessing of the king and is conducted under his authority and your leadership, Sir Matthew."

Matthew smiled broadly as he read the papers. He handed them to Sir John, who grunted. "Well, if we needed a sign that God was on our side, this is definitely it."

Sir Nicolas laughed as the papers were handed to him. "No doubt. The day the king blesses anything a Templar does and has him act in his name is indeed a day we have all witnessed a miracle." He handed the papers to Matthew who passed them back to Denys.

"You hang on to these, Sir Denys. If we're dealing with any troublesome noblemen, I think it's best they deal with one of their peers, so you'll be needing those more than I will."

Denys tucked them back into his inner pocket. "Agreed. Let's just pray we save far more lives than we take before this day is out."

"Amen to that."

Enclos du Temple, Templar Fortress
Paris, Kingdom of France

Thomas never failed to be awed by the size of the Templar fortress. It was an ostentatious display of wealth and power built so close to the Palais de la Cité, it appeared designed to remind the monarchy of France that the Templar Order was untouchable. He had never paid much mind to such things until he had met Sir Marcus and the others and become drawn into their encounters with the king. He had never known about the massive amount borrowed by King Philip to fight his wars in the north and his inability to service the loan. Working for Thibault had taught him all about interest and various other fees and payment types, though he was certain the king had secured better terms than most of her desperate clients.

Yet even a king could fall behind.

He wondered what would happen when the Templars lost their patience and demanded the king bring his delinquent account up to date.

A sergeant in his black tunic greeted them. "Are you Mr. Thomas Durant?"

"Yes, Sergeant. I've brought several others here by Sir Matthew's invitation."

The sergeant noted Thibault's presence. "You are all welcome to shelter here, and we've set aside a room for you, but should that shelter extend into the night, I'm afraid the lady will have to be transferred to the nunnery."

Thibault snickered at being called a lady. "This *lady* has no intention of spending a night at a nunnery. Should it become necessary, I'll return to my own home, thank you."

Thomas frowned. "Ma'am, that could be very dangerous."

"My men will protect me like they did earlier."

"If it weren't for Enzo, you'd be dead."

She patted Thomas' cheek. "Don't be silly. You would have protected me."

"Ha! I would be dead with you, and so perhaps would the boy. We must take this seriously. All of us are in danger until we find out what happens this evening."

She regarded him for a moment then sighed. "Very well. Let's see what the day brings."

They were led to a room with a large table surrounded by chairs. Food and drink were laid out on it, and it was a mad dash between Christian and Enzo to see who could reach it first.

The sergeant turned to Thomas. "Mr. Durant, should you require anything, there will be someone posted at the door at all times. I've been ordered to have any dispatches from the expedition passed on to you. There is a messenger corps with the battle group. It is due to arrive shortly at the staging area, at which time the first dispatch is scheduled to be sent. Any information we have will still be up to an hour behind actual events, so please make yourselves comfortable. It's going to be a long day."

The man left, closing the door behind them, and Thomas took a seat, pointing at the ground. "Tanya, sit."

Tanya sniffed the indicated floor space then promptly ignored his instructions, instead heading for the hearth of the large fireplace at the far end of the room. She curled up on the warm stone and Thomas shrugged. "Nobody's listening to me today."

Thibault batted a hand at him. "Nonsense, boy. We're all here, aren't we? Now, let us eat while we still have an appetite. I fear much of the news we receive later will starve us of any desire to dine."

Templar Commandery
Montereau, Kingdom of France

Marcus stood with Simon and Antley, poring over a map of the area. Antley indicated the village that Perrot called home, then a line of hills nearby. "The cave must be located here, not far from the village, like he said."

Marcus pointed at the town of Montargis, where they had their encounter with Satan's Soldiers. "We know this is a stronghold, but if Satan is indeed located in this cave, we have to assume it will be heavily protected as well."

Simon folded his arms. "If it is indeed Satan, does he truly need protection from mere mortals? I have no doubt we cannot kill him."

"Our mission is to drive him back to where he belongs, then make certain he never enslaves another soul through this gateway to the underworld."

"And just how do you think we'll accomplish that?"

"Faith. Never forget, God will be on our side. I intend to put my faith in Him to guide my sword and drive back the evil. We will be victorious. We *must* be victorious. Otherwise, all is lost if it is indeed Satan that we face."

Antley regarded him. "But you still have your doubts?"

"I do. I find it difficult to believe that God would allow this to happen.

There are no indications of the end times here. The sequence of events is wrong and the location is wrong, yet the conviction of the witnesses cannot be doubted. They truly believe they have spoken with Satan himself."

"Perhaps they've spoken with an imposter."

"Yes, this occurred to me as well, however, the voice they described is unlike anything they could imagine a man being capable of, but like I said, while I have my doubts, we must be prepared for the worst. Whatever is behind this, its source appears to be Perrot's cave. If we're to bring an end to this darkness spreading across the kingdom, getting to that cave is critical."

Simon pursed his lips. "How do you propose we get there? It's deep in enemy territory, and they'll throw everything they have at us if they know what we're attempting."

Marcus agreed. "If they are as well organized as we suspect, they likely have spies throughout the region, and certainly have eyes on this commandery. Anyone leaving here heading south will likely be followed."

"Not to mention Perrot," said Simon. "A farmer in his cart heading north, stops at a Templar commandery, then leaves heading south. They'll either suspect he's a Templar spy or has betrayed his oath to Satan. Either way, he'll be marked as a target."

"We'll have to identify their spies."

Antley leaned forward. "And how do you propose to do that?"

Marcus tapped his temple. "I have a plan."

The Summer Estates
Outside Paris, Kingdom of France

They had reached the staging area without incident and slightly ahead of schedule. No time was wasted as the enemy might have lookouts that could have already reported their arrival. The goal here was to liberate the children then take as many involved into custody as possible. But the priority remained the children, the innocent they were sworn to protect. The plan had already been discussed at length during the journey here, and it was agreed that the Hospitallers, the second largest contingent, would charge down the road to the opposite end of the line of estates in question, then set up a roadblock so no one could escape. The Lazarists and his own men would guard this end of the road along with the supply wagons, while the Templars would conduct the initial assault on Lord Archambaud's estate.

Sir Matthew raised his sword over his head. "To me, good sire! Beauséant to the rescue!"

He was echoed by those around him, and even Denys thrust his sword in the air, repeating the battle cry of the Templars. The Hospitallers charged first, racing down the road, and as the last man cleared the staging area, Sir

Matthew followed with the Templar Order, at least one hundred strong behind him. As the last man cleared, Sir Denys followed with four of his personal guard, the rest remaining behind. It was his job to convince any noblemen involved to surrender without incident, and as they galloped forward, he imagined what it must be like to be a Templar charging into battle against countless Saracens in defense of the Holy Land and the pilgrims it drew.

But he didn't have long to imagine. Lord Archambaud's estate wasn't far from the staging area, and they were soon upon it, the Templars spreading out across the front then charging up the grounds. As he reached the corner of the fence demarking the neighboring estate, he gasped at how swiftly things were moving. The inner gate was already opened and the Templars were pouring inside, surrounding the house while the bulk of the force headed up the right flank toward the barns, toward the prisons David and Jeremy had described. He couldn't see them yet, and they weren't his responsibility. Lord Archambaud was. As the Templars crested the hill at the rear of the property, shouts rang out and swords clashed, eliminating any doubt those in charge might have had.

He raced through the gates with his guard, then held position at the center of the courtyard as Templars poured through the main entrance. Shouts and screams from inside had him wincing. The Templars wouldn't kill the innocent, and so far, he hadn't heard a sword blade meet another. Staff members were hauled out and lined up, and he kept his eyes peeled for Lord Archambaud, but so far couldn't find him. He spotted the butler being escorted out by two Templar sergeants, the loyal servant clearly not pleased at being manhandled.

Denys dismounted and headed for the man, his guard remaining on horseback, covering him on either side as they advanced with him, their swords drawn. "Where is your master?" he demanded.

The butler said nothing.

Denys withdrew the papers from the king, displaying the royal seal. "In the name of the king, I order you to tell me where your master is!"

The defiant butler's eyes flitted toward the documents held in front of his face. "I do not recognize that man's authority over me."

"He is your king."

"He is no king of mine. Lord Archambaud is my master, and Satan is my king."

Gasps erupted from several of the staff members, clearly shaken by what had just been said. Denys stepped in front of one of them. "Where's your master?"

The woman trembled. "I don't know. All I know is he left in a hurry this morning."

Matthew rode up. "Did she just say he left this morning?"

Denys nodded. "Yes."

"Where did he go?"

Most of the staff shook their heads, though the butler remained defiant. Denys grabbed the man by the tunic. "This one likely knows exactly where his master has gone."

A sergeant raced up, hauling back on the reins at the last moment, bringing his horse to a skidding halt in the gravel. "Sir Matthew, the reports were correct. We have found…" The clearly troubled man paused, taking a breath as he struggled to control his emotions. "Well, sir, you have to see it for yourself. It's most disturbing, but I estimate at least two hundred children were being held. We're freeing them now."

Matthew made the sign of the cross. "Their condition?"

"From the brief look I got, I would say varying. You have to see the prisons they were held in. It's a miracle they haven't all died from disease."

"Resistance?"

"Minimal. It looks like only a caretaker force. There were at least two barracks that could hold far more than we encountered."

Denys frowned. "Then perhaps the bulk of the force left with Lord Archambaud."

"A force like that could be difficult to hide if they traveled together," said Matthew.

Denys agreed. "Yes. Not to mention the fact Lord Archambaud enjoys his comforts. He is most likely in his carriage."

Matthew pointed at David and Jeremy. "Take one of the staff members. Confirm if his chariot is still here."

"Yes, sir." The squires grabbed a stableboy from the lineup then headed toward the back.

Matthew turned to the sergeant. "How many prisoners do we have?"

The sergeant shifted uncomfortably. "I don't believe any."

Matthew's eyes widened. "None?"

"Well, sir, when the men saw what they had done to the children, no quarter was shown."

Matthew growled. "We need better discipline than that. We need prisoners to interrogate."

The sergeant lowered his voice slightly. "There is one survivor, sir, a beastly man who claims he's not part of this. He's an executioner hired by the estate."

Denys' eyes narrowed as did Matthew's. "I've never heard of an estate that employed an executioner."

"Neither have I." Matthew faced the defiant butler then addressed the sergeant. "Tell him we require his services before we set him free."

Defiance was replaced with terror and Denys smiled slightly.

They would soon have their answers.

Templar Commandery
Montereau, Kingdom of France

Marcus had a plan. It wasn't necessarily a good one, it was certainly a dangerous one, but it was a plan nonetheless. During their time in and around Montargis, he had observed that none of those in the black robes were ever challenged. They rode alone or in pairs, sometimes in larger groups. If his team were to wear the same robes, they should be able to travel within the lost territory unchallenged, and reach their destination with relative ease.

If they could get their small force with supplies to Perrot's farm, they could stage a surprise attack on the cave and find out the truth once and for all. Any number of things could go wrong, and if they were found out, they would be forced to fight their way out of the darkness and back to the commandery.

A tall order indeed.

Simon, of course, liked the plan. He just wanted some action. "How do you propose we get enough of these robes that they wear?"

Antley tapped his chin. "That might not be as difficult as you would think. We have a contract with a local seamstress who is well supplied. All she would need is one of the robes, and I have no doubt she could create as many as you want on short notice."

"She would have enough black cloth?" asked Marcus.

Antley shrugged. "Isn't that the advantage of black? Any color cloth can be dyed to be it?"

Marcus grunted. "You're asking the wrong man." He turned to his friend. "Simon?"

Simon gave him a look. "How in the name of God would I ever know anything about dying cloth?"

Marcus shrugged and tapped the man's tunic. "You wear black."

Simon rolled his eyes then turned to Antley. "You said all she needs is one of the robes to copy. I can think of only one way to get that."

Antley frowned. "As can I."

Simon addressed Marcus. "I suggest we go and acquire one of these robes. I suspect she won't be ready with them until tomorrow morning at the earliest, and by then, word will have reached Satan's Soldiers of what's happening at Lord Archambaud's estate. They might have increased their readiness by the time we get there."

Marcus agreed with his sergeant, who had come around on his own to Marcus' plan. "It may definitely prove more difficult, which is why there is a second part to my plan."

Simon cocked an eyebrow. "Oh?"

Marcus turned to Antley. "Do you know where we might acquire a load of manure?"

Archambaud Estate

Outside Paris, Kingdom of France

David winced at the sight of the twisted creature that walked laughing past him. Half his body was covered in scars, no doubt the result of what was a horrific fire sometime in his past. The butler had spewed everything within moments of being tied to the whipping post. All it had taken was a single flick of the whip next to the man's ear.

Lord Archambaud was heading for Montargis with over fifty men and carts loaded with weapons of war. He had left at first light after hearing the reports of a possible intruder overnight. David had cursed himself at that revelation. If he had managed to escape unnoticed, Lord Archambaud and his men would have been here.

The next piece of information to be revealed was all the estates involved in the area. Sir Matthew stepped over to the still bound butler. "One final question. Why is Lord Archambaud doing this?"

"He does as his master commands."

Matthew stared at him. "And who is his master?"

"The same master we will all have in time."

"And who is that?"

"Satan. He is my master and my lord's master."

Matthew bristled. "So then, your lord does this in the name of Satan?"

"Yes. And soon he will hold dominion over all your souls."

Matthew's sword swung full circle, removing the butler's head. "Satan will never hold dominion over me."

David's mouth was agape at the sight and he turned to see that Jeremy was as shocked as he was. Matthew cleaned his sword on the arm of the butler's body, still tied to the whipping post. He sheathed his blade then turned to the others.

"We have the list of the other estates. Leave a small contingent here to watch over the children and guard the household staff."

Denys stepped forward. "My guard can take care of that. I'll have them sent for."

"Excellent. Ten should suffice."

Denys agreed and passed the command on to Guillaume who had it executed by one of the others.

"Messenger!" shouted Matthew.

A man rushed forward, pen and paper at the ready. "Yes, Sir Matthew?"

"Notify the fortress that Lord Archambaud's estate has been taken with no casualties on our side, but that he was not found and is believed to be heading with a force of over fifty to Montargis. We have a list of other estates that we will now be liberating. Direct all arriving men toward the commandery in Montereau, along with all equipment and supplies we can spare to prepare for the upcoming assault. Also have them prepare for the arrival of at least two hundred children. Let Mother Superior coordinate that." He paused. "And have them send additional transports for the children."

Denys cleared his throat and stepped closer to Matthew, lowering his voice. "Sir, perhaps it's better to keep the children here. I doubt you have proper accommodations for so many at the fortress."

Matthew regarded him for a moment. "You haven't seen where they were kept yet, have you?"

Denys shook his head.

Matthew jerked his chin at one of the sergeants. "Show him."

Denys was led away into one of the barns, and he returned a changed man. "You are right. Of course, no child can remain in such conditions. I shall open my estate to as many as we can hold until arrangements can be made."

"Thank you, Sir Denys, you are most generous." Matthew turned to the messenger. "See that this gets to the fortress as quickly as possible."

"Yes, sir."

Denys interrupted. "May I make use of your messenger?"

Matthew shook his head. "Not this one. I want him out of here immediately." The messenger folded up the piece of paper, sealing it with wax. Matthew pressed his ring into it and the messenger was off. "Messenger!" Matthew shouted again, and another appeared. He presented him to Denys. "Dispatch any messages Sir Denys requires, as if it were I myself sending them."

"Yes, sir."

Denys bowed slightly. "Thank you, Sir Matthew." He stepped off to the side, dictating a message to his wife, warning her of what was to come.

David made a decision that no squire should make, but he and Jeremy lived under exceptional circumstances, and he prayed Matthew would understand. He stepped forward, leap-frogging the entire chain of command. "Sir Matthew, may I speak with you?"

Matthew smiled slightly. "Permission for you and Jeremy to join Sir Marcus in Montereau is granted."

David grinned. "Thank you, sir." He turned to Jeremy who stared at him in shock at the balls he had just displayed, and their good turn of fortune. While the work here was important, it would be taken care of regardless of whether two squires participated. Their position was with Sir Marcus, and everything they had seen, everything they had heard, told him the greater danger was where their master was.

Now they had to reach him in time to help.

Enclos du Temple, Templar Fortress
Paris, Kingdom of France

Thomas read the dispatch handed to him moments before. Less than two hours ago, the combined forces of the religious orders had taken Lord Archambaud's estate. The man hadn't been there, but they had liberated over two hundred children who were to be brought here.

He handed it to Thibault to read, then turned to Christian. "You'll be happy to hear that over two hundred children were just liberated from where you were held."

The boy looked up from petting Tanya. "Is that a lot?"

Thomas' eyes glistened, and he noticed Thibault turning away, biting her knuckle. "Yes, it is a lot. It's far too many. But thanks to you and your brave escape, they'll all be safe now."

Thibault dabbed her eyes dry. "So many innocents," she murmured. "And how will they possibly reunite them with their families?" She waved a hand at Christian. "How many are like him who have no idea where they are from? And how many more are there at these other estates? We could be dealing with hundreds. This is going to be a massive undertaking."

Thomas agreed. "It's too bad my father wasn't alive."

Thibault's eyebrows rose. "Why's that?"

"Well, as a forger, he was a remarkable artist. He could draw likenesses of the children that could be shown around the towns and villages. Perhaps parents or relatives or neighbors might recognize the children and they could be reunited. Otherwise, they are heading for an orphanage and a horrible life."

Thibault smiled. "You're a brilliant lad, even when you don't realize it."

Thomas' eyes narrowed. "What do you mean?"

"Your idea is fantastic. Your father isn't the only artist in Paris. Enzo, get me the man at the door."

Enzo rose and opened the door, the guard standing outside stepping in. "How may I be of service?"

Thibault rose. "I need to speak to whoever will be in charge of reuniting the children with their families."

The guard stared at him, puzzled. "Children?"

Thomas handed the man the dispatch, obviously out of the loop due to the post he manned. His eyes widened and he passed the pages back.

"It says here Mother Superior will be in charge. I will send word that she come here to see you as soon as possible."

"Thank you. And I'll have need of a messenger. There are many people to reach out to."

"Of course, ma'am." The guard left and Thomas turned to Thibault.

"Who are you sending messages to?"

"My men and the other leaders I was speaking with earlier today. I want every artist in this city rounded up and brought here. We have children arriving shortly. The sooner we get this started, the better."

238

Archambaud Estate

Outside Paris, Kingdom of France

Charlotte stared at the scene in front of her. It was heartbreaking. The children had all been liberated from their cages, and she understood now why the Templars had massacred all involved—it was clear they had been horribly mistreated. When it was evident it would take hours before they could relocate them, she had taken action, putting the remaining staff to work.

The children were now being stripped out of their filthy clothes. The laundry had been fired up and the clothes were being washed in bulk while the children's hair was clipped and they were scrubbed down. Many of the teenage prisoners had insisted on helping, and it was heartwarming to see the bond formed under such adversity, the older children acting as protectors for the young.

Sir Denys rode up and dismounted beside her. He surveyed the compound, awed by what he was witnessing. "This is remarkable. Did you do this?"

"It was the least I could do. This was my father's doing, and it is up to a member of his family to make it right, and I am all that is left."

"This is in no way your responsibility, but I understand your feelings on the matter." He sighed. "I only wish there were more like you at the other estates."

She turned to him. "What did you find?"

"We swept the entire area, even the estates not mentioned by the butler, just in case he was mistaken or lying. We found another six estates with setups like this, though none as big. Some had as few as a couple of dozen children, others as many as one hundred. I think in the end we may have liberated about five hundred. It's...sickening."

"And those responsible?"

Denys cursed. "All fled early this morning, like your father. We interrogated some of the prisoners and they confirmed that they are all heading for Montargis. Sir Matthew wants to secure this area and expand the search, as well as have all the children transported to the fortress before morning. We'll then head for Montargis. You are, of course, welcome to use my carriage and join us."

"No. I have nothing to say to my father, not after seeing this. He's dead to me. I will go to the fortress with the children, and not rest until every one of them has been reunited with their families."

"Should I encounter your father, do you want me to deliver a message to him?"

She stared at the children, still wide-eyed with fear, then nodded. "Yes. Tell him I hope he burns in Hell for eternity with his new master, and that I will spit on his grave every opportunity I get. Oh, and that I renounce his family name. From now on I will be known by my mother's maiden name."

Denys bowed. "You have my word, miss, that should I have the opportunity, I will deliver your message to him, word for word." He paused. "And when this is over, where will you go?"

She tensed and stared at the ground. "I don't know. I have nowhere to go."

Denys stepped closer and put a comforting hand on her shoulder. "Milady, you are welcome to stay with my family for as long as is necessary. You will not be alone and destitute if I have anything to say about it."

She stared up and him, her eyes filled with tears, and smiled.

Perhaps there still was good in this world.

North of Montargis, Kingdom of France

Marcus shifted in his saddle. He could ride for hours and never let it bother him, but sitting, waiting, doing nothing, could drive him mad. They were on the edge of enemy territory and had been waiting for the perfect target for over an hour. Most of Satan's Soldiers were traveling in pairs or more, and the few they had seen alone on horseback had come when too many witnesses were on the road. They had to do this with no one noticing, otherwise suspicions would be raised at why a man's robes were stolen.

"How much bloody longer do we have to wait?" muttered Simon from his position about ten paces away, both of them hidden in the trees lining the edge of the road.

"Patience, my friend. God will provide us with all we need."

"Patience my ass. Whoever had this saddle before me must have had the narrowest ass outside the Holy Land. I feel like I'm sitting on a rope."

Marcus chuckled then pointed down the road. "I think we have a candidate."

Simon turned and spotted the rider in question. "I don't care how many witnesses there are, I say we take him."

"Fortunately, the road appears clear."

Simon looked at him askance. "Wait. Did you spot him before or after that patience nonsense?"

"After, I assure you."

"I don't believe you."

Marcus readied himself and Simon became all business as he dismounted. The lone target sauntered past Simon's position and Marcus urged his horse forward, emerging from the trees and blocking the man's path. "Oh, pardon me. I didn't see you there."

The startled man peered out from behind his hood, not noticing Simon sneaking up behind him. The sergeant grabbed the man from his saddle and threw him to the ground. He shoved a dagger between the man's ribs, piercing his heart as a hand was slapped over the man's mouth, silencing any scream. Marcus grabbed the reins of the man's horse and led it into the trees as Simon dragged the body off the road and out of sight. He cleaned his blade on the grass then set to work removing the man's robe.

Marcus removed the saddle from the now ownerless horse then secured its lead to his steed. He hid the saddle in some bushes and made certain it wasn't easily visible. He turned to Simon, still struggling to get the robes off. "You're still not done?"

"If you'd care to lend your expert hand, you're more than welcome. I, for one, have little experience in stripping a dead man from his clothes."

"That's your first mistake. You're supposed to strip the clothes from the man, not the other way around."

Simon growled at him then finally freed the last appendage from the garment, holding the robe high in victory. Marcus shook his head and motioned for Simon to toss him the robe. He did, and Marcus rolled it up as Simon hid the body under a pile of leaves and branches. Unless someone purposefully came through here, he wouldn't be found for days. Marcus stuffed the rolled-up robe in one of his saddle bags as Simon mounted his horse, and the two of them emerged from the trees, heading back toward the commandery.

"I think that went rather well," commented Simon.

"It would appear so," agreed Marcus as he glanced behind them to find a couple of commoners walking the road in the distance. "Let's pick up the pace. I want to get this robe into the seamstress' hands as quickly as possible."

"Agreed, but let's make sure one of us remembers to tell her that the hole in the chest isn't meant to be there."

Marcus gave him a look. "I'm sure she'll figure that out for herself."

Enclos du Temple, Templar Fortress
Paris, Kingdom of France

Thomas stood to the side and stared in awe and horror at the organized chaos. Carts and carriages had been arriving for hours, each carrying another load of liberated children of all ages. Once unloaded, they would switch coachmen and horses, then leave to pick up more. He had lost count of how many were here, but it was easily three hundred. Those from Lord Archambaud's estate were in the best shape, thanks, apparently, to his daughter Charlotte's efforts. Those from the other estates were being cleaned up by the nuns, then sent off for a hot meal.

Young Christian was behind the line of tables set up to feed the children, his duty to hand each a piece of bread at the end of the line. He was wide-eyed with wonder at it all, and had even met some of those he had been held captive with.

"Renaut!"

Thomas spun toward the shout and saw Christian rushing around the table to hug an older boy.

"Christian! Is that you?"

The older boy embraced Christian and the two of them hopped up and down with excitement as Thomas walked over to join them.

"Christian, who's your friend?"

Christian beamed a huge smile. "This is Renaut! My brother!"

Thomas' chest tightened with the good news. "This is wonderful. Are you all right, Renaut?"

The boy nodded. "Yes, sir. I made it through better than most. They didn't punish the older boys as much since we could work harder."

Thomas frowned. "Well, I'm happy you are well and reunited with your brother."

"When can we go home?"

"Not right away. There is some business that needs to be taken care of, and we need to figure out where you're from."

"We're from Gien. Well, our farm is just outside it."

Thomas grinned at Christian. "There you go! Now we know where you live. We can get you home all the quicker."

Christian's jaw dropped. "Gien! I can't believe I couldn't remember that!"

The gates swung open and a small cart entered with an armed Templar escort, much different than what had been arriving all evening.

"Mother!" cried Christian who sprinted toward the cart, a woman sitting with the coachman leaping down, joy on her face as she held out her arms toward the boy, Renaut rushing to join them. The heartfelt reunion brought tears to Thomas' eyes as everyone looked on, the first family reunited.

Thibault joined him, her eyes glistening. "It is a wonderful sight, is it not?"

"Incredible."

"Amazing how one little fact known by one brother, but not the other, brought two together with the possibility of being returned home."

He eyed her, for her tone suggested a hidden message. "What do you mean?"

"I mean look about you. Have you not noticed what is going on?"

Thomas stared out at the courtyard, but couldn't spot what Thibault was referring to. "I'm sorry, but what is it that I'm missing?"

"Look at them. They're in groups. Two, three, ten. Almost all of them are in groups."

"Isn't that natural? I mean, wouldn't they not want to be alone?"

She pointed at the crowd of children. "Look at their faces and mannerisms. These are all children who know each other."

"Perhaps they met in the prison."

"No, some of them are from Lord Archambaud's estate, but many are from other estates, and they're all mingling together as if old friends. I'm willing to bet that there are more reunifications happening out there than we realize. I'm willing to bet there are siblings, cousins, neighbors, and more reuniting out there. Remember, they're all from the same area of the kingdom. It makes sense, doesn't it?"

Thomas watched the children in this new light, and it suddenly became obvious. There were definitely clusters out there of boys and girls who absolutely knew each other, and that increased the likelihood of at least one in each group knowing where they came from. "We might just get these children home quicker than we hoped."

Thibault agreed then pointed at the artists gathering against the far wall, drawing sketches of the children in the firelight. "We need to get them to focus on the boys who are still alone. They're the ones that will be the challenge."

Thomas smiled at her excitement. The woman accused of having no heart certainly had one tonight, and it was on display for the entire world to see.

Approaching Montereau, Kingdom of France

David smiled as they cleared the forest, the town the commandery was located in just ahead. They had set a brisk pace yesterday evening, taking advantage of the fading light to cover as much distance as possible. He had been determined to reach Sir Marcus before his master went off on another mission, so they had ridden through the night, only stopping to rest the horses.

And they were both feeling it, since a nighttime ride was always more stressful.

"I can't believe I'm saying this, but I can't wait to get home."

David glanced at Jeremy. "Really? I thought you were craving action."

"Oh, it's not that, it's Beatrice's cooking and my bed in the barracks. I guess I'm getting comfortable there."

David agreed. "Aye, I guess I feel the same. I miss the children as well." He grinned. "Now that's something I thought I'd never say."

Jeremy laughed. "I guess we're one big family." He frowned as they entered the town. "We have to win this, don't we?"

"I'm afraid so. Whatever is going on, whether under the direct guidance of Satan or by those who serve him in name only, they must be stopped, or the kingdom could be lost, and those at our farm will have uncertain futures, to say the least."

They rode up to the commandery, the proud red and white flag of the Templar Order fluttering in the breeze, and tied up their horses. David stepped inside and was greeted by a sergeant manning the front desk.

"Squires, what brings you here today?"

David bowed. "Sergeant, we are David and Jeremy. We seek our master, Sir Marcus de Rancourt, or our sergeant, Simon Chastain."

The man jerked a thumb over his shoulder. "They're out back, readying for a mission. We weren't expecting you until later."

"We rode all night."

The sergeant regarded them for a moment. "Were you two involved in the operation yesterday?"

David nodded.

"So, it's true?"

"If you mean that we liberated hundreds of children from captivity, then yes. It was…disturbing."

"I guess so."

"Unfortunately, those responsible escaped justice. Apparently, they left for Montargis yesterday morning, before we arrived."

The sergeant's head bobbed. "Yes, we had a large party travel through here a short while ago. That must have been them. The timing would seem to fit." He jerked his thumb over his shoulder again. "You better hurry if you want to catch your master. He's not expecting you yet, so might leave."

"Thank you, Sergeant." David sprinted down the hall with Jeremy behind him. He threw open the door at the far end and stepped outside, immediately recoiling at the sight that greeted him, and reaching for his bow. A dozen men in the black robes of Satan's Soldiers confronted them. How they had managed to get so close to the commandery was beyond him, but the alarm had to be raised.

"Stand down, squire!" shouted a voice he recognized as he fit an arrow in his bow. His arm darted out to stop Jeremy as Simon and Marcus removed their hoods.

"Thank God! I thought we had just stepped into the den of the enemy!"

Marcus chuckled. "That's exactly what we hope anyone who sees us will think. I'm pleased you made it in time. The last dispatch we had indicated you were on your way."

David shook his head in wonder as the message, sent after they had left, had arrived before they did, the Templar messenger network, especially in the Kingdom of France, incredibly efficient. Outposts, commanderies, and hired stables, all within half an hour's ride with fresh horses and riders at the ready, meant none of the usual delays. A well-rested rider could make extremely good time, especially one with the courage to let his horse do the work when riding at night. It meant a day's ride of a man with a horse-drawn cart or carriage could be covered in less than a couple of hours.

Marcus pointed to a wagon. "Rid yourselves of anything that identifies you as a Templar and put on those robes."

"Where are we going?" asked David as he pulled off his brown tunic.

"We're heading deep behind enemy lines to quite possibly do battle with the Devil himself."

Palais de la Cité

Paris, Kingdom of France

Sir Denys stood in front of the king, this his second audience in as many days. He presented the regent with a joint communique from the heads of the three holy orders that had participated in yesterday's operation. King Philip finished reading it, then placed it on his desk. "Five hundred and twenty-one children."

"Yes, Your Majesty, a shocking number."

"Indeed it is. And they are being well tended to?"

"Yes, Your Majesty. I've seen them for myself. They've all been brought to the Templar fortress and have been cleaned up and fed. Attempts are already being made to identify where they are all from, and local artists are drawing sketches of the boys they haven't been able to identify a hometown for."

Philip's head bobbed. "A brilliant idea. I assume these drawings will be circulated in an attempt to find people who recognize the children."

"Yes, Your Majesty, that's the hope. The fear, of course, is how many of the parents have been killed or will be killed in the upcoming confrontation.

We may end up with many orphans."

"Yes, that is definitely a possibility. I trust that you'll keep me informed on the situation as it develops."

Denys bowed. "Of course, Your Majesty."

"Now, let's speak of this upcoming confrontation. What can you tell me?"

"The three orders and my own personal guard are marching to the Templar commandery in Montereau. We will marshal our forces there, then march on the town of Montargis, which appears to be their stronghold and where all the noblemen that escaped yesterday morning apparently headed for."

"And what size of force are you expecting to face?"

"Certainly in the hundreds, perhaps even over a thousand. We simply don't know. Sir Marcus de Rancourt and his sergeant penetrated the enemy lines in disguise and counted over two hundred of what they're calling Satan's Soldiers inside the town. One of the townspeople told them that the troops were being billeted at farms in the surrounding area. We have no idea how many there are outside of the town."

"And do you believe it is indeed Satan behind this?" There was some hesitation in the king's voice, a hint of fear.

"Your Majesty, what I saw with my own eyes was pure evil. I have never seen anything like it. Hundreds of children held in tiny cages, forced to live in their own filth while slaving all day to enrich men that you and I work with on a daily basis, men who might have different opinions than us, but I always thought to be basically good. How so many could be taking part in such a thing, I have no idea, but where there is evil, there is the Devil."

"Is he in a cave outside the village of Gien?"

"I can't say, but there's only one way to deal with this, and that is with force. We require every possible resource to combat whatever it is behind this, for if this evil is allowed to spread, I fear for the very future of our kingdom."

Philip regarded him for a moment, his finger tapping rapidly on his chin. "The proof that something is amiss is irrefutable, and the fact that all of those behind this enslavement of children have fled to the same location, a location we already have reports on, indicates we must act." He rose. "Assemble the Court. The Kingdom of France is going to war."

Approaching Montargis, Kingdom of France

They were fourteen, now that David and Jeremy had joined them, plus one terrified farmer. Perrot was alone in his cart, and his story if challenged was that he was returning home after successfully selling livestock. Sir Antley had provided the man with a sufficient sum to make the story believable, and if by some stroke of bad luck he ran into someone who remembered he had been traveling with his wife and children, the story was that the children had fallen ill while visiting a cousin. His wife had stayed behind to tend to them, and he had returned to the farm so he could pay the weekly tribute. Every indication was that this entire operation was obsessed with tribute, with taking a cut of every bit of commerce in the area.

To address their concerns over possible spies, a Templar squire had been disguised as Perrot and sent with his wife Marie and their two daughters to Paris under escort. Anyone that might have been watching for him should have either followed, or reported back what they saw. Perrot had then left from the rear of the commandery, his face covered, well in advance of the rest of the contingent. It was essential that Perrot made it back home for two reasons. One, he was the only one who knew where the cave was, and two, his cart hid their equipment, buried underneath a pile of manure, a gift from his cousin to help fertilize his fields, or so the story went. Chainmail and armor for the knights, sergeants, and horses were all in that wagon, which was why it now had two horses pulling it instead of one, the weight substantially higher than normal.

Everyone was traveling in pairs, all wearing their newly acquired black robes, their hoods pulled up. As they approached Montargis, they blended in with others, the genuine Satan's Soldiers surrounding them. It was intimidating to say the least. None of his men wore armor. All they had were their weapons, their defenseless horses, and their skills, his entire team hardened warriors with years of experience on the front lines in the Holy Land.

One of the dispatches they had received from Thomas indicated that Mrs. Thibault believed many of those they faced were recruited from the street gangs in Paris. There was no indication that anyone they faced had true experience in battle, but numbers still mattered, and they could be outnumbered a hundred to one. Everything hinged on Perrot getting through the roadblock ahead, so the farmer was out front, now in line at a much more rigorous checkpoint than when they had encountered it yesterday.

Marcus just prayed Perrot could hold it together long enough to make it through.

Perrot drew a breath, the reek of the manure behind him filling his nostrils, something only a farmer could appreciate. It meant a good crop, it meant his family would be fed, it meant he would have extra in the harvest to trade for the things they needed.

Though none of that was true now. Now that load of manure represented more than any load probably had in history. It could be the key to defeating Satan, to stopping his incursion in the land of man where only God should hold dominion.

There was no possible way they could search the cart without unloading it, and he prayed the stench would limit any questioning. He was waved forward by a man in the dark robes that filled the area. Scores of the enemy surrounded him, and he was terrified. He pulled back on the reins, bringing the horses to a halt, then applied the brake.

"State your business."

"I'm returning to my farm after visiting with my cousin," he said, his voice quavering. He patted the purse hidden under his cloak. "I return with tribute for our master."

His challenger eyed the bulge, his eyes widening slightly at the clinking of coins. "And how did you come by such a sum?"

"I auctioned one of my milking cows and several chickens at the auction yesterday."

The man jerked a thumb over his shoulder at the town. "Here?"

"Yes, sir."

"Did you get a fair price?"

Perrot shrugged and forced a smirk. "Does the seller ever? I got enough to pay my tribute to our master."

The man nodded. "Very well." He stepped back and motioned for Perrot to proceed. Perrot released the brake and flicked the reins, and he prayed those whose scrutinizing eyes were upon him wouldn't notice the difficulty the horses had in getting them moving for a mere load of manure. Nothing was said, and they slowly picked up speed when someone yelled.

"Halt!"

He nearly soiled himself. He turned toward the voice to see if the order was meant for him. His heart stopped as he spotted a finger pointing at him. He pulled back on the reins and applied the brake once again.

"Where are your wife and children?"

He gulped, recognizing the voice of one of the men that had challenged him during their escape. He shouldn't have been surprised. There were dozens here. He had rehearsed this question with Sir Marcus. "They're at my cousin's. If you recall, I said after the auction we were going to visit my cousin. My children fell ill, so my wife stayed with them, and I decided to go back so I wasn't late in paying my tribute."

The man dismounted and drew his sword as he approached. Perrot's eyes bulged as his heart hammered. "I swear, I'm telling you the truth."

"And where did you pick up this load of manure?"

"It was a gift from my cousin. He had more than he needed, and he knew that I had to sell two cows recently, which meant I would be low. It was a great kindness, one that will help with my crops and increase my tribute."

The man raised his sword and plunged it forward, into the manure, then withdrew it, plunging it once more. Perrot was in a near panic. If the blade struck any of the armor hidden underneath, he would be found out and killed, or worse, brought before Satan himself to be feasted upon by the demonic one before facing an eternity in Hell where he'd be punished far worse than any of the others. His mouth was clamped shut, but if he remained silent, he feared it would make him appear guilty.

"Sir, I don't know what you hope to find, but I assure you it's nothing but manure, and it's quite fresh as you can smell. All you're doing is soiling your sword and your hand."

The man withdrew his sword, noticing his hand covered in dung. He cursed and stepped back. "Move along!"

Perrot didn't have to be told twice. He released the brake and flicked the reins, once again praying no one noticed the straining horses, and moments later, he was rolling away from the roadblock once again, this time unchallenged. He closed his eyes and directed them upward toward Heaven.

"Please, God, forgive me for my sins. Please get me through this so that I may see my family once more and give Sir Marcus and his brave brothers the strength to defeat the evil that has possessed my soul."

Marcus and Simon said nothing as they waited in line, the only word said the entire time Perrot made his way through the roadblock was a curse uttered by Simon when the farmer had been stopped and one of Satan's Soldiers searched the manure pile. The man was clearly inexperienced, however. When searching something like that in such a manner, the searcher should remain on his horse so that he thrust his sword down into the pile. Instead, by doing it on foot, the sideboards forced him to pierce at an upward angle, meaning he found nothing but the manure they wanted him to find.

A Templar would never make such a mistake.

They reached the roadblock and were waved through, the black robes provided by the seamstress contracted by the Templars fooling the indoctrinated. They turned onto the ring road and passed the slow-moving Perrot. Nobody said anything as the road was crowded with unfriendly ears. Perrot getting past the roadblock had been the key to this operation proceeding. Now that he had made it through, it was essential to put as much distance between the town and themselves as quickly as possible.

Marcus and Simon picked up the pace to match the rest on the road, leaving Perrot behind. There was only one route to follow to the man's village, which Marcus had already memorized, as had all the others. When they were past the town and the heavy Satan's Soldiers presence, they would rest the horses and make a count of how many of their small force had made it through.

He just prayed that God remained on their side as they pressed deeper into this evil.

Templar Commandery
Montereau, Kingdom of France

Sir Matthew entered the commandery in Montereau and was greeted by Sir Antley. It had been a long ride, started at the crack of dawn. Squires and support personnel had been sent out yesterday by all three orders, and by the time the advance column had reached the outskirts of Montereau, camps had been set up to hold the troops, and anyone wearing the black robes of Satan's Soldiers were being arrested on sight and held in a corral. They had already captured a dozen when he passed, which was a good start.

There was no point in hiding anything anymore. Lord Archambaud and the other noblemen no doubt either left behind observers to watch for their arrival yesterday, or given orders to have updates sent twice a day, and when none arrived, they would know the truth.

A messenger had caught up with them with an update from Sir Denys. The king had committed the entire forces of the kingdom to combat those operating in the name of Satan, but there was no estimate as to when they might arrive and in what numbers. They would give them until morning, but then would have to attack without them. The longer those they opposed had to prepare, the bloodier this battle would be.

Antley showed him into his office and Matthew sat. "What is the latest from this end?"

"Not much, I'm afraid. As per the instructions sent out to all the commanderies and outposts in the region, we've had resources showing up in small numbers and have been redirecting them to the encampments. Perhaps a hundred men so far. Judging by the eagerness of those I've spoken to, I suspect every able-bodied man is on his way here. The opportunity to fight within the kingdom where none expected, is too tempting to pass up."

"A hundred men is a good start, and I think you're right, we can expect more as word spreads."

"And what of the king?"

Matthew threw up a hand. "It's unclear. I received a message from Sir Denys on the way indicating that the king had committed the forces of the realm, however, we have no idea when they're arriving and in what numbers. Depending on how far this problem has spread through the nobility, we may see very little help."

Antley frowned. "That's unfortunate. We know from Sir Marcus that there were over two hundred in the town that they spotted, plus a column moved through here yesterday that we suspect was led by Lord Archambaud, and it had approximately one hundred men and two dozen wagons."

"Some of those would have been loaded with supplies for the journey and for when they got there, but some of the prisoners we interrogated indicated there were loads of weapons and uniforms being sent."

"Yes, I read that dispatch. The uniforms have me curious. Aren't the black robes enough to distinguish them from anyone else?"

"One would think, though whether they're efficient for fighting, I cannot say. From what I saw of those captured so far, I would think they would encumber the ability to wield a blade."

"So, what now?"

"Scouts will be sent out tonight to gather intelligence while the bulk of the force rests and the horses are tended to. Our supply column should be here by morning. Hopefully more of our brothers will arrive through the course of the night, then tomorrow we will march on Montargis, secure it, then expand outward to sweep the area. Any word on Sir Marcus?"

"No, which I'm taking to be good news, for if they hadn't made it past the roadblock, someone would have reported back."

"You didn't send scouts to observe?"

"No, Sir Marcus didn't want to risk anyone being caught as it could raise the alert."

Matthew agreed with the decision, and Antley was right, no news was good news in this instance. "And when is he due to reach the farm near where this cave is located?"

"If all went well, they should be approaching it tonight."

Matthew frowned. "I don't envy the man. His is perhaps the most difficult task we face. And if what the enemy claims is true, that the cave is indeed a portal where Satan can deliver instructions to his minions, they will defend it to the last man. And if his powers extend beyond his realm, I pray God lends Sir Marcus and his team the power necessary to defeat this ultimate evil."

Outside Gien, Kingdom of France

Sir Marcus lay prone on the ground with Simon beside him. It was late evening now, the sun barely providing any light, and ahead lay the village of Gien that Perrot called home. But unlike most villages this size that would be dark but for the glow from fireplaces, candles, and lamps, the entire perimeter of the village was lit by torches, and figures could be seen passing behind them as if on sentry duty.

"Do you think they're expecting us?" asked Simon sarcastically.

"They certainly appear to be expecting someone. Likely, word has spread about the loss of the estates, and if whoever is commanding them has any experience whatsoever, they would have had lookouts along every major access road to this area, and would be aware of our column coming from Paris." He jabbed a finger at the village. "If the cave is indeed near here, they're going to defend this as we would defend Jerusalem."

"Well, we lost Jerusalem."

Marcus chuckled. "True. Which means they can lose this."

"What do we do now?"

"We wait for the others, then try to make our way around the village into

Perrot's farm. I'd like to be hidden on his farm before daybreak, even if he hasn't reached us yet."

Simon gestured at the well-lit village. "Assuming most of their force is behind those flames and not conducting random patrols, we should have little difficulty reaching the farm. These idiots have forgotten that while the fire might allow you to see the immediate vicinity, it not only reveals your position, it deadens your eyes to what lies in the distance."

Marcus agreed. Lighting the village the way their enemy had was a sign of inexperience. The flames likely served two purposes. One, to provide comfort in the dark, the other to capitalize on the visual imagery that this place was indeed commanded from the hellfire below.

Approaching Gien, Kingdom of France

Perrot was far more relaxed now than at the roadblock. As he put more distance between himself and Montargis, the surroundings became more familiar, so much so, that when nightfall came, he didn't bother stopping. He was so close to home now, he was too desperate to reach it to rest. As a result, he couldn't stop yawning, and his ass was killing him. Riding distances like this was uncomfortable for him. He was used to being on his feet, working the farm.

As he rounded the bend and the village came into sight, he gasped. The place he called home should be slumbering, but was instead well lit in a manner he had never seen before. He squinted into the darkness and could see men patrolling the perimeter of the village behind a line of torches, and he pulled back on the reins, uncertain as to what to do. The plan had been to simply ride through the village to his farm, no matter what time of day he arrived. This was, after all, his home, and there was no other way around, not with this heavy a load. He had to go through the village because of the cart, and the Templars needed their equipment, so abandoning it was not an option.

He clasped his hands in front of him and prayed for guidance, but as usual, his prayers went unanswered. A twig snapped to his left and he gasped as two men emerged from the shadows, both holding bows and arrows at the ready, though neither aimed at him. "Are you Mr. Roussel?"

Perrot nodded. "Y-yes, sir."

"My name is David. This is Jeremy. We serve Sir Marcus."

"Oh, thank God. I thought I had been found out."

"You're safe for now. We haven't spotted any patrols. They seem to be staying inside the village."

"What am I supposed to do?"

"Follow the plan. You live here. This is your home. You're returning from having sold your livestock and you have tribute for your master. Just remember your story and you'll do fine. It worked at the roadblock, it will definitely work here where people who know and trust you live."

Perrot drew a deep breath. "You're right. And besides, what choice do I have?"

"You'll be fine. Just remember your story. And don't be afraid to ask questions that would come naturally."

"Such as?"

Jeremy shrugged. "Oh, I don't know. How about, what's with all the fire?"

Perrot cracked a smile, perhaps for the first time in days.

"I suppose you're right. This is my home. I belong here, no matter what master they think I serve." He flicked the reins, urging the horses forward.

"Good luck, Mr. Roussel," said David as Jeremy bowed his head.

"And to you, gentlemen." Perrot closed on the village far more rapidly than he would like, but it was all in his head. As he approached the ring of fire, someone spotted him.

"Who goes there?" shouted a man from the dark.

"It's me, Perrot. What's going on here?"

"Perrot is that you?"

He recognized the voice of one of his neighbors. "Alain?"

"Yes, it's me. Where have you been? Jeban said he saw you leaving in the middle of the night the other day."

Perrot passed through a gap in the torches and brought his cart to a halt, applying the brake as several of his neighbors he recognized approached, the men in black hoods ignoring him. "Aye, that was us. We just wanted to get a jump on the auctions. You know how the prices are better in the morning."

Alain squinted. "Where's your family?"

"Oh, the children got sick so my wife stayed with them at my cousin's place. He's going to run them back when the children are feeling better." He patted his purse. "I wanted to get back in time to pay tribute to our master."

"How did you make out?"

"You know how it is, the prices aren't as good as they used to be, but it'll be enough. Our master will be pleased."

"Good, good." Alain waved a hand in front of his nose. "That's quite the load you've got there."

Perrot laughed. "A gift from my cousin to make up for the shortfall of losing two cows."

"Smells fresh."

"It is. And I can tell you it's been a distinct pleasure to be riding with it for over a day."

Alain roared with laughter then waved him through. "Go on, get home my friend. Rest and we'll see you tomorrow at prostration."

Perrot smiled. "Tomorrow it is." He released the brake then flicked the reins and the horses strained once again, Alain picking up on it immediately.

"Why are your horses having such difficulty?"

Perrot had prepared himself for this question, and it was all the more

266

fitting at this time of night. "I've driven them hard all day. They're exhausted. They'll both be getting a good rub down before I go to bed, I assure you." He kept going, the cart picking up speed, and Alain called after him.

"You should know better than to treat your horses like that."

"I know, my friend, I know, but tribute must be paid."

"Yes, tribute must be paid."

Perrot waved a hand as he left them behind. "Satan is my master, and I pledge my soul to him."

Roussel Farm

Outside Gien, Kingdom of France

"Someone's coming," said one of the sergeants, and Marcus handed the brush he was using on his horse over to one of the squires. He liked to brush down and tend to any horse he was about to ride into battle. It created a bond between horse and rider that could prove invaluable. When the steed trusted the rider in control, they were more likely to take guidance in the stressful conditions of battle without resistance.

Twelve of them were now in the barn on Perrot's property. All they were waiting for were David and Jeremy, who'd been left behind to watch for Perrot, and of course the man himself with the cart carrying all their supplies. Marcus peered through the gaps in the wood to see two riders approaching, their silhouettes recognizable to him at any distance. "Open the doors," he ordered. Two squires swung the doors outward as Marcus beckoned his personal squires inside. They picked up the pace and cleared the doors that then swung closed behind them. They dismounted and bowed to Marcus.

"What's the word on Perrot?" he asked.

David replied. "He's passing through the village now. He appeared to have a friendly conversation with those guarding the road, then they let him pass. He should be here any moment."

"Excellent. Let's make room. Get all the horses in the stalls and everybody out of the way. I want him to be able to pull completely inside the moment he gets here, then we have to get to work."

Simon stabbed a finger at him. "I am not shoveling shit."

Marcus laughed. "My friend, tonight we all shovel shit."

Clearing the other side of the village had been easy, a few pleasantries exchanged without stopping. Satan's Soldiers patrolling the perimeter had ignored him, and now as his farm lay directly ahead, if all had gone according to plan, the Templars should be in the barn, hidden from sight. He rode up the laneway, passing his darkened house, and headed for the barn, the doors swinging open as he approached. He caught sight of Sir Marcus in the pale moonlight and breathed a sigh of relief that he was being greeted by friend and not foe. He pulled in, two of the Templars grabbing the leads and guiding the horses all the way to the back.

The doors closed behind him and his shoulders slumped as his entire body shook with relief that the most difficult and terrifying journey he had ever made in his life was now over.

Marcus extended a hand and helped him down. "Any trouble getting here?"

"No, though I did run into several of my neighbors standing guard. I just stuck to the story we rehearsed and they appeared to have bought it."

"Good." Marcus turned to the others. "Let's get to work."

Squires, sergeants, and knights alike set to transferring the manure. Perrot stood aside, shaking his head at how quickly the work could be completed by a dozen strong men. What he would give to have that many laborers on his farm. Life would be so much easier. The manure was transferred into one of the vacant stalls—they couldn't risk anyone seeing these men working outside, and no one would believe he had come home from a long journey and done the work through the night. If all went according to plan, all this subterfuge should no longer be necessary before the sun set tomorrow, for either they would be freed from Satan's grip, or they would be dead.

Templar Commandery

Montereau, Kingdom of France

Sir Denys cursed the king, and it wasn't the first time he had done so. Nobody had shown up overnight and no messages had arrived indicating when they could expect troops to fight on behalf of the kingdom. Templars, Hospitallers, and Lazarists had continued to trickle in through the night, and they were now a substantial force in their own right.

But would it be enough?

His personal guard were the only soldiers there that didn't belong to a religious order. Sir Matthew stood at the head of the room, briefing the commanders of the various orders on what the scouts had observed overnight. "All indications are that they are expecting us and they no doubt have scouts just as we do. The roadblock is now fortified and they've begun erecting a barrier across the fields, though it's incomplete. Our scouts reported that a large number of the enemy left the town late in the evening, and it is believed they're billeted on farms in the area. That suggests their numbers may not be as large as we feared, and that the count observed in the town is a show of force meant to inflate their perceived numbers.

"But there is a significant change that was noted in our most recent scouting reports. The men returning from the farms are no longer wearing the black cloaks. Most are now equipped with armor, including chainmail with black tunics and surcoats with a coat of arms that the scouts couldn't make out. Inform your men that they're to target not only men in black robes, but also anybody wearing these new markings."

Denys cleared his throat. "Is there any indication of whether these men are actually trained?"

"Drills have been observed, so they are indeed training, however, how well trained they are and how experienced they are isn't known. We suspect few have significant, if any, combat experience."

"What about archers?" asked someone else in the room.

"The reports I've been reading indicate everyone's either carrying a sword or a lance. Almost nobody has a bow. However, for all we know, they have plenty of bows and arrows stored out of sight for when they're needed. Right now, their role has been intimidation of the townsfolk and the surrounding area. That's better done with mysterious robes and swords. When their role turns to defending their territory, we may find they're well prepared."

"So, what's the plan?" asked Denys.

Matthew indicated a map on the wall, the town clearly marked out. "Unfortunately, we don't have any support from the king or the nobles, so it will be up to us. Our aim is to liberate the town, secure it, then to swing through the area clockwise and counterclockwise, sweeping through the farms and mopping up the stragglers in the surrounding villages."

"That's a lot of territory to cover," said Sir John of the Hospitaller Order. "It's most unfortunate that the king has failed us." He pointed at the map. "For all we know, there are hundreds, perhaps more to be dealt with over a huge area, not to mention the fact that my understanding is the locals have

272

converted to Satanism. Depending on how fanatical they are and how firm in their new beliefs, we could be facing thousands."

Matthew agreed. "This is true, which is why we've sent Sir Marcus deep behind enemy lines with a strike force. He will be assaulting the cave from which the witnesses claim Satan delivers his instructions. If he's successful, we'll either prove that this was a hoax, or he'll silence the voice that inspires our opponent."

John inhaled deeply. "And should he fail?"

"Then God help us all."

Roussel Farm

Outside Gien, Kingdom of France

"I still say it smells like shit."

Marcus took a whiff of his chainmail and couldn't disagree. Everything smelled like shit. They had spent the entire night preparing then sleeping in the barn with a load of fresh manure. The sun had just broken over the horizon, and according to Perrot, morning prostrations were about to begin in the cave. It wasn't a daily requirement, merely a weekly one, but every day was busy, especially as the numbers grew.

Tribute must be paid.

The hope was to blend into the crowd. Last night, Perrot had shown them where the cave entrance was, just in case there was any confusion in the light of day. Marcus turned to the man tied to a support post. "Are you comfortable?"

Perrot shrugged. "As comfortable as one can be when bound, I suppose."

Marcus chuckled. "It's for your own good. I don't want you anywhere near that cave when the fighting begins, but people will be expecting you to be there. This way, should we fall, anyone who comes upon you will believe your story. You were jumped when you returned home last night, tied up, and left for dead."

"I pray you succeed, Sir Marcus. I pray all of you make it through this, for should you fail, then all is lost. I would prefer to die here tied to this post than to survive in the hell that would be created upon this earth."

Marcus' head bobbed at the man's words and he turned to the others. "You heard what he said. This fight is a fight we must win. The evil that comes from that cave must be stopped. Whether it is a fiction of man or the horned one himself, it must be stopped. We are fighting for the very future of this realm and victory is not an option. It is a must."

He pulled the hood up on the black robes hiding his armor, then mounted his horse as the others did the same. Jeremy fit a gag over Perrot's mouth before he and David opened the doors to the barn.

Marcus clasped a fist against his heart. "May the Good Lord grant us the strength and the wisdom to prevail today against the evil that has befallen His dominion." As he headed out of the barn, he stared out from under the hood and braced for battle.

A battle from which he likely wouldn't return if his opponent indeed was Satan himself.

Approaching Montargis, Kingdom of France

Sir Denys and his men watched from the rear as the column of almost five hundred knights, sergeants, squires, and support personnel marched toward the town of Montargis. It was an awe-inspiring sight, and he could only imagine what it must be like to witness the massive battles of the crusades where tens of thousands on either side maneuvered for advantage in a battle to the death. The bravery on display today was stirring, and while they were on the side of good, he feared they might not be on the side of the victors by the end of the day.

He cursed the king again. Not a single man had arrived to join in the battle despite his commitment to send the entire force the kingdom could mount. They were going up against Satan and his followers, whether Satan himself had taken possession of the enemy's souls, or they had been tricked into following him. He had seen religious fanaticism before, and in fact was witnessing it now in its purest form. These Christian knights, sworn to protect the innocent, were marching into battle because they believed God was on their side and that He would protect them from the evils they faced. And the same would be true with the enemy who believed that Satan was on their side and would give them the power to defeat any who opposed them.

It had taken almost two hours to reach Montargis and he had no doubt any element of surprise they might have had was gone, and as the trees cleared, revealing the town ahead, there would be no hiding themselves now. He couldn't make out much from his position at the rear, but they continued to press forward, and once he was clear of the trees, he could see the Hospitallers deploying to the left flank, the Lazarists to the right, and the Templar force spreading out like an arrowhead, the bulk of their force still on the road.

He signaled for his men to stop, his orders to stand fast at the forest's edge and to not move in until the roadblock was secured, at which point his force would hold it while the Templars liberated the town.

Somebody shouted ahead and the hundreds of men on horseback roared. Archers behind them loosed the first volley of arrows and Denys held his breath as scores of the deadly weapons sailed through the air in an arc, at the bottom of which destruction reigned. Another volley was sent and then another. He stood in his saddle to see the line of Satan's Soldiers spread out in front of the village, many behind makeshift barriers, some crying out as arrows found their mark.

There was another shout. This time he distinctly heard Sir Matthew ordering the advance. All three religious orders moved in unison, their colors on full display, the sun glinting off their armor as if blessed by the Holy Spirit. God, how he wanted to be there, how he wanted to be up there with those brave warriors as swords clashed and men screamed in rage and terror as the line of cavalry reached the barriers.

The armored horses pushed through and gaps quickly formed as the enemy line broke. The knights charged through, their blades swinging, slicing open their victims, piercing their armor, freeing them of limbs. It was brutal. It was the bloodiest thing Denys had ever witnessed, and as the gore stained the battlefield and the cries of dying men filled his ears, he no longer desired to be there, for he feared he could never live with the memory of what he would have done in the name of God against men, many of whose only sin was being terrorized into serving evil.

"Sir, the roadblock has been cleared," reported his marshal, Guillaume.

Denys drew his sword and raised it in the air. "Advance and secure the roadblock!"

They advanced rapidly toward their assigned position as the knights of the religious orders pressed forward, squires and sergeants eliminating any of the enemy survivors they left behind. As they reached their new post, slick with blood, the barriers cast aside, Guillaume gasped and pointed. "Sir!"

Denys turned to where his marshal was pointing and his jaw dropped as hundreds of enemy soldiers, most on horseback with armor and their new uniforms, emerged from the town.

This battle could yet still be lost.

Outside Gien, Kingdom of France

Marcus rode with Simon by his side, his team mixing in with Satan's worshipers as they headed for the cave. So far, blending in had been no problem, the black robes serving their purpose well and providing anonymity to those who hid behind them, friend or foe.

As they neared the cave, the crowd thickened and the numbers of Satan's Soldiers increased. Last night, he counted only six guards, but now there were dozens. It was rapidly changing the dynamics of the situation. They were fourteen, and the plan he had been developing was based on them fighting six, perhaps a dozen, to take control of the cave. He had expected civilians in large numbers as Perrot had advised him, but they weren't a threat, even if they chose to fight. But now with scores of the enemy in the area, he had to rethink things.

What was the goal? The goal was to discover the truth. Was this indeed a portal for Satan to communicate with his followers? The real question was, would they be battling with Satan and the powers he possessed, or merely his voice and the terrorized devotion it inspired? If they were fighting the power of Satan, then no blade could defeat him, only the power and glory of God. But that victory could take time, which meant they had to hold the cave, if they even managed to take it in the first place.

The opening was just ahead, and guards in black robes were directing people in and out in batches, those entering all carrying something, those exiting, their hands empty.

Tribute must be paid.

It all reeked to him. His logical mind asked what needs Satan would have of tribute, but he had seen exactly what it was used for—to raise an army of men. And that required money. The assault on Montargis would have already begun, so word would reach here within several hours at most. Whatever they were going to do, they had to do now without delay, for only more would be arriving.

He stared at the opening as it came into view, tucked behind an outcropping of rock, and he thought of the legend of three hundred Spartans holding back an entire army because they had the advantage of position. But the same was true of the defenders here. If he and his team revealed themselves too soon, it would give the defenders time to fall back inside the cave and prevent them from entering.

They had to get into the cave without raising suspicions.

A horse corral was set up nearby, meant for worshipers and Satan's Soldiers to leave their horses while heading inside for prostration. He guided his horse over to the entrance of the corral then dismounted as the gate was opened by what appeared to be a local who said nothing, instead staring at his feet. Marcus gently smacked his horse's hind quarters, sending it in with the others, and Simon did the same.

They both slowly headed for the entrance as the others of their team rid themselves of their horses. Marcus stood not twenty paces from where he needed to be, and steadied his heart, the excitement of what was to come surging through his veins. This could be the end of a long career devoted to

God and the Order, or could be his greatest victory.

All fourteen of his team were now off their horses, and it was beginning to appear slightly suspicious. There was no more time to wait.

This fight begins now.

Montargis, Kingdom of France

Sir Denys watched in horror as hundreds of arrows loosed from within the town rained down on the Templars directly ahead of him. Shields were raised and the trained men drew in their limbs, minimizing their exposure, but too many arrows found their mark on man and beast. The archers of the religious orders returned fire blindly, no targets in sight within the town.

"Continue to target the main force!" shouted Matthew from the midst of the melee.

The archers redirected their effort on targets of opportunity, of which there were plenty. The Templars were holding the line, the disciplined force using its years of experience against the superior numbers of the enemy, but they were losing too many. Wounded were stumbling toward Denys' position, helped by the less infirm. He checked behind them to see that there was no danger between the roadblock and the tree line. He turned to Guillaume. "Take ten men. Have them help the wounded and get them to the wagons."

"Yes, sir!" replied Guillaume, barking orders, half his force rushing forward to help the walking wounded—the dead would remain for another time. Denys feared if this continued much longer, the dead would far outnumber the living, and he damned the king once again as someone shouted that the Lazarists had fallen. He rose in his saddle and stared to his right, cursing at the sight of what remained of their right flank, retreating toward the tree line.

They were going to lose this fight.

There were simply too many, and they were too well prepared.

Outside Gien, Kingdom of France

Marcus bowed his head as he had seen the other black-robed soldiers do, and headed for the entrance. He noticed they were murmuring something and he strained to hear what it was, but the only words he could catch were, "my master." He flashed back to what Perrot had told him they were supposed to repeat within the cave. "Satan is my master, and I pledge my soul to him," he said, his skin crawling with the words.

Simon repeated them, and he prayed the others would think to do so as well. He passed through the entrance, immediately taken by the chill. Inside was damp with a peculiar odor filling the air that took him a moment to place.

Brimstone.

It was dark, the passageway narrow, but light flickered ahead, a dull orange glow cast over the stone. He breathed in deeply through his nose, the pungent odor almost overwhelming, but he had to steady his heart and pray to his Lord Jesus Christ as he repeated the hateful words that now echoed off the walls around them, his voice mixed with Simon's and others that lay ahead.

The passageway opened up into a large chamber with dozens inside, many lying face down on the floor. His expert eye swept the area from left to right, doing a mental tally of how many were inside with them, including how many were soldiers and how many were merely followers. He was directed to the rear of the room, and the chants grew noticeably in intensity as the near-circular room focused all the echoes of the devotees toward the center.

The chant ended and everyone on the floor rose quickly, filing toward an altar at the front of the chamber. Names were stated before tribute was handed over, everything recorded in a log, then the empty-handed headed outside.

Marcus mimicked the others that had arrived with them, lining up in rows in the center of the chamber when suddenly the entire room shook. The vibrations of the most terrifying voice he had ever heard surged from the bottom of his feet all the way up his legs and spine and into his mind.

"Who is it that dares enter my dominion?"

And for the first time in his life, he felt genuine fear.

They were indeed here to fight Satan.

And today they would die.

Montargis, Kingdom of France

Denys' marshal Guillaume had organized wagons from the rear and the wounded were now being loaded and hauled away from the battlefield. The Templars continued to hold their line, but their numbers were thinning and the orders shouted were no longer by Sir Matthew. Denys feared the worst for the man.

The Lazarists' line had completely collapsed, leaving the Templars' right flank exposed. Rather than thin their lines more, they had fallen back slightly, the line curving to prevent substantial numbers from outflanking them. But it would only last for so long. The enemy had recognized the weakness, and he could see from his own position that scores of the black-uniformed opposition were heading toward the now weakened flank.

This battle was already lost. Someone had to order the retreat, but with Matthew down, he feared no one dared give it, the religious zealotry he had feared they would face from their opponents, now on full display. These men were fighting for God against Satan, and they were willing to die for the cause rather than live to fight another day.

This could lose them the war.

He stopped one of the Templar sergeants. "Who's in command?"

"I don't know. I saw Sir Matthew fall."

"Who would take command if he falls?"

"Any one of the knights. Just listen for whoever's shouting orders."

"Thank you, Sergeant." Denys let him go and peered into the chaos. The arrows from the enemy had stopped as the Templars engaged their opponents in hand-to-hand combat, leaving no way for the archers hidden within the town to target only their enemy. It had helped limit the unchallenged casualties, but even as each Templar Knight bested two or three of the enemy, more continued pouring into the battle, whereas those on the side of God had no reinforcements, abandoned by their king and his cowardice.

He spotted a knight shouting an order and urged his horse forward. Guillaume cursed from behind him, barking orders at his personal guard to accompany him, and the small group surged forward into the battle, swords drawn. Squires had killed the enemy that riddled the ground behind the knights and sergeants on horseback, leaving few threats. He soon reached the front line, and the Templar Knight who appeared in command spotted him.

"Sir Denys, it's not safe for you to be here!"

"It's not safe for any of us," replied Denys. "We are losing this battle. The order must be given to retreat so we can regroup and fight another day. We've lost our right flank, and the Hospitallers are faltering on our left. It's only a matter of time before we're surrounded. We need to leave now while we still can, otherwise there'll be nobody left to defend the realm."

"This is a fight to the death, sir, and God is on our side. We will prevail."

A horn rang out behind them, a trumpet call he would recognize anywhere. The entire battlefield came to a momentary halt as everyone turned toward what could only be described as the horn of the Archangel

Gabriel, crying out over the battlefield. Denys' chest ached with hope as he beheld thousands of troops spreading out across the battlefield with the king's colors flying proudly at the head of the army he had promised.

Victory would be theirs this day, for those who fought in the name of God were about to damn the Devil from the lands God held dominion over.

Outside Gien, Kingdom of France

The evil that surrounded Marcus was palpable. He could feel it in the damp air that forced the sweat from his skin, in his nostrils filled with the putrid stink of the brimstone and torches, through the vibrations Satan's voice pulsed up his body, through his ears overwhelmed by the whispered words that echoed so loudly. Satan, whom he had never doubted was real, was indeed here, and it was the most terrifying thing he could imagine.

How they would be victorious over the lord of the underworld was beyond him. His faith faltered, his confidence that God and the Good Lord were at his side wavered. But he had to get control of his fear. Satan was here. Perrot had been correct. Everything they had been told was true, which made victory all the more important. This incursion into God's dominion had to be halted, and they were the only ones that could do it.

He inhaled deeply, ignoring the sting in his nostrils, the pain in his lungs. He lay down on the floor as the others did, and turned his face toward Simon, whose eyes reinforced his own fear as Satan's voice rumbled on in Latin. Marcus ignored the words, instead focusing on the task at hand as he slowly calmed his hammering heart.

"How many of ours have made it inside?"

Simon shook his head. "I don't know. I spotted two others, so there are at least four of us."

"That will have to do. We have to secure the entrance so no more can get in."

"That could mean no more of our own."

"We'll have to risk it. As soon as the ritual is over, we take action."

Simon nodded and the chants stopped. Moments later, everyone rose and Marcus gave the signal by gripping the hilt of his sword. Simon did the same as Marcus' eyes traveled around the room, mentally counting how many of the black-robed figures also gripped their swords.

There were eight of them.

This was it. They had to act now. He stepped toward one of the guards then drew his sword, the sound of others unsheathing around him echoing through the chamber as Marcus' blade swung, removing his target's head. Panicked worshipers surged toward the exit as Marcus advanced on the next guard before he could react. Blades swung around him, the element of surprise on their side, and within moments, the black-robed guards were no more, and the civilians there for prostration and payment of tribute had fled through the narrow entrance.

Marcus pointed at the gap in the wall. "Secure the entrance. Only our people get through."

As if on cue, David and Jeremy rushed inside, followed by two more.

"Report!"

David pointed from whence they had come. "Two sergeants are holding the front entrance. It's confusion outside at the moment, but they'll regroup."

"Understood." Marcus pointed at the altar. "See if that can be moved, we might be able to block the entrance with it. No matter what happens, from this point forward, nobody gets inside this chamber until we force Satan back to the pits of Hell."

Montargis, Kingdom of France

The enemy lines collapsed quickly with the arrival of the promised army. Thousands of troops on horseback and foot marched forward as the Templars quickly fell back, leaving the enemy exposed. Hundreds of arrows rained down on them, quickly thinning their numbers. As scores of the enemy fell in quick fashion, those that remained fled back toward the town, pursued by the reinvigorated Templar force, backed up by the thousands of new arrivals.

Denys spotted Matthew lying on the ground, an arrow through his shoulder. Two squires attended to him, and the man raised a weak hand as he spotted Denys coming toward him.

"Better late than never, I suppose," said the warrior monk.

"Yes, I feared all was lost."

"How goes the battle? I can't see anything."

Denys delivered a professional assessment as he scanned the battlefield. "The Hospitallers have firmed up and are now advancing on our left flank, backed by at least five hundred men. The Templar front has reached the edge of the village with at least a thousand men backing them." He turned to the right flank. "What remains of the Lazarists have been joined by what must be a thousand men. The town should be encircled shortly and then we'll burn them out if we have to. Victory will be ours, Sir Matthew."

"Glory be to God," said Matthew as he winced, one of the squires pulling the arrow through.

"Will he be all right?"

The squire nodded. "He should be. I just need to cauterize the wound to stop the bleeding."

Matthew grunted. "But will I be able to swing my sword?"

"God willing, sir, yes, but I make no promises. Your ability to wield the sword is in God's hands now."

Matthew grunted. "As I suppose it always was. Now, finish with this wound. I have a battle to command."

Outside Gien, Kingdom of France

David roared as he pushed with all of his might, the heavy stone altar top finally moving as he and Jeremy executed Marcus' orders. But it was simply too heavy. "We're going to need more hands here!"

Simon and another sergeant stepped over, and between the four of them, they lifted the stone top and carried it toward the entrance. Simon, fully armored, led them through the narrow opening as shouts erupted from the entrance and swords clashed.

"Order them to fall back as soon as you're ready to position the stone!" shouted Marcus.

Simon merely grunted under the strain of the slab as they pushed deeper through the passageway leading to the outside. The sounds of the battle grew as they were enveloped in darkness, a hint of sunshine ahead, and David became painfully aware he had nothing but a dagger to defend himself with, his bow left behind in the cave.

They reached a bend and Simon turned back toward them. "It opens up past here. Let's set it up here."

David set down his end and the sergeants pushed the opposite end up toward the ceiling. It was the height of a man and could prove a good barrier if they could somehow lock it in place. He noticed a protrusion in the wall on the right. "Push it toward me. We can wedge the corner up there."

The two sergeants pushed harder as David and Jeremy guided it into the slot.

"It fits perfectly." David gripped at the opposite edge and yanked then pushed. The slab wouldn't move. There was barely enough room for a man to squeeze by, and it would limit the enemy to sending one at a time.

Simon attempted to squeeze through with all of his armor. "This isn't going to work."

"Let's just slide it out of the slot and get our people on this side, then we can reposition."

Everyone hauled at the slab, tilting it back out then toward David and Jeremy, who supported it while the sergeants squeezed past.

"Fall back!" shouted Simon, his order echoing through the passageway. The sound of the battle changed, the clinking swords stopping as footfalls echoed. "Hurry!" shouted Simon, beckoning to someone.

David couldn't see anything, his view blocked by the slab. Two squires rushed past them followed by two sergeants.

"Now!" shouted Simon.

David shoved with all his might, twisting the slab back into position as the roar of the pursuers filled his ears. The slab locked into place with a satisfying thud, then everyone stepped back. One of the knights took up position in the protected corner, his blade held high. A sword jabbed through the opening, followed by the arm holding it. The knight's blade dropped, severing the arm, a scream erupting on the other side. The enemy turned to slamming against the slab in an attempt to break through. The knight pressed his body against it, providing it with some support.

"We should be able to hold this for a little while, but it's too crowded in here for a proper defense." The man pointed to the two squires that had been fighting at the entrance. "You two stay here." He indicated another knight. "We'll hold this. The rest of you go do what we came here to do."

David shuddered at the thought as they hurried back toward the cavern. They might have delayed the horde from outside that wanted their heads, but they had also blocked themselves in with Satan.

If God weren't on their side, they were not going to survive.

Montargis, Kingdom of France

Sir Denys led his men deeper into the town and was sickened by the carnage. Scores of the enemy were dead or dying. He didn't mind that, if they were all truly evil, but he had his doubts, as some of those he saw could barely be called men. The fighting was far enough ahead that his men were merely protecting the rear as the mass of combined forces swiftly pushed through the town.

He spotted one of the enemy in the new uniform, dead, face down in the mud. He dismounted and his guard surrounded him as he flipped the body over and gasped at the coat of arms emblazoned on the man's tunic, a coat of arms he hadn't been able to see from his previous vantage point.

Guillaume noticed it as well. "Is that what I think it is?"

Denys continued to stare at the coat of arms. He was certain it was what he suspected, but it was covered in mud and he had to be certain. "Canteen!" he shouted, thrusting a hand in the air.

One of his men dismounted, handing over a canteen. Denys poured it over the dead man's chest, wiping away the mud, revealing the pristine coat of arms of Charlemagne.

And suddenly everything made sense.

Outside Gien, Kingdom of France

"How dare you violate my sanctum! Surrender now, and I may spare your lives, defy me, and I will possess your souls for eternity, and you will suffer like no one before you."

Marcus held his sword in front of him, struggling to control his fear. He had no doubt the voice he was hearing was that of Satan. No man could ever make himself sound like this. But this had always been a possibility. The fact they had made it this far and secured the entrance, at least temporarily, without any casualties on their side, meant God stood with them and Jesus Christ wielded a sword of righteousness by his side.

And that was all he needed to be victorious over the ultimate evil.

"Reveal yourself, you coward! Your words mean nothing to me!" he shouted back as he slowly circled the room, eying every shadow for a sign of the beast.

"Mere mortals can't bear the sight of me. You would die in terror the moment you laid your eyes upon me! Surrender now and I'll allow you to leave, defy me and I shall reveal myself as I welcome your souls into the ranks of the condemned."

Marcus pressed his back against the far wall as the nine others with him continued to slowly turn, watching for any sign that the Devil might make good on his threat. "I fight on the side of our Lord Jesus Christ. He gives me the strength to resist you. While the sight of you might fill the sinner with fear enough to kill him, my heart is filled with love for my Lord. My body brims with the strength God gives me to resist evil in all its forms. Again, I challenge you, reveal yourself!"

Simon, in the center of the chamber, turned toward him, his eyes narrowed.

"Your god holds no dominion here. This is my domain and mine alone."

Simon approached as Satan continued his rant. Simon pressed his mouth to Marcus' ear. "When you were speaking and you faced the wall, your voice almost sounded like his."

Marcus eyed him. "What do you mean?"

"I mean, you sounded almost as evil as he did. Just not as loud."

Marcus stared at his sergeant then turned toward the wall. He pointed at where he had been standing. "You try it."

Simon took his position as Marcus headed to the center of the chamber, Satan still spewing his venom. Marcus gestured at his sergeant to say something.

Simon faced the wall. "Listen, asshole, if you promise I don't have to shovel shit for eternity. I may consider your offer to surrender."

Marcus' jaw dropped. His sergeant's words were distorted, turned into a deep rumble, nowhere near the intensity of the voice they had been hearing, but the effect was obvious to him and the others in the room as they all stared at each other in shock. Simon joined the group now collected in the center of the room.

"What's going on?" asked Jeremy. "Are we all becoming possessed by being in here?"

Marcus dismissed the idea. "No, I've heard of this. If a wall or a room is shaped just so, someone can whisper in just the right point and the sound is carried, even amplified. Something's happening here that's distorting the voice, making it sound demonic." He stabbed a finger in the air. "That's not Satan we're hearing. That's a man, and I'm willing to bet I know who that man is."

Montargis, Kingdom of France

Denys hailed the king's representative on the battlefield. "Lord Garnier!"

Garnier spun on his saddle. "Sir Denys, it's good to see you survived until our arrival."

"Thanks to the Templars and the others."

"Yes. If you'll forgive me, sir, I have a battle to fight here."

"Yes, but are you aware of who you are fighting?"

"Those who would serve Satan, I am told."

"No. This has nothing to do with Satan." He jumped off his horse and grabbed one of the bodies lying on the ground. He tore off the tunic and held it up. "This is who we are fighting. This is what it's all about."

Garnier's eyes narrowed, puzzled, then his mouth was suddenly agape with recognition. "That's the coat of arms of Charlemagne!"

"Exactly. Three centuries ago, King Philip's family ousted power from Charlemagne's. This is all a play to regain the throne. We aren't fighting Satan at all. We're fighting Lord Archambaud, who is a direct descendant of the Carolingian Dynasty."

"But what about this cave I've heard tell of where Satan speaks?"

302

Denys shook his head. "I have no idea, but it must be a trick of some sort." He stabbed a finger at the coat of arms. "This is what it's all about. The throne. This is a rebellion against the king designed to look like something else. When we defeat those who oppose us, Lord Archambaud and the others who joined him in this must be brought to justice."

Garnier bristled. "If what you say is true, they shall all pay with their heads." He turned in his saddle. "Get me a messenger! The king must be informed of this at once." He turned to Denys. "You have done well today, Sir Denys. You shall be mentioned in my dispatches. You and the Templars may have just saved the king's throne."

Denys bowed deeply. "I am but a loyal servant."

Garnier dictated his message to the king and Denys returned to his horse, wondering how the Templar leadership would feel if they knew they were helping preserve the throne of one of their greatest rivals.

Outside Gien, Kingdom of France

"We need some relief!" shouted someone from down the corridor, the clashing of swords not having ceased during their discovery of the trickery. Marcus pointed at one of the knights and a sergeant. "Go relieve them." He jerked his chin at two squires. "Join them. Hold that line no matter what happens."

"Yes, sir," replied the knight, and they disappeared down the passageway, the four weary men manning the passage appearing a few moments later as the battle continued at the chokepoint they had created.

"How goes it?" asked Marcus.

One of the knights responded as he leaned against the wall. "You can only hack off so many arms without getting tired."

Marcus chuckled. "Perhaps serving in the Kingdom of France has made you soft."

The knight laughed. "It has. If I make it out of this alive, I vow to redouble my training." He jerked a thumb over his shoulder at the battle. "The stone is holding, but I saw the hints of a crack. If they put their backs into it, they could be breaking through shortly."

"Then we have no time to waste. We believe that voice that continues to rage at us is nothing but trickery. The shape of this chamber makes a man's voice sound evil. We need to find this man. He's obviously hidden somewhere. Search every bit of these walls, floor to ceiling, every nook, every cranny, every crevice. Test its strength with your sword. He has to be hidden here somewhere."

Marcus faced the wall and drew his dagger, tapping at the wall from as high as he could reach until he was on his knees, then repeating it a hand's width to his left. The others all spread out, doing the same. He listened to the rants, the same threats repeated, the same demands to surrender made, the same claims over their souls. But as they continued their meticulous search, there was one thing this so-called Satan revealed—he couldn't see them. Surely, he would have said something about the futility in what they were doing, but he had said nothing, instead, merely getting angrier and angrier as Marcus ignored him, no longer responding to his taunts.

There was no point. This was but a man, and he was quite certain he knew who he was.

"The stone is breaking!" shouted somebody from down the corridor.

Marcus cursed as he stepped over to the entrance and shouted, "Hold for as long as you can then fall back to the cavern!"

"Yes, sir!"

A thought occurred to him. They hadn't found anything yet in the cavern, and something as obvious as another passageway should have been clearly evident with all the firelight. All they had found were crevices and small gaps enough to fit a blade in but little more. There was only one place in this cavern they hadn't searched yet and they didn't have a clear view of.

The passageway.

"My followers grow closer, your defeat is inevitable. My legion will skin you alive for your insolence!"

Lord Archambaud paused, cocking an ear, again hearing nothing in response. Whoever was in the chamber had stopped speaking, and now he heard only the occasional shout, the last indicating his followers were breaking through the tunnel.

The question was, who were these men? It was obviously an organized, disciplined effort, and that could only mean his secret had been discovered. But how much was known to his enemies? Did they know of the Satan hoax? He didn't think so. The responses from his challenger were certainly addressed to Satan. Were these religious warriors here to fight the demon he was impersonating? A small group of warrior monks perhaps, that had somehow discovered this location?

They had wiped out the Templars a week ago in Montargis. It was plausible that they investigated and somebody talked, but the Templars were no match for the army he had raised. This was a plan decades in the making, slowly plotted behind the scenes as he gathered supporters to oppose the king. It was delicate work, painfully deliberate work, for if the wrong person was approached, if the wrong thing was said or overheard, it would be his head.

But a casual remark made by Father François two years ago had sparked a memory from his youth. "The reason we see so much evil on Earth is that man fears Satan, but not Jesus Christ, who is all loving. Satan commands a good man to do his bidding out of fear, and that man will do evil on this Earth, secretly praying that all will be forgiven by the Good Lord on his deathbed." It had been an interesting conversation that followed.

The Carolingian family had been unfairly ousted from the throne, and it had taken generations for their descendants to regain their stature in the Court. But now was the time for the Carolingian family to reclaim the throne from the incompetent Philip, whose follies on the battlefield and ineptitude with the kingdom's finances had them deeply indebted to the Templar Order, among others.

But raising an army was difficult, and almost impossible for it to go unnoticed. But this idea that good men would do evil out of fear had reminded him of a youthful adventure when he visited lands his family once controlled to the south, and a cavern in the hillside with a unique characteristic. His cousin had him stand in the exact location he now stood, and speak in barely a whisper. His voice was magnified and twisted into a demonic growl that had him almost soiling himself the first time he had heard it.

It was a terrifying experience, forgotten for over thirty years, remembered at the dinner table one night with Father François, and it had set a plan in motion, a plan, that as it began to work, terrified even him at how successful and twisted it had become.

But as his wealth grew from the scheme, and his followers multiplied, it became clear he would be successful, and the ends justified the means. Philip had to be ousted, replaced by him in order to save the kingdom from its king's ineptitude. Once he was in power, he could release those he had fooled from the terror that now ruled them. He would claim he defeated Satan's armies in the name of God, freeing all those who had been kidnapped, though not before killing all the witnesses, which unfortunately now included his daughter.

He had sent her and his wife away to protect them from what was to come, so there'd be no chance they might stumble upon his secret, but with his wife's death and his daughter's unexpected return, that part of his plan had been shattered. It had disappointed him when he found out she would have to die to maintain his secret.

But unfortunately, his secret was out. She had escaped, and that same night, someone had infiltrated the grounds. His reports indicated a force of

Templars and other religious orders had raided the estates and a Templar force was headed their way, likely already engaging his troops. But he had far more than they suspected, and his superior numbers would make quick work of the Templars, then they would march on the capital and surprise an unprepared king.

He would use the wealth he had been accumulating for years to bribe the other noble families into backing him, and soon the kingdom would be his, regardless of the stories Templars would tell of the children held on his estate. He would deny them as the rantings of an order owed money by a king now dead, a debt he intended to never pay.

The plan could still work, he just needed to make it out of this current situation alive.

Marcus felt his way along the walls, both hands outstretched, running along the cool rock. He took his time to run his hands up and down, not wanting to miss any openings high or low, for he might only have one chance at this. The fighting ahead was desperate, someone shouting moments ago that the slab had split in two. The line would fall back soon.

His left hand found a void and he stopped, his heart hammering as he investigated and smiled. There was a narrow opening. He tried to fit through it but couldn't. "Jeremy!" he shouted, and his squire responded.

"Sir?"

"Get down here!"

Footfalls echoed and Jeremy was soon at his side.

"Get me out of this armor."

Jeremy set to work, expertly removing the chainmail.

Marcus handed him a dagger. "Come with me." He squeezed through the opening, his sword extended in front of him, and he wriggled his large frame several paces until it opened up slightly. He could see a flame flickering ahead and a man's voice whispering the rantings they had heard since they arrived.

A man's voice, not a demon's.

Marcus smiled as he rounded a bend and spotted a man, silhouetted by a lone torch, whispering at the wall in front of him. "Lord Archambaud, I presume?"

The man spun toward him then reached for the sword on his belt. Marcus stepped forward and slammed his fist into the man's nose, shattering it, knocking him out cold.

"They're through!" shouted someone behind him, and he turned to Jeremy, putting a finger to his lips.

"They likely don't know this is here."

It would only be a matter of time before his entire team was slaughtered, and even if his brothers were successful in Montargis, they were hours at least away from rescuing his team.

Then a thought occurred to him, and he stepped over to the wall where Lord Archambaud had been standing, struggling to formulate the words necessary to end this once and for all.

He closed his eyes and steadied his breath, sickened by what he was about to say.

"For those of you who serve me and call me master, I salute you. The battle is over and we are victorious. I order you to lay down your arms and return to your former lives. I release your souls and those of your loved ones back to God and his dominion. My work here is done, and so is yours. Again, lay down your arms and return home, your souls and those of your loved ones are free. Take this message to all my followers throughout my dominion. My time here is done."

He paused and listened. He could barely make out anything being said in the cavern until Simon's voice came through distinctly.

"Well, you heard your master, lay down your weapons and go home!"

A sword clinked, then another, but there was still fighting in the passage to the outside. Someone shouted, "Satan has freed us! Satan has freed our souls! Lay down your arms and go home!"

More swords clattered on stone and a few moments later, Marcus smiled as Simon had no doubt figured it out.

"Oh, master, can I please go home now? I've got shit to shovel."

Marcus laughed. "Is it all clear?"

"Yes, sir. The enemy is gone."

"Excellent. Secure the entrance. I'll be out in a moment."

"You should clear your throat. It sounds like you've got something caught in it."

Marcus laughed then pointed to Jeremy who led the way as Marcus dragged Archambaud's unconscious body. They squeezed back out into the main passageway to find the others heading for the entrance. Simon was bringing up the rear with a torch, and stopped as Jeremy helped Marcus back into his armor.

"You should have heard yourself. It's going to take me a few days to be able to look you in the eye and not think you'll possess my soul."

"It was that effective, was it?"

Simon shuddered. "Unbelievably. I can see why so many were so easily fooled. I could tell it was you because I could recognize your voice slightly, but it was so inhuman, so demonic that you could have put Angeline behind there and I might have bowed down to her and pledged my soul."

Marcus' head bobbed as he tested his armor. "That makes sense. There's no way Lord Archambaud was here the entire time. Others would have been speaking on his behalf, playing the role. My guess is he came here to have a little fun from time to time, and today he was here hiding out from our forces, just in case things went wrong in Montargis. That would explain the additional forces here."

Simon held out the torch, staring at Lord Archambaud with disdain. "What are we going to do with him?"

"Tie him up and hold him here until our forces arrive. While the people here have surrendered, we don't know what's happening outside. The plan was for a force to be sent here as soon as Montargis was secured. If they were successful, then they should reach here either by evening or early tomorrow. We'll hole up here, and if it becomes absolutely necessary, we'll let the people in the chamber and I'll pretend to be Beelzebub once again."

Simon gave him a look. "Just don't let it go to your head."

Marcus ran his fingers through his hair and shrugged. "No horns yet."

Enclos du Temple, Templar Fortress
Paris, Kingdom of France

Marcus passed through the gates of the Templar fortress at the head of the Templar column, at the right-hand side of the wounded Sir Matthew. The commander of the Templar Order in the Kingdom of France would survive, and from what Marcus knew of the man, he would fight hard to make a full recovery so that he might one day wield the sword on behalf of their savior. The relief column had arrived at the cave late in the evening, and Marcus and his men had spent the night camping at Perrot's farm, the man delighted to hear one of the dispatches that had arrived with the column, indicating his wife was safe at the fortress with all their children, including Christian and Renaut.

Lord Archambaud had been handed over to those acting on behalf of the king, and he was already in a dungeon awaiting execution. Several of the other noblemen involved had been captured, several others killed, but there were still at least two missing, though any power they once had was now gone, and the threat they posed minimal.

The king had ordered the cave sealed so that it couldn't be used again to trick his people, and cartloads of children were already leaving the fortress, returning the most innocent of the victims to their families, dozens of carts passed on the way here.

"Sir Marcus!"

Marcus turned to see Thomas waving. Tanya bolted and Marcus dismounted as she leaped up, putting her paws on both his shoulders and licking his face. He jerked away laughing, then patted her hard and pushed her back to the ground.

"I think she likes you," said Matthew.

"I think so."

Matthew dismounted and two stableboys took their horses away. "It would appear the Templar Order is once again in your debt."

Marcus dismissed the notion. "One can hardly be in debt to the order he has pledged his life to serve in the name of our Lord."

"This is true, but you and I both know you have other responsibilities now."

Marcus sighed as Simon, David, and Jeremy joined him, Jeremy rolling on the ground with Tanya. "Yes, I suppose I do. I always thought my brothers would be my only family, but now I suppose I have two families."

Matthew placed a hand on Marcus' shoulder and gave it a squeeze. "My brother, your family is our family. Should they ever need anything, should anything ever happen to you, know that the Order will embrace them and see that they are well taken care of."

Marcus' chest ached with the commander's words. "I am honored, sir, and if you ever have the time, I extend to you an invitation to come and spend a couple of days at the farm and meet this growing family you've adopted."

"It would be an honor."

"I'm afraid, however, if you do take me up on my invitation, all I can

313

offer you is a bed in our barracks."

"It will be a pleasure to sleep among brothers and share in the simple life I once knew before command placed such a burden on me."

Simon leaned forward. "Well, sir, if you're looking to embrace the simple life, I will be more than happy to lend you my pitchfork so you can join in on the shit shoveling."

THE END

ACKNOWLEDGMENTS

A few years ago, someone named Wessel Gordon emailed me. He told me he was a huge fan, was interested in becoming a member of my proofreading team, and pointed out a continuity error in a book published many years ago.

I can't remember if I replied.

I get a lot of requests to join the proofreading team, and if you're an author, you will know from experience that many people are simply looking for a free lunch. My team has been with me for years, and some of them I know personally, the rest through hundreds of emails over the past decade.

But Wessel persisted, always providing me with new feedback, and eventually it became clear that he was indeed a fan, and was buying the books since he was sending me genuine feedback, so I decided to give him a chance.

And it breaks my heart that after only two books, he became so sick that he was unable to do the work he had been so eager to do. He provided me and several others with regular health updates, and none of them were good, then the updates stopped.

Another member of the team, also in South Africa, reached out and told me Wessel had finally succumbed.

A tragic loss.

Rest in peace, Wessel.

His obituary is after these acknowledgments should you care to learn a little more about his difficult life.

Now for a fun fact. The cave in this book is real. Years ago, I came across it in my Internet travels, and made a note that it would make a great idea for a book. Now, all these years later, I can't find the article to share with you, but it does exist, and it's in France. If you can find it, please let me know!

As usual, there are people to thank. My dad, as always, for the research, and of course, my wife, daughter, my late mother who will always be an angel on my shoulder as I write, as well as my friends for their continued support, and my fantastic proofreading team!

To those who have not already done so, please visit my website at www.jrobertkennedy.com, then sign up for the Insider's Club to be notified of new book releases. Your email address will never be shared or sold.

Thank you once again for reading.

THE TEMPLAR DETECTIVE AND THE SATANIC WHISPER

Obituary for Wessel (Schalk Willem) Gordon

17/01/1971 – 14/05/2022

R.I.P.

Wessel was born on Wednesday 17 January 1971 in Welkom in the Free State, South Africa with a disability known as Spina Bifida.

Joppie and Ina, his parents, moved to Oberholzer, after which Wessel went to the Hope school in Johannesburg at the age of 3. From there on to the Martie du Plessis School in Bloemfontein and then to the Elizabeth Conradie School for the physically challenged in Kimberley where he matriculated.

He participated extracurricular in gymnastics, bridge, weightlifting, and wheelchair races

Wessel had a rich general knowledge through his love of reading. He appeared on TV in the program Who Wants to Be a Millionaire and also had an intense interest in history.

He especially enjoyed proofreading novels for various authors including J. Robert Kennedy. This activity allowed him to be in another world and forget his illness for a while. He became involved in the stories and related to the characters.

Wessel also loved animals, and dogs in particular. There wasn't a breed he didn't know.

Rest in Peace, Wessel. You are always in our hearts.

Milton Keynes UK
Ingram Content Group UK Ltd.
UKHW012217080923
428346UK00012B/271/J